The Lights of Lilly Pilly Creek

Abbie L. Martin

Book 3 - A Lilly Pilly Creek Ghost Mystery

THE LIGHTS OF LILLY PILLY CREEK

ISBN: 978-0-6457139-8-5
Abbie L. Martin paperback edition / December 2023
Abbie L. Martin books are published by Abbie Allen Publishing

CHAPTER 1

As she read aloud the first pages of her grandmother's diary, Jones saw a translucent figure twirl into view. She did her best to ignore the female form with long, red hair moving across the room.

"September eighth 1990. Today, Jones Margaret was born. A gorgeous bundle of joy for her new parents, Kitt and Margot. Baxter and I were her first visitors, and I cried when I saw my only son holding his new daughter. In honour of the newest member of the Eldershaw family, I thought today should be the day I resume my journaling after a rather long hiatus."

Jones looked up at her sister, tears in her eyes. The auburn-haired figure of Autumn, wearing a striped red blouse, tweed pants and brown loafers, had now stopped her pirouettes and beamed at her sister.

"Oh, Jones," said Autumn. "Granny started writing the day you were born!"

Jones nodded, smiling but unable to speak. When they'd decided today, just two weeks before Christmas, would be the day they finally opened their grandmother's lockbox, Jones wasn't sure what to expect. As she slowly turned the key and lifted the lid, she'd heard her ghostly sister squeal in delight. It was stuffed to the brim, full of cherished mementos. Jones had felt her chest tighten, a hint of apprehension creeping in as she contemplated what they may uncover. The sisters seldom allowed themselves to step into the past, rarely able to speak of all the people they'd lost. Neither their grandparents nor their parents were with them. And Jones was lucky her sister was still here, even though she was a ghost, seemingly tethered to the building they stood in.

"Go on," said Autumn. "Keep reading."

Jones tucked her brown hair behind her ear and continued. "Kitt kept The Memory Bank closed today, of course. But Baxter and I have said we'll open up for them this week, so they don't have to worry about it. It's going to be fun to go back. I wonder if we'll remember what to do! And how much will things have changed?"

"So, they were still living in Lily Pilly Creek?" said Autumn.

"Yes, they must have been," said Jones.

Jones had no recollection of her Granny and Poppy living in Lilly Pilly Creek. Her strongest memories were of their summer holidays spent at their grandparent's beach home in Port Vincent on the Yorke Peninsula. And, of course, they often came to stay at the family home in Lilly Pilly Creek, the home they'd lived in before Jones and Autumn's parents moved in.

"How many journals are there?" asked Autumn, hovering over the table where they'd pulled everything out.

Jones ran her hand over three piles of journals in front of her. "It looks like eleven," said Jones.

"We've got a lot to get through!"

At that moment, the pair heard a noise coming from the garden at the rear of The Memory Bank.

"Sounds like Lorne or Flick have arrived," said Jones.

"Do you think they'll get the garden finished before the Christmas

Party?" Autumn asked, moving over to look through the window, waiting for one of the gardeners to appear.

"They've promised they would," said Jones. "I think the main thing left to do is put in the water fountain."

Autumn clapped her hands together. "Oh, what a good idea that was," she said. "Even if I do say so myself."

Jones laughed! As always, Autumn was the designer of the two. Just as she had contributed brilliant ideas to the recent renovation inside The Memory Bank, Autumn had played a pivotal role in the new garden's design. Lorne Fox and his daughter Flick had brought it all to life over the past month.

"It's Flick," said Autumn, watching as a woman wearing navy trousers, a long-sleeve top and heavy work boots appeared through the rear gate.

Jones pushed herself up from the table. "I'd better put all this away before customers arrive," she said, glancing at the clock to see it was quarter to nine. It wasn't easy to get everything back neatly into the lockbox, but she finally slid it into its compartment in the lockbox room just as it was time to open.

The Memory Bank was an institution in Lilly Pilly Creek. It was a combination of a gift shop, a stationery and art store, and a cosy bookshop. Yet, what set it apart, and the inspiration for the name, was the imaginative use of the old bank's lockboxes by customers to store their treasured memories. It was their grandmother's idea. The same grandmother whose lockbox they'd only recently discovered had remained in the Bank.

Starting with their grandparents, it had subsequently been run by their parents, then later only their dad after their mum died when Jones was three and Autumn one. When Autumn finished high school and university, she had managed it with their dad until his own untimely death. Now, it was Autumn and Jones who had teamed up. However, the wider world wasn't aware that Autumn was currently haunting The Memory Bank (with Jones's full support) after she'd been dramatically pushed down the Bank's spiral staircase by her conniving ex-boyfriend.

It seemed year after year, The Memory Bank's history got more dramatic.

Jones pushed this startling thought out of her mind, locked her grandmother's box securely away, and went to open the wooden front door and officially start the day.

"Jones, could I speak to you for a moment?" said a female voice behind her. Jones pulled back the Bank's front door and turned to greet Flick with a smile.

"Absolutely!" said Jones. "How's it going?"

"I just hoped we could chat about the final plantings and double-check before I put them in the ground." Flick wore her honey-coloured hair in a high ponytail, her tanned skin glowing red. She had already been hard at work.

"Was it the plants for the herb garden?" Jones followed Flick through the large glass doors that slid back to reveal the new garden. She was thrilled with all the work Flick and her father had put in. Jones had asked the Foxes to create something that blended the cottage gardens her mother had loved with the native plants of the Australian bush that surrounded them. She wanted the space to be inviting in both the warm and cooler months, allowing people to socialise or take a moment of quiet reflection. The sisters knew it was a lot to ask, but Lorne and, in particular, Flick had been more than up to the task.

There were now only a few final touches to be made, and one of those was the placement of plants in the area Jones was calling 'The Secret Garden'. This secluded garden area had been suggested by Atlas. It was separated by a trellis that would eventually be covered in jasmine and would contain a small lounge and the water feature.

Flick walked to the corner where Jones had asked if they could plant some herbs. A selection was laid out in front of them. Autumn loved the herbs they'd chosen after pouring over the catalogue together. The sisters had decided to choose herbs that had intriguing names and were renowned for their medicinal properties. Some of their favourites were Fairywand, Toothache Plant, and Elderflower, in honour of their family name Eldershaw.

"How can I help?" asked Jones.

"What I want to know is, as we have a few of each plant, do you want them grouped, or do you want it to appear more like they've self-sown?"

Autumn had been hovering next to her sister but then floated directly above the vacant garden plot and turned to face her sister.

"Hmmm," said Jones, pondering the question. "Grouped-" Autumn vigorously shook her head. "Or self-sown?" At this, Autumn declared "Yes! Most definitely self-sown." Of course, only Jones could hear her, but she appreciated her sister's input.

"Self-sown," said Jones. "Most definitely self-sown." Jones turned to Flick, whose face made it clear she approved of their choice.

"Excellent!" she said. "I'll get cracking."

"Thank you, Flick," said Jones. "We love everything you've done." Autumn raised her eyebrows at her sister, worried using the word 'we' would strike Flick as unusual. But Jones was sure Flick would think she meant Atlas, who, with perfect timing, had just walked to join them.

"Working on the herb garden today?" he asked.

Although Atlas was an employee of The Memory Bank, he did also, as of a few weeks ago, have his own business office inside the Bank, and was as invested in this garden as Jones and Autumn.

"Yes," said Jones. "Your secret garden is almost done!" Atlas smiled. It was a comment he'd made in passing when they'd all been distracted by the poisoning of bride-to-be Iris. Yet Jones had tucked it away in her mind and ensured his idea was included when she sat down to plan the garden.

"Just letting you know, a few customers walked in behind me," said Atlas, indicating the inside of The Memory Bank.

Jones nodded and, leaving Flick to the herb plants, returned inside, first picking up the coffee Atlas always brought her, before greeting their customers. She was pleased to see two of her regulars, Gladys and Neha, who were renowned for their art supply buying abilities.

"Good morning, ladies," said Jones. "How can I help you today?"

"Were you in the new garden?" asked Gladys. "When can we see it? Won't you give us a sneak peek?"

"You'll have to wait just like everyone else," said Jones. "At the Christmas Party!" The women pouted dramatically but smiled just the same.

"Did you know I have a special visitor staying with me today?" said Neha.

"I did, actually," said Jones. "Plum is coming to say hi just before we close."

Plum was a close friend of their mother's who'd always made an effort to keep in touch with the girls. It had been a while since she'd visited, but she was coming back to Lilly Pilly Creek for a few days to catch up with her old school friends, one of them being Neha. Plum had made sure to arrange a time to visit The Memory Bank as soon as she arrived in town.

"Oh wonderful," said Neha. "I know she can't wait to see you and everything you've done with the place."

"I'll leave you to look around," said Jones. "And I won't dare tell you there may be some new brushes on the far table." Jones winked at the ladies, who grinned at her before moving in that exact direction.

Jones turned around, looking for her sister. She was surprised to see Autumn behind the counter, staring intently at something. Slowly climbing up on a stool next to her, Jones leant forward to find out what Autumn was staring at. A pencil.

"What are you doing?" asked Jones.

Autumn didn't respond. She stared at the pencil, not moving a muscle of her transparent figure.

Jones peered at her sister and then back to the pencil. She felt like Jane in Mary Poppins as she watched Bert attempt magic. Jones promptly said, "Is somethin' s'posed to happen?" in her best cockney accent.

Autumn couldn't help but let out a laugh.

"What on earth are you doing?" Jones tried again.

"I was trying to move that pencil!" Autumn replied.

"With your mind?"

"Of course!" Autumn retorted. "How else would I move it?"

She was right. Autumn's ghostly abilities may have enabled her to walk through walls, but they didn't allow her to move or touch anything. Except for the glass window she'd previously somehow managed to break, saving Jones's life in the process.

"Are you having any luck?"

Autumn punched her fist down at her side in frustration. "No, nothing!"

"How long have you been working on this?"

"Oh, at least a few weeks," she sighed. "I was sure it would be easier than this. I'm sure Patrick Swayze worked it out much quicker in Ghost."

Jones laughed at Autumn's reference to one of the few resources they had to help them try and understand their current situation. "But he had help, remember? From that subway ghost."

"Yes of course," said Autumn, bringing her hand to her forehead. "If only we lived in New York City. The big apple is crawling with ghosts."

"Obviously!" said Jones. "Crawling with ghosts in the entirely accurate Patrick Swayze and Whoopi Goldberg movie."

"Surely it was based on a true story." The girls laughed. They were continuously referring to fictitious books and films for source material. They knew it was ridiculous, but unfortunately, they were yet to find a definitive guide on *'What to do if you return to earth as a ghost.'* Autumn was going to have to write that one day.

"Well, keep trying!" said Jones. "I'll get back to running the Bank."

"I hope you're not mocking me," said Autumn. "Can you imagine what we'll be able to achieve together once I work out how to move things? The Eldershaw Detective Agency will take off!"

Jones smiled at her sister and left her to her pencil.

CHAPTER 2

Plum by name and Plum by nature. As their mum's closest friend strode into The Memory Bank just before five that afternoon, it became apparent Jones's godmother had truly embraced her name.

Her bobbed hair, which had previously been grey, was now a lovely shade of purple. She wore a white t-shirt, dark jeans and silver ballet flats topped off with a long, flowing, wispy jacket, the colour of lavender. To complete her look, Plum wore bold purple glasses. She was stunning.

"Oh Jones," said Plum. "Dear Jones," and she pulled her into a long, comforting hug. When they were both ready, Plum pulled back, still gripping Jones by the shoulders, and looked deeply into her goddaughter's eyes. Jones was surprised to feel her eyes water and quickly spoke to avoid dissolving into tears.

"Thank you so much for coming," said Jones. "What do you think?" Jones stepped back and waved her arms around her.

Spinning slowly, attempting to take in every inch of the renovations, Plum turned back to Jones. "Absolute perfection! Margot would have adored it!"

Plum strolled through The Memory Bank, picking up candles, swiping her hand along bookshelves, and inhaling the scent of the flowers that Jones had recently taken to displaying. She had become a connoisseur of the roadside stalls around Lilly Pilly Creek and took Autumn on drives to select bunches each week.

"Has Plum always been this amazing?" Autumn asked, following the woman around the Bank. As she floated, in an instant Autumn changed her blouse from a red stripe to a deep aubergine, clearly showing an affinity with Plum's style.

"Just don't change your hair," Jones thought but resisted saying aloud. She didn't want Plum to think she was losing her sanity. Jones knew one of the driving forces for her Godmother's visit was to check on her.

"Oh, the Christmas tree!" said Plum. "This is gorgeous!"

Plum had walked over to the current centrepiece of The Memory Bank. At Flick and Lorne's insistence, a massive Christmas tree had been installed in the centre of the main space. Jones thought they may have gotten a little carried away, but Autumn adored it.

"You've got to live a little! Especially at Christmas time!" Autumn had told her.

Autumn had also been the one to suggest they get creative with the decorations. Instead of filling the tree with baubles, they'd covered it in antique keys. They were known for their lockboxes, after all. They'd used as many old keys as they could find along with some new ones to add extra shine. It was so clever. What surprised them the most was the customers who came in and handed over their own keys to add to the tree.

"I thought you wouldn't mind a few more," they'd say, dropping the keys into Jones's hand. Of course, Jones didn't mind at all and would hurry to find some twine so she could hang them up.

The centrepiece was amazing, and Plum's appreciation thrilled her.

"Come and look at the garden!" said Jones. Together, Jones and

Plum strode over to the new pride and joy of The Memory Bank.

Seeing Plum walk through, running her fingers through the foliage, Jones finally had her first glimpse of what this garden would add to the Bank. As soon as you stepped in, you felt calmer. Watching Flick watering, Jones realised once the water feature was added, the sound of flowing water would bring a sense of tranquillity to the space. She was pleased she had finally committed to its creation.

"How wonderful," Plum said, walking back to Jones. "It's just divine."

"I'm so pleased," said Jones. "Flick and Lorne have done a wonderful job."

"Oh," said Plum, turning to Flick. "Are you Lorne's daughter?"

Flick looked up and smiled. "Yes, do you know him?"

"We were at school together," said Plum. "And on a few committees when we were older before I moved."

Flick nodded.

"I'm Plum," she said, extending her arm to Flick. Flick wiped her hand on her pants before taking Plum's hand.

"Nice to meet you," Flick smiled.

"Well, Jones," Plum said, turning to her goddaughter. "I think a drink is in order? What's next door like?"

Plum referred to Hugo's wine bar, immediately next door to The Memory Bank. It was still relatively new to Lilly Pilly Creek, so she wasn't surprised Plum had never been.

"It's lovely," said Jones.

"The wine bar or the owner?" Autumn chimed in.

As always, Jones ignored her sister when others were around and went to grab her keys and bag. Atlas had already left, so it was up to her to turn off the lights, set the alarm and lock the door.

"Flick, are you ok to lock the back gate when you leave?" Jones said, about to secure the glass doors.

"Sure!" said Flick. "I won't be much longer. I'll see you at the Progress Association meeting."

Jones twisted the latch and walked to the front door, where Plum and Autumn were waiting for her. Punching in the alarm numbers, Jones guided Plum out the door and twisted the heavy key in the lock.

"What do you fancy?" asked Jones. "Bubbles?"

"As long as it's Bird in Hand," said Plum. "My favourite."

Plum linked arms with Jones, and they made their way to Hugo's.

As she pushed open the door, Jones tried to appear nonchalant, but quickly scanned the room, looking for the man himself. Although nothing had happened as yet, it seemed imminent that Jones and Hugo would finally go on their first date. Autumn was immensely frustrated at how slow the two of them were, but there was absolutely nothing she could do about it.

"There he is," whispered Autumn into Jones's ear, pointing towards the rear courtyard, strung with glowing lights.

Jones smiled. The bar sounds disappeared as she watched him in his element, pouring wine and chatting with customers. Tonight he wore a check shirt, sleeves rolled up on his tan arms, and a pair of brown corduroy pants, his signature tea towel slung over his shoulder. It was only a moment before Hugo seemed to sense her eyes on him and looked up. They stared at each other momentarily before he smiled and waved, signalling that he would meet her at the bar.

"Is that him?" said Plum, startling Jones.

"The owner?" Jones asked. "Yes, that's Hugo." She knew her cheeks were pink, but she didn't care. They made their way to the bar, and before long, Hugo was there.

"Good afternoon, ladies," Hugo said, charming Plum with his smile.

"Hugo," said Jones. "Please meet Plum, my godmother."

"Lovely to meet you, Hugo," said Plum, shaking his outstretched hand. "This is a delightful wine bar. Just what Lilly Pilly Creek needs!"

Hugo grinned. "What can I get you?"

"Plum has specifically requested a Bird in Hand sparkling," said Jones. "A bottle, please."

"Certainly! I'll bring it over. Will you be outside? There are still a few tables left."

On a warm evening like tonight, Hugo knew the outside area was her preference. Jones led the way. She found a table on the gravel overlooking the gum trees that lined the bubbling Lilly Pilly Creek. Jones turned her head and saw her sister floating down towards its banks. It wasn't her usual practice. It was almost as though she was being drawn to the creek. If their life had been a traditional ghost story, this moment may have been a little eerie, but for Jones, it was a peaceful and beautiful sight, watching her translucent sister floating above the earth, alone and happy.

Jones turned back to Plum. "It's so nice to have you visit."

"I'm just sorry I haven't been back sooner," said Plum.

Hugo arrived, carrying the bottle in a silver wine bucket along with two crystal champagne flutes.

"As requested," Hugo said, lifting the bottle of wine with a flourish and then casually popping the cork.

"A glass of wine on the banks of Lilly Pilly Creek," said Plum, watching as the pink-tinged bubbles fizzed in their glasses. "Oh, this brings me back." Jones saw Plum had closed her eyes, stepping back in time for a moment.

Jones glanced up at Hugo. They shared another smile.

"Shall I bring a cheese platter?" Hugo asked Jones.

"That would be great," Jones nodded. Hugo moved away, and Jones reached for the two glasses, placing one in front of Plum.

"In memory of Margot, Baxter and Autumn," Plum said, lifting her glass. "To friends and family."

"To friends and family," Jones responded quietly, clinking her glass against Plum's. The pair smiled as they took a sip.

"That's the stuff!" said Plum, her accent slightly broader than usual. Plum then laughed and took another long sip. "Oh, it's good to be back. Not quite the same without your mum. But I am looking forward to spending some time with you, Jones. You do remind me of her, you know?"

"Of Mum? Do I?" Jones was shocked. Whenever anyone spoke of her parents, they always said Autumn was a perfect blend of the two, and that Jones was more similar to her granny.

"Absolutely," said Plum. "Your calm thoughtfulness, for one. And the way you've stepped up and taken over The Memory Bank when you could have easily walked away. That is Margot through and through. They would have been so proud of you."

Jones smiled slightly, staring at her hands. She realised at that moment how important it was that her parents be proud of her. Even now, when they were both gone.

"But how are you, Jones?" Plum asked. "Really?"

Her eyes quickly shot up to Plum's, surprised at the question. She felt her hands shake a little and gripped her glass. Taking a deep breath, she responded. "It has been hard. If I'm being completely honest, it's been incredibly hard. But there are also some very good things in my life, and I'm happy." Jones knew she sounded cryptic, but she had no plans to share with Plum that she wasn't quite as alone as everyone thought.

"Yes, I've noticed," said Plum, tilting her head towards Hugo. "What's going on there?"

Jones was confused for a moment before laughing. "Oh, that's not what I meant!"

"Oh sure, Jones," said Plum. "Come on. Tell me!"

Shaking her head but unable to take the smile off her face, Jones told Plum the story of Hugo. She revealed that ultimately there wasn't all that much to tell. Even though he had both saved her life *and* accompanied her in a thunderstorm as they ran through paddocks, chasing a killer.

"And you're telling me you still haven't gone on a date?" Plum exclaimed. "You two need to get your acts together."

Jones expected to hear her sister pipe in. It was at times like these that Autumn usually made her opinions known. Jones knew she would be in full agreement with Plum. However, Jones looked up to see Autumn still floating along the riverbank, slowly moving in the direction of The Memory Bank. Jones thought Autumn must be intentionally leaving her alone with Plum. She wondered what Autumn was expecting the two of them to talk about. Did she believe Jones may reveal Autumn's existence to their mother's oldest friend? Did she want her to?

With perfect timing, Hugo arrived with the cheese platter. Plum took her opportunity.

"Now, Hugo," she said. "Jones and I have been talking, and she's been saying she's feeling a little cooped up. She needs to go out and do something, get out of Lilly Pilly Creek. And we thought you would be the perfect person to accompany her. What do you think?"

Jones's face was the colour of beetroot, her mouth agape. Hugo was at a loss for words, staring at Plum before looking towards Jones. Yet, a true professional, he regained his composure quickly.

"Absolutely!" he said. Jones was shocked by his conviction but very pleased, unable to stop a smile from forming.

"Actually," said Hugo, turning to Jones. "I have been invited to a private wine tasting near Gumeracha in a couple of days. Would you like to join me?"

Jones took a quick sip of wine before replying, "Yes, that sounds lovely."

"It's settled!" Plum clapped her hands and leaned forward to take a slice of aged cheddar, popping it in her mouth.

"I'll touch base tomorrow," Hugo winked at Jones and walked away.

"Plum!" said Jones. "You are something else!"

"Well," said Plum. "How do you think your dad finally asked out your mum? Baxter was useless until I intervened. And as they say," Plum lifted her hands to the sky. "The rest is history!"

Jones laughed out loud, secretly thrilled to learn this snippet of history about her parents.

"And with that," Plum said, glancing at the gold watch on her wrist. "I had better make a move. Neha is expecting me for dinner."

"Sounds lovely. I might sit here and eat this cheese platter for dinner," said Jones. "I've got a Progress Association committee meeting tonight."

"The Progress Association? Is that still in formation?" asked Plum.

"It sure is," said Jones. "I think it was quiet for a few years, but it's well and truly back in full swing. We've resurrected The Christmas Lights Competition as well."

It surprised Jones to see Plum's face blanch.

"You have? Wasn't that cancelled?"

"I think so," said Jones. "But that was years ago. Thirty years ago exactly, I believe. Which is why we've chosen this year to relaunch it." Plum had bit her lip. "You seem bothered by that. Why?"

Plum shook her head. "Oh, it's nothing. It's just-" Plum paused. "Well, did they tell you why it was cancelled?"

Jones frowned. "No, actually, they didn't."

Plum leaned forward and took Jones's hands in hers.

"There was a break-in at The Memory Bank," she explained.

"There was?"

"Yes," said Plum. "A woman was found unconscious in the lockbox room. Someone had whacked her on the head."

Jones gasped.

"Somehow, they'd gotten their hands on the keys and knew which boxes to grab," Plum continued. "And do you know what?"

"What?" Jones leaned in even further.

"One of those lockboxes was your Granny's. It contained her jewellery."

"Her jewellery?" said Jones. "But The Memory Bank doesn't store any valuables."

"No, it doesn't. But at the time your granny did decide to store some of her jewellery there. Because it was their building, she thought it was just as protected as a safe in their home. Unfortunately, she was wrong."

"Did they ever find out who did it?"

"No. It scared the community because it happened on the night of the Christmas Party, when half the town was in The Memory Bank. They realised it was likely someone they knew, and never finding out who could be so brazen and violent? Well, your parents refused to host The Christmas Party the next year, and the Progress Association decided to cancel the Christmas Lights competition. It all fizzled out after that, and no one could face restarting. Until now."

"Yes, until now," said Jones. "I had no idea. That must have scared everyone."

"Your mum and dad had only recently taken over The Memory Bank. Your grandparents had retired. I think they were still living in town. Your parents used to rent a small cottage up on Waratah Crescent," Plum said, as she took another piece of cheese. "I don't think it was long after that they moved into the main house, and your grandparents moved to the beach house. But I know for a while they were thinking of changing their plans. Staying in town to help with The Memory Bank. It freaked out everyone."

"I had no idea." Jones shook her head and finished the wine in her glass.

"It's probably time to move on," said Plum. "No doubt everyone overreacted in the end."

"But what about the jewellery? Was it ever found?"

Plum shook her head. "Not that I know of," she said. "And your grandmother was so disappointed. One of the items was her gorgeous opal earrings. She loved those. They were long and big, and everyone commented when she wore them. They were her statement piece. Gone forever."

Plum pushed herself out of her chair. "How about we carry these things over to the bar?" Plum raised her eyebrows with a smile. Jones laughed but followed her lead.

Plum had only been in town for a matter of hours, and already she was making her presence known.

CHAPTER 3

Jones had to drag herself away from the comfort and conversation of Hugo's bar. Recently it had been a regular location for her, seating herself at the bar with a wine and something to eat, chatting with Hugo when he wasn't serving customers. She knew after all these weeks it was a little ridiculous that neither of them had taken the next step. Jones knew she was indebted to Plum for sorting them out. She found she was rather excited about the upcoming wine tasting.

However, The Progress Association Committee meeting was beckoning, so after saying goodbye to Hugo, she left the bar. Autumn retreated inside The Memory Bank, and Jones made her way up the Main Street to the only pub in town. The Creekside Inn was the regular venue for their committee meetings.

She entered the pub and saw one of her newest friends, Mr Manowski, sitting at the bar. She gave him a wave and continued through the ladies' lounge and along a passageway.

Inside one of the rear rooms, she found the usual motley crew of committee members. Iris Wainwright had already arrived and Jones made her way to sit next to her. Ever since Jones had helped Iris create a memory box for her wedding *and* discovered who was responsible for poisoning and nearly killing her, they had become firm friends.

Prue, the committee chair, was sitting at the head of the table with papers laid out neatly in front of her. For all the negative things that could, and indeed *were,* said about Prue Timberley, the local real estate agent and property investor, she was very effective at running meetings. Prue nodded at Jones as she took her seat.

Rex Keegan, an electrician who had taken on a lot of the heavy lifting of getting the Lilly Pilly Creek Christmas Lights competition to life, sidled into the room, quickly followed by Colin Fletcher, who always had a beer in hand. Jones wasn't quite sure what Colin did, if anything, but he was a long-term committee member, and even if no one had worked out what he brought to the group, he was there. He just was.

Tara Galati of the Galati wine family came in and sat next to Prue as the Committee's Secretary. The pair were quite a force on the committee, but it was thanks to their drive that they had relaunched the Christmas Lights competition this year.

"Who are we waiting for?" asked Prue as everyone found their seats.

Jones glanced around and noticed that Flick hadn't arrived. "Flick isn't here yet," she said. "She was just finishing up at The Bank when I locked up, so I don't think she'll be far."

Prue, prompt as always, glanced at her watch. It was seven exactly. Time for the meeting to start. "We can't wait," said Prue. "We have a quorum, so we'll put her as an apology for now."

Tara dutifully took attendance, and they reviewed the minutes of the last meeting. Then it was time for correspondence in.

"Unfortunately, we've had some letters from unhappy citizens," Prue explained.

"Unhappy about what?" Colin said gruffly before taking a gulp out of his tinny.

"The lights," explained Prue. "I'll read one of the delightful letters aloud."

To whom it may concern

After 30 years of tasteful Christmas lights in Lilly Pilly Creek, we have once again been inundated with gaudy and impractical lights which, not only make Lilly Pilly Creek look like Lunar Park, but I am subject to having spotlights directed at my bedroom until late in the night, causing detrimental effects to my sleep and mental health. I implore the committee to reconsider the resumption of the Christmas Lights Competition and return our town to the haven of taste it once was.

"Bah!" scoffed Rex. "And who was that from?"

"Anonymous," said Prue.

"Anonymous!" said Jones. "They don't even have the nerve to sign their name?"

Prue attempted to maintain a straight face but as she looked at Jones a slight smirk appeared. "Obviously, we can't respond to them directly, so all we can do is take it on notice. Does anyone want to discuss this?"

"They can shove it up their-"

"Colin!" Prue reprimanded but joined in the laughter of the group. He'd attempted to say what they were all thinking. After all the effort they had put in to get the Christmas Lights Competition up and running again, they weren't inclined to indulge the complaints of one Lilly Pilly Creek resident.

"Unfortunately, that's not the only letter we've received," said Prue.

Jones raised her eyebrows, wondering what this one would be about. Prue, however, was interrupted.

"Sorry, so sorry," said Flick, rushing into the room and slamming the door closed a little too loudly. "Sorry, continue. Don't mind me." Flick was puffing and dropped into her chair with a thump. "Is there any wine?" she said, glancing around. Usually, there were wine and soft drinks on the table, and she wasn't disappointed. Tara reached for a bottle of her Sangiovese and poured Flick a glass. Jones stared at her, surprised, as Flick drank almost the entire glass in one go. Looking up, it shocked Flick to see everyone staring at her. "Oh, sorry, keep going. Just ignore me."

It took a moment, but Prue found her poise and continued.

"The second letter," Prue turned her head towards Jones. "Is from someone complaining about the choice of venue for the Christmas Party and awards presentation."

Jones tried to keep a poker face but was feeling decidedly miffed that someone wasn't happy The Memory Bank would be hosting this event.

"Does it say who this one's from?" asked Iris.

"Yes," said Prue. "Molly Shepherd."

"Ahh," said Colin and Rex together, nodding their head in complete understanding.

"What am I missing?" asked Tara. Prue, Jones and Iris looked equally confused.

"Well, she's the reason we cancelled the Christmas party in the first place," said Rex.

"She is?" said Prue.

"She got whacked on the head and left for dead, right there in The Memory Bank," explained Colin.

"What! It was Molly Shepherd?" gasped Jones. In one night she'd discovered that The Memory Bank was the scene of a crime all those years ago, and now she discovers the person rendered unconscious in her Memory Bank was local farmer, Molly Shepherd. "Left for dead?"

"Colin's exaggerating a bit," said Rex.

"No, I'm not!" said Colin. "She was in awful shape. In hospital for a week. And to be honest, I don't think she's ever been the same since."

"Well, you should know," said Rex.

"How dare you!" shouted Colin, abruptly standing as though to threaten Rex.

"Gentlemen!" Prue said sternly. "Sit down." As always, Prue got the response she wanted. Colin sat back down, although continued to glare at Rex. "What I want to know is if this is something we need to be concerned about. Should we speak to Molly?"

"Perhaps," said Rex, and Colin shrugged in something of agreement.

"*I'd* like to speak to her," said Jones. "If that's ok?"

"Is that safe Jones?" asked Iris.

"Molly's harmless," said Jones. "At least that's my impression." Jones looked around the table, seeking confirmation.

"Doubt old Molly would bring you any harm," said Colin. "But she can be feisty, so don't expect her to back down."

"So we all agree that Jones will contact Molly to discuss her letter?" clarified Prue.

Everyone nodded in agreement. "Tara, can you please note that in the minutes?"

Tara nodded, typing away.

The remainder of the meeting continued, without any further surprises. The time was set when everyone would arrive to help set up at The Memory Bank on the day of the party. Rex the electrician also confirmed he would install a surprise light feature to mark the official opening on the night. Even Jones was unaware of what he had planned.

Once the meeting was formally closed, just before eight o'clock, everyone stayed to chat and drink glasses of wine or soft drink. Or in Colin's case, another beer. Jones stood with Iris and Flick. She chatted away with Iris but Flick was very quiet, drinking her third glass of wine, and often appearing to drift away into thoughts of her own.

"Iris," said Jones. "You look so much better. How are you feeling?" It was only a few weeks ago that Iris was hospitalised, poisoned by none other than her brother Charlie. Fortunately, Jones had discovered the truth before anyone else was harmed, but Charlie was not so fortunate.

"So much better," said Iris. "I was back out in the paddocks this week, checking the herd. Drew was very relieved to see me back in the ute!"

"That's wonderful. Have you rescheduled the wedding?" Jones asked her.

"We're looking at late March. Just finalising things with Tara." Iris and Drew had planned to hold their wedding at Tara's winery, where her future brother-in-law was the head chef. Jones was slightly surprised to hear they were going with this option again. In particular, because Tara was Drew's ex and still seemed to hold a candle for him. But Jones was pleased everything was working out for Iris. She deserved it.

"Jones, I'm going to head off," said Flick, downing the last of her drink and sighing. "But the water features have come in, so I wondered if you wouldn't mind popping into the nursery before you open tomorrow? It would be nice to make a decision and get the installation underway."

"Sure," said Jones. "Not a problem. Is eight thirty ok for you?"

"Perfect," said Flick, then glanced at her watch. "I need to get home to bed, I think." She ran her hand through her hair, certainly looking tired.

"Are you ok, Flick?" Jones asked.

"Yes, yes," Flick said, nodding her head. "I just think I'm exhausted from the warmer weather. I'll be fine. See you in the morning." She placed her wine glass on a table before quietly making her way out of the meeting room.

Jones watched her leave, sure that there was something more than the heat causing Flick to seem so out of sorts. She wondered why Flick had been so late to the meeting, and if something had happened since she'd last seen her. Or perhaps it was as simple as receiving the delivery of the water features late in the day. Jones would make sure she checked in properly with Flick in the morning.

CHAPTER 4

The summer weather certainly seemed to have hit Lilly Pilly Creek and Jones was enjoying picking her outfit for the day. She had chosen a mid-length striped skirt paired with sandals and a crisp white t-shirt. Yet, as was her tradition, her t-shirt was decorated with a quote. Today's was *"Let go of people who bring you down, and surround yourself with those who bring out the best in you." - Taylor Swift*

No matter how warm it was, Jones would never start a morning without a cup of Sybil's coffee. With a spring in her step, Jones made her way to the coffee van which today was parked out the front of one of the empty shops in the Main Street. Jones spotted a new sign on the window. 'Butternut Cheesery Flagship Store Opening Soon.'

"A cheesery!" Jones exclaimed in greeting to Sybil.

"I know!" said Sybil. "Perfect for Lilly Pilly Creek."

Sybil placed a milk jug under the steam wand and cranked it. "Any food today, Jones?"

"Do you have any more of that zucchini slice?"

"Sure do!"

"I'll take two slices please," said Jones. "Breakfast and lunch."

"How's the plans for the big party going?"

"I think we're getting there," said Jones. "Rex says he has some sort of surprise and he's not even telling me."

"Typical Rex," laughed Sybil. "But he usually delivers."

"By the way, Sybil," said Jones. "Have you heard of anyone complaining about the lights?"

"No, not at all," said Sybil. "Why?" She raised her eyebrows. Usually, Sybil was delivering the local murmurings. Today Jones was the one with information to impart.

"We've had an anonymous complaint sent to The Progress Association," said Jones. "Nothing we can do about it, obviously, but we were concerned there may be more than one person with issues.

"Not that I've heard," said Sybil. "I say ignore them. Don't let one bad apple, well…you know." Sybil had obviously seen Jones's t-shirt choice for the morning.

Jones smiled, coffee and zucchini slice in hand, and headed to Foxglove Nursery. The nursery was tucked just off the Main Street. Jones had sought advice from the knowledgeable staff while choosing plants for the new Memory Bank garden, as well as when endeavouring to revive her mother's cottage garden.

She tried to open the shop door, but it was still locked. Neither Lorne, Flick nor one of their team had arrived. Jones glanced at her watch and saw that it was only just eight-thirty. She leaned back against the wall, savouring her coffee and then pushed her nose into the paper bag so she could snatch a bite of the zucchini slice.

"Sorry! Sorry" said Flick. "I seem to be running late a lot." Flick jogged down the street, her backpack swinging from side to side as she ran. Coming to a jarring stop at the shop door, Flick yanked the bag from her back and dropped it to the ground. It took her a moment of rifling to pull out what she was looking for. A set of keys to the nursery.

Flick pushed the door open and a bell rang, alerting the empty shop to their arrival. She turned the lights on and walked over to the shop counter. "The water features are out the back in the warehouse. I wanted to ensure that no one else would see them before you made your selection."

Jones followed Flick to the rear of the building where there was a roller door. Flick took her keys and got down on her haunches to unlock it.

"That's strange," said Flick.

"What is it?" Jones tried to figure out what caught Flick's attention.

"The roller door is unlocked," she said. Rising, she pulled the door up and open. "And the lights are on?"

She glanced from side to side with confusion before making her way into the warehouse. "Dad! Dad, are you in here?"

Jones cautiously followed Flick. It was a large shed, very high, with tall stock shelves lining two walls. The remainder of the floor space was divided into bays storing a variety of items. From that vantage point, the entire warehouse was easily visible. She let Flick wander through, checking on things, knowing she would spot if anything was out of place.

Just as Flick was making her way to a stack of compost bags, she let out a guttural scream and vanished from view.

"Flick," Jones was dashing towards the place she'd been. "Flick! What is it?" Jones pulled to a rapid stop as she discovered what had affected Flick so much. There on the floor was her dad, Lorne Fox. Around his head, a halo of blood.

Flick crawled away, dry retching and making sounds usually only heard from an animal. Although the man looked well and truly dead, Jones apprehensively shook his shoulder as she pulled out her phone. It made no difference. The man was heavy and cold. Jones called the police and then went to sit next to Flick. She was lying on the floor near hay bales, eyes closed, her face ashen, making what can only be called whimpers. Jones put her hand on Flick's leg, the closest thing to her, and took some deep breaths.

It didn't take long for Sergeant Schmidt, or Christopher as he'd requested Jones call him, to arrive once Jones had called triple zero. A paramedics' team wasn't far behind, but they just did a cursory once over, confirming Lorne Fox was very much deceased.

Christopher didn't so much as raise an eyebrow in acknowledgement that yet again Jones was at the scene of a major crime in Lilly Pilly Creek. He just listened to what she had to say and then went over to speak to Flick. More officers arrived and began taking photographs, walking through the warehouse and shop searching for clues.

Jones had been instructed not to leave, so she'd found herself a spot outside in the nursery. She sat on a garden bench placed underneath the cool branches of a Robina tree. She was grateful for her second zucchini slice, if not for her hunger pangs, which had well and truly subsided, but at least for the distraction. If only she could ask Sybil to bring her another coffee. Or perhaps a gin from Hugo's. The sight of Lorne Fox lying on the ground like that was an image she wished she could erase.

From what she recalled, it appeared Lorne had fallen and slammed his head on something very solid. And yet Jones couldn't recollect seeing anything of that description in the immediate vicinity. Only bags and bags of compost, potting mix, and mulch. She didn't like to admit it, but it appeared more likely that something, someone, had struck the man. And based on the police activity she was observing, Christopher was considering the same possibility.

It was a shock to Jones, although, as she pondered further, it wasn't a complete surprise. Lorne was a man known for rubbing people the wrong way. She couldn't say she had ever heard of a confrontation with Lorne getting physical, but she wouldn't put it past him, at least in his younger days. But in his fifties? Jones was struggling to picture it. Then again, maybe it wasn't Lorne who got physical. Maybe whoever had whacked him over the head had let their own temper get the better of them. Jones wondered if they would ever find out. She wished Christopher would come back so she could pick his brain.

Jones glanced at her watch. It was nine-thirty. Oh no! She was well and truly late opening The Memory Bank. She had no way of contacting Autumn to explain what was going on, but maybe, just maybe, Atlas had already arrived. He had his own office for 'Wayfinder Labs' but didn't have set hours. Although Atlas did have shifts at The Memory Bank, and also helped out at a pinch when Jones needed it, this morning Jones was meant to open up. She wondered how many customers had already popped past, questioning where she was.

Rubbing her hands on her skirt to push off the crumbs, Jones stood, deciding she would make sure she did indeed have to stay, or if she could talk to someone later. If they insisted she stay, she would make a quick phone call to Atlas to see if he was around. If she was honest, there wasn't anything much Jones could provide in the way of insight. She had absolutely no idea what was going on or who would want to hurt Lorne Fox.

"Jones!" Christopher was standing under an archway. "There you are. Can I just get you to come with me? I need you to walk through what exactly happened this morning."

"Oh sure," said Jones. "But hasn't Flick done that?"

"She's ah, not handling things very well," said Christopher. "I haven't been able to get much out of her."

Jones followed Christopher to the front door and told him everything, from her arriving a few minutes early to Flick rushing up moments later. She even mentioned the quip about running late again.

"Again?" asked Christopher.

"She was just having a joke," explained Jones. "Flick was late to last night's Progress Association Committee meeting as well."

Christopher murmured and noted this down. Jones furrowed her brow but then continued her explanation as he looked back up at her. She showed how Flick had dumped her backpack on the counter, which was still in the same place. Jones then demonstrated how Flick had crouched down to open the door but was surprised to find it unlocked. She then went on to tell him about the warehouse lights being on and tried her best to recall the path Flick had walked before discovering her father.

"Well, that's been a big help," said Christopher.

"It has?" Jones didn't think she'd told him much at all.

"Yes," said Christopher. "I think that's all we need, but of course, you know I'll be in touch if I think of anything else." With this, he allowed himself to smile at her. Jones grinned back. They had both been through this a few times.

"Well, I'm going to open up the Bank, if it's okay to leave?"

"Not a problem," Christopher nodded. He turned and walked towards Flick, who was now sitting on the hay bales, her head in her hands, surrounded by police officers.

Jones took one last deep breath before leaving. This was not the morning she had expected.

CHAPTER 5

"What is it, Jones?" Autumn made a beeline for her sister, sensing something was wrong. Today she was wearing one of her favourite long red dresses and the skirt floated behind her like a kite's tail.

"You won't believe this!" said Jones. "I've just seen a dead body!"

"Another one?" said Autumn.

"Well, technically I've only seen dead bodies at funerals," Jones corrected her sister, guessing at the accusation in her question. "But yes, it's Lorne Fox. He's dead!"

"Really? What happened?" Autumn followed Jones as she found a chair at one of the customer tables and massaged her temples.

"He was just lying there. Blood all around his head."

"Blood!" Autumn whizzed in front of Jones. "You don't mean…."

Jones was nodding, but it took her a moment to say it out aloud. "Yes, I think Lorne Fox has been murdered."

Autumn gasped.

"I didn't even think to ask," said Jones. "Is Atlas here?"

"No, I haven't seen him. I began to worry when neither of you was here by opening time," said Autumn. "A few people tried to get in, but they just shrugged and walked away."

"I'm not sure if I can face anyone today," said Jones.

"You don't have to!" said Autumn. "You can keep the Bank closed. Everyone will understand.

"I can't believe this is happening again!" moaned Jones.

"Again?" asked Autumn. "You mean, like being on the scene of

Iris's collapse?"

"Of course, I mean that," said Jones, lifting her head and rolling her eyes at her sister. "What will Christopher think? What will *everyone* think?"

"Well, hopefully, everyone will be smart enough to realise you're just unlucky."

"Extremely unlucky!"

"Perhaps not as unlucky as Lorne," said Autumn.

"Ahhh!" Jones cried out, before closing her eyes and laying her cheek flat on the table.

They heard a rattling at the front door and both looked up, startled.

"Oh Atlas," said Jones. "It's only you." She pushed her palms into her eye sockets, attempting to push away the beginning of a headache.

"Only me!" Atlas cried with a smile on his face. Then he took in Jones before him. "Are you okay? Oh, the door was locked. What's happened?"

"You are not going to believe this...." Autumn started, anticipating Jones retelling the story. And she did, almost word for word, as she'd told Autumn.

"Again!" Atlas said.

"Haha," said Jones. "I'm a little sick of that joke."

Atlas narrowed his eyebrows but didn't seek any sort of clarification. Instead, he handed Jones the flat white he never forgot to deliver and, sitting next to her, began speculating about what may have happened to Lorne.

Jones drank almost half the cup of coffee before she joined Atlas in attempting to guess the reasons behind the apparent murder.

"Maybe he'd just aggravated the killer one too many times," suggested Jones.

"Probably a customer seeing you found him in the warehouse," said Atlas.

"Yes, good point." Jones took another sip of the coffee. She stared up at the ceiling, trying to remember if she'd heard of anyone with a particularly strong grievance against Lorne or Foxglove Nurseries. She couldn't think of anything. "Poor Flick."

"I'll say," said Atlas. "Jones? If you don't mind me asking, why were you at the nursery this morning?"

"Picking out a water feature," she answered. "At least I was meant to be. Who knows when that might happen now."

"What if the garden isn't ready for the Christmas party?" Autumn called out from somewhere in the bookstacks.

"I guess that's the least of my worries," said Jones. "Or at least it should be. It would be the last thing on Flick's mind. I wonder what she's going to do now, without her dad?"

Atlas and Jones sat quietly for a moment, and Autumn remained silent. She, of all people, knew what it was like to lose a father with whom you worked. If only Autumn could speak with Flick and empathise with her. Jones supposed she should talk with Autumn about her experience. She couldn't recall having ever taken the time to understand what that had truly been like for Autumn.

"Jones, I've just remembered something!" Autumn called out.

Jones looked up to see her flying towards her.

Looking to her side, she checked to see what Atlas was doing. Still sipping his coffee, Jones made sure to sit still and wait. He eventually finished his coffee and threw his cup in their recycling bin. "Think I'd better start some work," he said. "Unless you need anything?"

"No, I'm fine, Atlas, thanks. I'm going to see how I feel and will either open up or go home."

Atlas nodded and went into his office, closing the door.

"I heard them!" said Autumn.

"Heard who?" Jones hissed, turning to look at her sister, who was now making a strange midair zig-zag movement.

"Lorne," said Autumn. "And his killer!"

"Seriously? Where? When?"

Jones was confused. Had Autumn been near the nursery that morning? Last night? Why? Yes, Autumn had been venturing out of The Memory Bank by herself more and more, but it would have been a tremendous coincidence if she happened to be outside the Foxglove Nursery at the exact moment a murder was taking place.

"Last night," said Autumn. "When you were with Plum."

"You heard them arguing from Hugo's?"

"I heard Lorne Fox arguing with someone at the back of the Bank."

"The Bank? What *our* Bank?"

"Of course our Bank," said Autumn. "What other Bank is there?"

"Ok, sorry," Jones shook her head. "I'm just trying to understand. Explain. What exactly did you see and hear? And when?"

Autumn floated over to the table and sat down in a chair opposite

Jones. She rested her elbows on the table and clasped her hands together under her chin.

"I didn't see anything. But I did hear something. When I was down by the creek." Autumn closed her eyes, recalling the scene. "It was really quiet. Lovely. I'm planning to spend more time down there."

Jones smiled at her sister and nodded encouragingly.

"And because it was so quiet when I heard the arguing, it startled me," Autumn explained. "I'm *sure* it was Lorne. He's very loud when he's angry. But the other voice," Autumn shook her head. "I'm fairly confident it was female, but I can't be sure."

"Did you take a look?" Jones asked, assuming her sister would have headed directly over to see who was making such a racket.

"Of course, but by the time I got there, Lorne was alone, angrily packing things into his ute. Then he slammed the tailgate shut and flattened it out of there."

"And you think it was his murderer?" said Jones.

"I mean, it makes sense, doesn't it?" Autumn shrugged her shoulders, unable to provide a better answer.

"It does," said Jones. "But if we've learnt anything since the founding of The Eldershaw Detective Agency," Jones raised her eyebrows with a smirk. "It's that what makes sense isn't always the truth."

Autumn nodded her head, her eyes rolling slightly, annoyed at Jones's logic. "Sure, ok. But it *has* to be significant. Should we tell Christopher?"

"How?" asked Jones. "I don't think I'm going to be able to bluff my way through this time."

"True. I guess the whole bar saw you at Hugo's at the same time you'd be claiming you overheard the argument," said Autumn. They both sat and thought.

"Maybe we're going to have to find out who he was fighting with, ourselves," said Jones.

"Like an investigation?" Autumn looked up, a smile on her face.

"Exactly. Like an investigation." Jones couldn't help but return Autumn's smile.

CHAPTER 6

Jones decided she couldn't face opening the shop. She told Atlas to keep the door locked. He needed to concentrate on his work. Lilly Pilly Creek would understand. No doubt everyone already knew that she was with Flick when they found her dad's body.

Jones didn't even go via Sybil's coffee van. She was too drained to hear all the gossip Sybil would share with her. No doubt it would be significant, but that could wait. For now, Jones just wanted to be home, alone.

She curled up in bed with a cup of hot, sugary tea and a packet of TimTams. Jones tried to block the vision of seeing Lorne Fox lying on the cold, hard ground of the warehouse. It was shocking and tragic. More so when remembering the awful cries of his daughter, Flick. You would never wish a daughter to find her father like that.

Jones had brought home with her some of the photo bundles from her grandmother's Memory Box. Some were black and white, tiny, with thick white edges. Others the bubbly and hazy Polaroid photos of the eighties. There were photos of the Eldershaw family in this very house, sitting around a birthday cake or a group of cousins pushed together for a quick snap. Many had half a head chopped off, and Jones recalled the jokes about Granny's photography skills.

What Jones noticed was how many photos there were at Christmas time inside The Memory Bank. Reviewing those photos again, Jones saw that year after year the Christmas Light Competition awards were being presented right there in the Bank.

"This *was* a long-standing tradition," Jones thought. And yet one unconscious lady and stolen jewellery had stopped all that for thirty years. Was it possibly an overreaction? Was it just a good excuse to no longer host the awards, or was there more to it? Jones felt her journalism senses tingle. Was there more to the story than met the eye? And why had no one ever really explained to her what had happened until Plum arrived?

Jones leant back against the bedhead, and with the warm cup of tea clasped in her hands, began to ponder how she might find out what happened. Would the answer be inside her grandmother's lockbox? She felt her weariness dissipate as the intrigue of a long-lost story took over her mind. Perhaps she was getting delirious, but Jones couldn't ignore the quiet but distinct bell ringing in her head. There was more to be learnt about the Christmas Party robbery, and Jones was going to find it. For one, why did they never catch the thief? There would have been a crowd of people at The Memory Bank that night. Was there simply too many for anyone to notice one individual sneaking off with their loot?

She shook her head. This wasn't the mystery she should focus on when she had just discovered a dead body.

"Jones, just because you were there, doesn't mean you need to solve the case," she reminded herself. She pulled another TimTam from the packet and took a large bite of the smooth yet crunchy chocolate biscuit. Of course, she knew herself. Knew she couldn't help but investigate, especially now that Autumn had overheard an argument. That was going to be tough to reveal to the Police without sounding crazy. The fact of the matter was, it would be irresponsible of them to ignore this key piece of information. Jones needed to look into this, somehow, as it may be the break the case needed.

"But how would we even start?" Jones shook her head, finishing her TimTam and taking one last gulp of her tea. The idea made her brain fuzzy, and she realised the shock of the morning was now settling in. Placing the cup on her side table, Jones slid down into her bed, pulled up the covers, and let herself fall asleep.

"Jones! It's just Wren!"

Jones shook her head, confused. Did she hear someone calling? Just when she'd fallen asleep. Laying still, she listened again.

"Jones," the voice called again. "I'm leaving you some dinner in the fridge."

"Wren? Is that you?" Jones called out.

"Yes!"

"Hang on, I'll come down!" As Jones sat up in bed, she looked at the clock and was surprised to see she had slept for the entire afternoon. Shaking her head, Jones found her Ugg boots and made her way to the kitchen where Wren was closing the fridge.

"Gosh, are you ok?"

Jones frowned. Did she look that bad?

"I'm fine. I was just asleep."

"Oh, sorry!"

"It's okay. It seems I've slept the whole afternoon."

Jones pulled up a stool at the breakfast bar and Wren leant against it.

"After what you went through this morning, I'm not surprised. Wine?"

Wren had pulled out a bottle and was holding it up. Jones nodded.

"So you heard?"

"Of course!" laughed Wren, finding the cupboard with Jones's wine glasses. "Everyone's heard. This is Lilly Pilly Creek. I saw Atlas at Hugo's and he told us everything. You poor thing. Anyway, Hugo whipped up some tea for you, and I've just popped it in the fridge."

Jones smiled. Hugo had made her tea. Wren smirked as she poured the wine, but didn't comment.

"The entire bar was talking about it, trying to speculate who might have done in Lorne."

"Done in? That's a bit crude isn't it?"

"Well, it seems the list of suspects is rather long." Wren took a seat next to Jones and took a long sip of her wine before continuing. "Lorne has put a lot of people offside throughout the years. Pretty much no one was surprised he'd been murdered."

"Seriously! They thought he was so disliked that any number of people could be suspected of *killing* him?" Jones took a sip, not taking her eyes off Wren.

"Well, when you say it like that, no. Not really. Most said he drove people bonkers, but he was harmless enough." Wren shrugged. "I think it was just the beers and wine talking, and you know what small towns are like. Everyone trying to work out what's happened."

Jones took another sip. "Gee, this is good. What is it?" She pulled the bottle over to read the label. Haunted Cellar.

Haunted! Seriously? She didn't know why the universe was constantly sending messages about the fact her sister had returned as a ghost. First ghost mushroom hunters and now a haunted winery. She couldn't deny it though. This was some good wine.

"No idea," said Wren. "Hugo recommended it. We know he's got good taste." She couldn't resist a little wink at her friend.

Jones shook her head but appreciated the comment. She wasn't wrong. If this wine was anything to go by, Hugo had excellent taste.

"So, when are you two finally going to get together?"

"Well, now that you mention it." Jones glanced sideways at her friend.

"What!" Wren's eyes went wide. "What's happening? Why didn't you tell me?"

"There was the minor incident of me seeing a dead body this morning," said Jones.

"That is absolutely no excuse!" Wren joked, but took a gulp of wine and leaned in. "Tell me."

"It's all Plum's fault. She forced Hugo to invite me out."

"Forced him. Sure!" Wren laughed.

"Well, he wasn't exactly in a position to refuse."

"Tell me every word."

Jones went over the conversation between Plum and Hugo, Wren listening like her lawyer self, mulling over every phrase.

"So, you're telling me that as soon as Plum mentioned him taking you out, he immediately had a suggestion for what you could do?"

"Ah, I suppose so." Jones shrugged.

"He had *clearly* been thinking of it! Thank goodness for Plum. He just needed a kick up the butt."

"Wren!" Jones shook her head, smiling at her friend as she drank her wine.

"Well, he did," said Wren, pouting. "I'm just annoyed I didn't do it first. But progress is progress. So, what are you going to wear?"

"I have absolutely no idea," said Jones, shaking her head, her smile fading.

Wren swung off the stool, grabbing her glass and the bottle of wine as she did so.

"Well, let's go! Show me your wardrobe!"

Jones laughed and shook her head at her friend, who was now striding down the timber hallway.

If there was one thing for sure, Jones could always rely on her best friend.

CHAPTER 7

"So who exactly did Wren identify as possible suspects?" asked Autumn that evening.

Jones, having slept all day and then eating Hugo's delicious meal of slow-cooked lamb shanks with mashed potato, decided she would visit Autumn. She wanted to take a closer look at their grandmother's journals.

"I don't recall any specific names," said Jones. "Only that he had rubbed a lot of people the wrong way over the years."

"Well, that's not new information. He is a bit of a grump." Autumn tonight wore red tartan pyjamas and reindeer slippers. She was giving off a snowy white Christmas vibe usually not seen in Australia.

"Yes," said Jones. "A grump who is fortunately very good at designing gardens."

"Or his daughter is," said Autumn. "I bet it's Flick that's the brains behind the operation."

Jones lugged her grandmother's lockbox out and placed it on The Memory Bank's counter.

"Let's go out into the garden!" said Autumn.

Jones looked through the glass garden doors and saw a beautiful sight. The sun was setting, throwing pinks and purples across the pavers. Jones smiled, and leaving the lockbox, went to unlock the doors. Autumn floated through the glass as Jones pushed the door open before returning for the lockbox.

Jones flicked a switch near the doors, and strings of lights burst to life. It looked like a fairy garden. Setting the lockbox down on one of the new outdoor tables, Jones sat with a pleased sigh.

"This is just lovely out here," said Jones. "I'm so glad we went to all this effort."

"Not much effort on my part," said Autumn. "Although I can't deny it, I have some pretty great ideas."

Typical Autumn, never one to shy away from patting herself on the back. But she was right. Much of the design out here came from Autumn's creative brain. Unfortunately, Jones had to take the credit gracefully in front of Flick and Lorne, but the sisters knew the truth.

With the sounds of crickets and frogs surrounding them, and a few cockatoos finding the best perch for the night, Jones clicked open the lockbox.

"What exactly are we searching for?" asked Autumn, twirling gently amongst the plants.

"I thought I would search for an entry about The Christmas Party," said Jones. "The *last* Christmas Party."

"Oh, good idea," said Autumn. "Seems a popular topic. And considering it was the reason they cancelled the whole thing, it would be a good idea for the hosts of this year's party to know what went on."

"I was thinking the same thing," said Jones. "It seems strange that only Plum gave us a hint of what actually happened."

"Let's dive in," said Autumn. "It will distract us from the latest town drama."

Jones reached into the box and pulled out the pile of journals. On the front cover of each was a year in gold lettering. "So, exactly thirty years ago would be……this one!" Jones pulled out a maroon diary and turned the pages to December.

"Look at this!" said Jones, pointing to a page. In capital letters, their grandmother had written 'THE LIGHTS HAVE BEEN STOLEN!'

"The lights?" Said Autumn. "I didn't know someone stole decorations." I thought it was jewellery?"

"Let me read," said Jones.

"The lights have been stolen. Someone came into the lockbox room and stole *my* lockbox. The one with all my jewellery, including the Lights. I was stupid to have left them here. I thought of all places, they'd be safer here than at home. My mother's brooch, some of her rings and a few other pieces were stolen too. But I can't believe my opal earrings are gone. The earrings Bax gave me on our first Christmas."

"The lights were earrings?"

"Must be," said Jones. "I wonder why she called them the Lights?"

Autumn frowned. "Maybe because they were opals. The gorgeous rainbow colours, I guess it almost looks as though they're lit up."

Jones nodded and continued reading. "They found Molly Shepherd in the room. The thief had bopped her on the head so she doesn't remember anything. She's not even sure why she was there in the first place. And it was so busy at the Christmas party no one saw anything. Well, people saw a lot of things, but I guess too much champagne flowing meant they didn't remember anything useful. I just can't believe someone from Lilly Pilly Creek is so brazen to walk into our Bank and steal from us! It seems they managed to get into the safe with all the keys, and knew exactly which one to grab. Probably me prattling on as usual and giving away the number. I'm so angry with myself." Jones glanced up at her sister before she read the next line. "And I'm haunted by the fact that our precious Memory Bank no longer feels safe. I don't think I'm ever going to trust anyone in this town again. At least, not until I find out who did it."

"But they never did," said Autumn sadly.

"Sounds like Granny was a bit of a detective, too," said Jones.

"Do you think she made notes in her journals?"

Jones had the same thought and was turning through the next pages to see what she could find.

"Colin Fletcher! Granny thought Colin had stolen them."

"Really? The same guy on the Progress Association Committee with you?"

"The very one," said Jones. "And now that I think about it, he had quite a bit to say last night."

"He did?" said Autumn. "Like what?"

"Mostly that Molly Shepherd wasn't the same afterwards. But…."

"What? What is it?"

Jones shook her head. "Oh, probably nothing. It's just-"

"What!"

"Well, Rex said something like 'you should know' when they were talking about Molly. I don't know. It almost seemed like Granny wasn't the only one who thought Colin did it."

Autumn's mouth was wide open. "Maybe Granny was a detective

after all!"

"But if he did do it, why was he never caught? Never charged?"

"Does Granny say anything else?" asked Autumn, nodding her head towards the journal.

"Not much that I can see. I might have to take the next year's one home as well and read it." Jones rifled through the pile, identifying the correct diary.

"I wonder if anything was in the newspapers?" suggested Autumn.

"Oh yes, that's a good idea," said Jones. "Maybe the Library has an archive of the Lilly Pilly Creek Chronicles."

"Did there used to be a town newspaper?"

"Yep! I did a project on it at University. I think I interviewed the last editor. Now, who was that again?" Jones closed her eyes, trying to think. "I have no recollection. Hopefully, I can find my old report on my computer somewhere."

"You know who'd remember," said Autumn. "Sybil."

"Of course! I'll ask her first thing."

CHAPTER 8

Jones never needed an excuse to head to Sybil's coffee van each morning. However, today she was moving at a brisk walk, anxious to identify the editor of The Lilly Pilly Creek Chronicle. And of course, no doubt Sybil would have some inside word on Lorne Fox. She was likely bursting to speak with Jones as well.

Jones could feel in the air that it was going to be a hot one. The cool Adelaide Hills air was already dissipating just after eight. Jones felt the hint of sweat on her back as she walked. She wore pale pink linen shorts, and a navy singlet that said "No space of regret can make amends for one life's opportunity misused!" - A Christmas Carol

Despite the previous day's trauma, Jones felt surprisingly light on her feet. She had a mission. Find the editor of the old Lilly Pilly Creek Chronicle. Jones recognised that the journalism blood ran deep and the thrill of hunting a story would never leave her. She was pleased to see Sybil once again parked outside the future-planned cheesery.

"Morning Sybil," Jones called. Sybil's head shot up from the jug of milk she was steaming and her eyes went wide.

"Jones!" she called out, apparently oblivious to the gaggle of customers she was shouting over. "Are you ok?"

Jones walked up close to the van. "I'm fine Sybil, I'm perfectly fine."

"I'll chat in a minute. Cappuccino two sugars!" Sybil called. An old man with a walking stick stuck his hand out to grab it and thanked Sybil with a nod before shuffling off.

Two men in their cycling lycra were up next, and then a woman wearing painting overalls. Finally, it was Jones's turn and as Sybil prepared her usual flat white, Jones filled her in.

"Well, you know what they're saying," Sybil said, leaning over the counter.

"No, I have no idea," said Jones.

"It was one of his ex-wives," she said, swirling the milk jug over Jones's coffee cup.

"One of them! How many does he have?"

"Two," said Sybil. "And both marriages ended very badly."

"How recent was the second one?"

"Oh, maybe three years," said Sybil. "But it could be either of them. I think he owes both of them money, and it's like pulling teeth. Plus, he's just a pain-in-the-butt human being overall. I've never really liked the guy."

"But do you think one of them disliked him so much they would have killed him?" Jones took her coffee from Sybil.

"Honestly, if I were married to him, I'd be surprised that I hadn't already killed him," Sybil said as she crossed her arms and leaned back on her rear counter.

"Sybil!" Jones was shocked.

"Jones, you didn't know him. He was one of those chauvinists who thought he knew everything."

"He seemed to get on with his daughter Flick, though?" Jones said.

"Perhaps," Sybil shrugged. She didn't look convinced.

Jones turned to walk away and then remembered she had

something to ask Sybil.

"Do you remember who the last editor of The Lilly Pilly Creek Chronicle was?"

"Of course!" said Sybil. "It was Dorothy Riley. She's still alive, you know."

"That's good," said Jones. "I was hoping to speak with her."

"She's in the nursing home now," said Sybil. "Up near the medical centre. Finds it hard to get around these days, but she's still got all her marbles. She's a fascinating woman to talk with."

"Thanks, as always!"

As Jones walked away from the coffee van, she had thoughts racing through her mind. Had Lorne Fox been such an awful husband, that even after divorcing him, one of his wives still hated him enough to resort to whacking him over the head? Sipping her coffee, Jones shuddered, thinking how bad it must have been to live with him. If she and Autumn were going to investigate, she would have to question a wider pool of people. However, Jones couldn't deny the idea that one of the wives was the culprit fit in with Autumn overhearing Lorne fighting with a female.

As Jones walked in the direction of Hugo's she was pleasantly surprised to see the man himself leaning against the front windows.

"Hi!" he smiled. "You've been to Sybil's, I see."

"Don't I always," Jones smiled, lifting her coffee cup.

"Well, it is the best coffee in town."

Jones smiled and had another sip, not taking her eyes off him.

"I was hoping I'd catch you," said Hugo. "I wanted to check if you're still up for joining me at the wine tasting tonight?"

Jones smiled, recalling Plum's scheming. "Of course!"

Hugo grinned and put his hands in his pockets. "Excellent. We need to be there by seven, so did you want me to pick you up about six thirty?"

"Yes, that sounds great," said Jones. "Where exactly are we going?"

"Oh yeah," he smiled. "We're going to Haunted Cellars."

"Really?" She felt her heartbeat quicken just a little at the word haunted.

"Do you know it?"

"No," Jones shook her head, trying to play down her surprise. "It makes sense, seeing as that was the wine Wren brought over last night. It was delicious, by the way."

"Just wait 'til you try the good stuff!" Hugo nodded his head as he thought about it.

"I can't wait," said Jones. "And six thirty works well. From my house?"

"Absolutely! I'll see you then."

They had yet to perfect their goodbyes, especially as it usually happened when Hugo was standing behind his bar. Jones just waved, lifted her coffee cup again, and continued on. The spring in her step intensified. Finally, she was going on a date with Hugo.

"What is up with you?" Autumn asked as Jones walked into The Memory Bank and made her way to the counter.

"What?" Jones didn't make eye contact with Autumn, instead

draining her coffee cup and bending deliberately slowly and deeply to put the cup in the bin.

"Seriously? Are you ok? Are you in shock from yesterday?"

"I'm ok," Jones casually turned away. "I just ran into Hugo outside."

"Ah ha!" Autumn clapped and spun up towards the ceiling. "That explains it!"

Jones shook her head as she watched her sister flip and spin in the air, smiling at her antics. It was nice to see her so happy.

"Yes, but also, you'll never guess where we're going." Jones said.

"Where? Tell me!" Autumn whizzed down to face Jones.

"A winery called Haunted Cellars."

Autumn shrieked a little. "Seriously!"

"I'm dead serious," said Jones. "Sorry, I mean, yes, I'm serious. It is called Haunted Cellars. Wren brought over a bottle of their wine last night and it was delicious."

"Well, sounds like fun. I'm sure it means absolutely nothing."

"But can you imagine if it *was* haunted?" asked Jones.

"Just because you can see *me*, doesn't mean you can see all ghosts," Autumn winked and slowly floated upwards. "Or that there are even other ghosts to see. I could simply be a figment of your imagination."

"Do you really think that?" Jones frowned, confused by her sister's comment.

Autumn smiled. "No, I do not. But I wouldn't let the quirky name of a winery bewilder you. Go out and have fun!"

"You're right," Jones nodded. "Now, on to more important things."

"What could be more important?" Autumn whooshed down.

Jones tilted her head. She could have sworn she felt a little breeze as Autumn landed.

"What?" her sister asked.

"Nothing." Jones looked perplexed. "Only, I thought I felt you just then."

"Felt me?"

"Yes, when you moved past me. Or the air moved past me. But I'm sure it was just my imagination."

Autumn stared at Jones and then at the space around her body. "Perhaps." She didn't move for a moment, pondering what Jones had said, then shook her head. "So, what were you going to tell me? What is so important?"

"Right, well, the word on the street-"

"So Sybil's coffee van," Autumn chuckled.

Jones laughed. "Of course. Sybil says most people believe it was one of Lorne's ex-wives who killed him."

"Wives? Plural?"

"That's exactly what I said. Sybil tells me Lorne has been married twice. The last one ended about three years ago. I'm guessing the first one was Flick's mum."

"I think I know Flick's mum. Well, knew her," said Autumn.

"You do?" said Jones.

"I'll try to remember, but I think there was a lady who used to come into The Memory Bank that was probably her. I just don't remember her name. She wouldn't have been using the surname Fox at that time, I'm sure."

Jones took a seat behind the counter and rested her chin on her hands.

Autumn floated as though lying on a sunbed and travelled throughout The Memory Bank.

They heard keys rattle in the door and turned their heads.

"Morning!" a familiar voice called.

"Hi, Atlas!" Jones responded.

Atlas strode in bearing coffees as always, but this time there was something wedged between the two paper cups.

Although she'd only just finished her cup, Jones gratefully took the second flat white and began sipping.

"This was on the doorstep," he said, handing Jones an envelope. Written across the front in all capitals was one word.

JONES.

CHAPTER 9

The envelope was pale blue and had been hand-delivered, as it was without a stamp or any other mark. Jones tore it open.

Autumn was hovering behind, reading over her shoulder.

I wish to implore you to reconsider holding the Christmas Lights Party at The Memory Bank. The tragedy of the last Christmas Lights Party should not be forgotten, nor made light of, and I think it very disrespectful to consider the resumption of the Party at the same venue. Jones Eldershaw, in memory of your parents and grandparents, please, move the party.

"It's not signed!" said Autumn.

Jones handed it to Atlas to read. He wouldn't know that this was the second such letter, the first read out at The Progress Association committee meeting. Jones explained this to Atlas and why she thought this letter was also written by the same person. Molly Shepherd.

"Tragedy?" Atlas asked. "What does she mean?"

"Oh, don't you know?" said Jones.

"Know what?" Atlas sat on a stool next to Jones, his face an expression of panic.

"The thing is, the last time the Christmas Lights competition was held, at the Awards party, Molly Shepherd was attacked and found unconscious in the lockbox room."

"What!" Atlas clearly couldn't believe what Jones was saying.

Jones nodded. "Yes, it was the reason they cancelled the lights competition the following year. And it just never resumed."

"And so you think Molly Shepherd is the one who has written

this?"

"I do," said Jones. "Although, it might be worth checking with Prue to see if the handwriting or paper or anything matches. It would be unlikely to be anyone else, but I guess you never know."

"True," said Atlas. "But it is disappointing for people to be so unsupportive."

"I can understand, I guess," said Jones. "It would bring back some awful memories."

"Yes," said Atlas. "Maybe a bit of a slap in the face to her. I mean, most of the town has probably forgotten about it or didn't know about it at all. But I imagine it doesn't feel like thirty years ago to Molly."

Atlas was right. Being violently struck and in hospital for weeks afterwards was something you didn't just get over. Ever. Jones realised it was important for her to talk to Molly, and listen to her. Maybe after hearing what she had to say, Jones might realise Molly was right. Perhaps they shouldn't be holding the party in The Memory Bank after all.

However, Jones thought that before she met with Molly, she'd like to get as much information as possible. And Jones realised that Dorothy Riley, the immediate past editor of The Lilly Pilly Creek Chronicle, was the woman to help her.

Jones signalled Autumn to meet her in the stacks.

"I'm going to visit Dorothy Riley at lunchtime," she whispered.

"Who?" Autumn looked utterly confused.

"Dorothy Riley," explained Jones. "The editor of The Lilly Pilly Creek Chronicle. Well, the last editor. Sybil reminded me. She was the one who helped me with my project. I'm hoping she knows where the archives might be now. Do you want to come?"

Autumn beamed. "Absolutely!"

"What do you think? About Molly's letter?"

"I think she has a lot of nerve!" Autumn's face was furious. "Why didn't she just come and speak to you herself?"

"I suppose she doesn't want to come to The Memory Bank. I wonder if she's ever returned?"

"Well, a phone call then," said Autumn. "It's not that hard."

"Maybe it's hard for her," said Jones.

"You are being very understanding," said Autumn. "For someone whose Christmas Lights Awards Party is under threat."

Jones scoffed a little. "Let's not get too dramatic, Autumn. I mean, yesterday I saw a dead body. Losing the Christmas Party isn't a big deal."

"Well, it might not be to you!" Autumn burst out before shooting through the stacks and away.

Jones's mouth gaped. What was that all about? She almost called out Autumn's name but clamped her hand over her mouth at the last minute. What would Atlas have thought? Her ears pricked, and she realised they also had customers. There was nothing for it. She would have to speak to Autumn later about what had made her so upset. For now, Jones needed to take off her deerstalker and put on her shop owner hat.

Moving into the main area of The Memory Bank, it pleased Jones to see Plum.

"There you are!" she cried, spotting Jones from across the room. Plum looked as striking as ever. Today she wore a full purple skirt with a white short-sleeved blouse, and a small geometric purple and green scarf tied at her neck.

"Plum!" said Jones. "How has it been at Neha's?"

"Lovely!" said Plum. "Neha's husband Rakesh is an amazing cook. Last night we ate curry in the garden and drank a few too many bottles of wine."

"That sounds lovely," said Jones.

"But Jones, how are you?" asked Plum. " I came to the Bank yesterday, but it was closed. I didn't want to disturb you at home. Is it true? You were there when they found Lorne?"

"Yes, just me and Flick," she said.

"That must have been awful," Plum put her arm around Jones. "Are you sure you should be back at work?"

"Yes," said Jones. "I'm ok, really. But look at this." She handed Plum the letter.

"The nerve!" Plum said when she'd finished. "Some people just won't let anything go."

"I'm wondering if it might be from Molly Shepherd. She wrote a letter to the Progress Association as well."

"She did?" Plum looked up, surprised.

"Yes, it was read out at the committee meeting on Monday night."

"I wouldn't have thought she would be so vicious as to demand the party be cancelled," said Plum. "She always seemed like someone who just got on with life."

Jones shrugged. "Who knows? But I'm thinking I need to talk to her in person. Do you know where exactly she lives?"

"She has a farm on the other side of Lilly Pilly Creek. She breeds Alpacas."

"Alplacas? Really?"

"Oh yes," said Plum. "Alpacas are all over the Adelaide Hills now, but Molly was one of the first to have them. I don't know much, but I think she's quite good at it."

"Thanks," said Jones. "So what are you up to today? Or are you leaving?"

"No, I'm going to stay until the Christmas Party. Neha is insisting and now, well after what you've told me, I think I should. You know to reach out if you need any help."

"Of course Plum," said Jones. "But don't worry. You just enjoy your mini break in Lilly Pilly Creek. Go wine tasting or something!"

"Speaking of wine tasting," said Plum, her eyes twinkling. "Is tonight the big night?"

"It sure is!" called Autumn from across the room.

Jones frowned for a moment. She could have sworn she saw Plum's head move, almost as though she'd heard Autumn. Jones would need to talk with her sister. Perhaps she was getting some powers neither of them had noticed.

She looked back up at Plum. What had she asked? Oh yes. Jones's smile returned.

"Yes, I'm going out with Hugo tonight," said Jones.

"Wonderful!" Plum beamed. "That's lovely. Now, I'm going to visit one of my friends in Birdwood and I need a housewarming gift for them. What do you suggest?"

Jones toured Plum around the tables of gifts in The Memory Bank. She showed her the candles, journals, and the new pottery items recently added to the collection, made by a local artist. Plum settled on a book on the history of the Adelaide Hills's first settlers, and two coffee mugs for the husband and wife.

"These are perfect Jones!" said Plum, as Jones handed them to her in one of The Memory Bank's calico bags after carefully wrapping the mugs in tissue paper.

"Thank you!" said Jones.

As Plum walked out, Wren walked in.

CHAPTER 10

"Now, I should not be telling you this," said Wren as she hustled Jones to a quiet corner. Autumn was hovering near them, listening to every word. "I've just seen Rex Keegan at the police station."

"Rex?" asked Jones. "What was he doing there?"

"Constable Partridge was taking his statement."

"His statement?"

"Yes." Wren was nodding and raising her eyebrows, trying to ensure Jones understood. "His…statement…"

Jones furrowed her brows, desperately trying to understand.

"For Lorne's murder!" an exasperated Autumn said.

"What!" said Jones. "You mean they think Rex could be responsible for Lorne's death? Why?"

"I'm not entirely sure. I just thought maybe *someone* should keep their ear to the ground." Wren winked.

Jones nodded slowly, showing she understood.

"Anyway," said Wren. "I'd better get back to my office and do some work."

"I'll follow you out," said Jones. "I'm going to visit Dorothy Riley. I'll just let Atlas know."

Atlas was happy to sit behind the counter and assist customers. "Thanks, Atlas," said Jones. "I'm not sure how long I'll be."

"All good," said Atlas.

Jones grabbed her handbag and, with Autumn by her side, made her way out of The Memory Bank.

"Are you ok Autumn?" Jones asked her when they were by themselves. She hadn't forgotten Autumn's anger earlier.

Autumn waved her sister away. "Yes, I'm sorry," she said. "I'm just looking forward to the party. You know I need things to come to me."

"Of course," said Jones. She felt silly to not have understood. "And if we moved the party, you'd miss out on all the fun."

Autumn smiled and nodded before changing the subject.

"Do you think you should call Dorothy first?" Autumn asked as she floated next to Jones.

"I thought it might be best to just arrive in person," said Jones. I mean, what if she's hard of hearing or something? That might just confuse her more."

But Dorothy Riley was most certainly not hard of hearing. If it wasn't for the wheelchair with a canister of oxygen attached to it, you would have wondered why Dorothy was in a nursing home at all.

After one of the staff members informed Dorothy of her presence, Jones, accompanied by Autumn floating next to her, was escorted down to Dorothy's room. Despite hospital-grade laminate floors and an adjustable bed, Dorothy had made the room feel homey. Lots of photos were on the walls, fresh flowers in a vase, and a small bookshelf bursting at the seams. There was even a framed picture of Dorothy on the front page of The Lilly Pilly Creek Chronicle upon her retirement. And the closure of the newspaper.

"So lovely to have a visitor," said Dorothy. "And someone who's still out and about in the world. It's nice to see you again, Jones. How many years ago was it that you interviewed me?

"Gosh Dorothy, I think maybe ten years ago or so. I can't remember." Jones thought back to her younger self at university, arriving to conduct her interview. Dorothy had lived in a big house on the hill back in those days. Paddocks surrounded it and her son had been out baling hay the day she had visited. Jones presumed her son and his family now lived in the gorgeous old house. At least she hoped it remained in the family.

"How *did* you go with that assignment?" Dorothy asked, filling her kettle from the small sink in her room.

"Very well, from what I can remember," said Jones. "It's a long time ago!"

"And yet I imagine you are here today to pick my brain. What if I can't remember what *you* want to know?" Jones looked up at Dorothy and was relieved the see the older woman was smiling. Autumn giggled. Dorothy Riley had a cheeky streak, it seemed.

"I'm sure your memory is a lot better than mine!" Jones retorted as the kettle bubbled and fizzed before finally clicking off. Dorothy began to prepare the cups of tea.

"I like to think if it's up here," she said, tapping the side of her head. "I'll find it when I need it."

Jones nodded and accepted the offer of milk and sugar.

As they sipped, Dorothy talked about the people in the photos around the room, sharing stories about her family and friends. "Thankfully, many of my friends are still alive and well enough to come and visit. When you're the editor of a newspaper, fortunately, you make friends of all ages throughout the years."

"Do you miss it? Being an editor?" asked Jones, finishing the last of her tea and standing to put it in the sink.

"Yes," said Dorothy. "I do actually. But unfortunately, that was taken out of my hands."

"Why did they close the paper?"

"Money," said Dorothy. "Isn't it always? I did my best, but the internet came along and small newspapers just weren't as relevant anymore. At least, that's what they told me. But I still wonder how much we've lost by not sharing all the local stories."

Jones paused and thought about this. She was right. The local stories didn't get published in the bigger papers, even the bigger regional papers. There was so much that wasn't recorded anymore, because the small newspapers no longer existed. Dorothy had a point. It was sad to have lost such an important part of the town's history.

"Dorothy," said Jones. "Do you know where the archive of the newspapers is? Did they ever get digitised? Or the hard copies kept?"

"No, they never got digitised as far as I know," said Dorothy. "But don't *you* know where the papers are?"

Jones was confused. Why would *she* know where the papers were?

"What do you mean?"

"Well, all the old newspapers, spanning back nearly a hundred years," Dorothy adjusted herself slightly in her wheelchair. "They're in The Memory Bank."

"They are?" asked Autumn, who had been sitting on Dorothy's bed, listening to everything.

"You're telling me all the original copies are at The Memory

Bank?" asked Jones.

"Yes dear," said Dorothy. "Didn't you know?"

Jones shook her head. "I had no idea."

"I suppose that makes sense," said Dorothy. "With your dad gone and Autumn passing so suddenly, who was there to tell you?"

"But why haven't I come across them? Where are they?"

Dorothy smiled and sipped her tea.

"They're in the secret room, dear," the woman said.

"How does she know about that?" Autumn burst out.

"Have you discovered the secret room yet?" Dorothy asked.

"Yes, I have," said Jones. "But how do *you* know about the secret room?"

"Ah, well, that, my dear is, a secret." Dorothy smiled and sipped her tea.

"That Dorothy Riley is a sneaky character," said Autumn as they floated back to The Memory Bank. Jones was in a hurry until she realised they weren't going to be able to hunt for the newspapers until the Bank was closed and they were alone. It was a secret room, after all. Or, as Autumn liked to call it, her escape room. They didn't want anyone else to know about it.

"She is indeed," said Jones. "But in the best possible way, I think."

"I wonder what else she knows?"

"I can only imagine," said Jones. "But it seems you have to know the right questions to ask before she'll reveal anything."

"Spoken like one journalist to another, I would say," said Autumn, sliding through the front door before Jones had a chance to pull it open.

"Now we just have to wait until closing time to check out these newspapers," said Jones.

"You may need to wait," said Autumn. "But I'm headed to the escape room."

And with a grin, Autumn slipped through the wall.

CHAPTER 11

Jones was miffed, of course. Autumn was going to be able to discover the location of the newspapers before she could. However, she appeased herself with the knowledge that Autumn may be able to *see* them, but she couldn't touch them until Jones got there.

In the meantime, when there was a lull between customers, Jones decided it was finally time to phone Molly Shepherd.

"Jones Eldershaw? From The Memory Bank?" Molly asked when Jones introduced herself.

"Yes. How are you, Molly?" Jones felt very awkward and had to admit she was glad to be having this first conversation over the phone. She was very apprehensive about how Molly would react to being contacted.

"Well, I suppose I'm ok. I presume you received my letter?"

"Well actually," said Jones. "I've received two?"

"Two? What are you talking about?"

Jones was surprised. She had just assumed the unsigned letter was also from Molly.

"I only sent one letter to The Progress Association," said Molly. "If you've received two letters, then it's not from me."

"I must be mistaken," said Jones. "I was wondering if I could come and visit you, and talk through your concerns. Would that be ok?"

"You'll come out to the farm?"

"Sure, if that's okay with you? I thought I might pop over tomorrow morning?"

"Fine by me, but I'm putting the hay out first thing."

"Perfect," said Jones. "Can you text me your address?"

"I'll send you directions, as I'll be in the Wattle Flat paddock tomorrow."

"Thanks, Molly, I look forward to seeing you then."

Molly grunted in response and hung up.

Jones walked over to Atlas, who was still at the counter, ringing up a man who had bought a selection of the local history books.

"I'm trying to work out where my great-grandfather built his first house," the man was explaining to Atlas. "There's no local history group here, is there?"

Atlas looked across at Jones, who shook her head. "No, I don't think there is," said Jones. "That is surprising actually."

"Well, you know what you should do then," said the man with a wink as he left.

Did he mean Jones should start up a local history group? It wasn't a bad idea, but Jones still struggled with the idea of creating something that may cement her Lilly Pilly Creek. She still had her job waiting for her at The Advertiser newspaper back in the city. Jones hadn't given that up yet, not knowing how long Autumn would be around. She worried she may not have the same allegiance to The Memory Bank if and when Autumn was no longer a fixture. Did she love The Memory Bank or was it just the fact that she was there with her sister? As it appeared to be the only place Autumn could remain for long periods, Jones simply could not leave. She had no choice but to stay. However, if that all changed, where would Jones's heart lead her? Lilly Pilly

Creek or back to Adelaide?

"Nothing like adding more to your list of things to do," Atlas said once they were alone at the counter.

Jones laughed. "Exactly what I was thinking! Although it is a good idea. I wonder why we don't have a local history group. Surely there used to be one?"

"Meanwhile, is there anything you need me to help with for The Christmas Party?"

"What day is it? Wednesday?" Jones felt the week was getting away from her.

"Yep," said Atlas. "Three days to go."

"The main thing is, are we going to have to finish up the garden for Flick?" said Jones. "Shall we go out there and see what was left to do?"

Atlas and Jones headed out into the garden. The warmth hit them as soon as they opened the doors, but it was a lot cooler than the temperature on the street. It was amazing how cooling a garden was. Jones walked around to the last place Flick had been, the herb garden.

"Looks like there's still a few pots to plant," said Atlas. "I could do that."

"That would be great Atlas," said Jones. "And I'm going to assume we won't be getting the water feature this week. Maybe we can perhaps leave a few plants in pots in that area for now?"

"Good idea," said Atlas.

"What I do keep thinking about is, are any old decorations stored here? It would be nice if I could discover some of the decorations my parents and grandparents used."

"That would be brilliant," said Atlas. "The perfect link to the past."

"Hello!" They heard a male voice calling from inside The Memory Bank.

"I'll go," said Jones, leaving Atlas to assess the planting.

"Christopher!" said Jones. "Hi!"

"Hi Jones," said the local Police Sergeant. "I'm here in an official capacity, I'm afraid."

Jones nodded. "How can I help?"

Christopher glanced around to see who else was in the Bank.

"Atlas is in the garden, but otherwise we're quiet," said Jones. Except she knew that wasn't the truth. As she spoke, Autumn emerged from the escape room and hovered next to Christopher.

"What I wanted to know is when Lorne and Flick were working here, did you notice anything unusual?"

"Do you mean between the two of them?"

"Yes, it could be, or anything else?"

Autumn nodded her head at her sister. Jones knew exactly what Autumn wanted her to tell him.

Jones looked to the ceiling, thinking. How was she going to phrase this?

"There wasn't much I noticed, at least not between Flick and her dad. I do think at one time I overheard Lorne arguing with someone, a female. But I couldn't tell you who it was. I didn't see them and I couldn't make out the other voice except to tell you it did sound female."

"Nice one," said Autumn.

Jones was just hoping Christopher didn't ask too many questions.

"When was this?"

"I'm pretty sure it was the night before Lorne died," said Jones.

Christopher took notes. "And what time?"

Jones felt her chest tighten. What on earth was she going to say?

"Gosh, now you're testing me. It was after we were closed, but I'm not sure."

Christopher nodded. "But before The Progress Association committee meeting?"

Of course, Christopher knew she'd been there. "Yes, it was. And I had a drink at Hugo's just before that. So it was probably just as I was about to leave to go to Hugo's, but I can't for the life of me remember what time that was."

"Who were you with?"

"When I heard the argument?"

"Well yes, that, and when you were at Hugo's."

"Oh, well, I was by myself when I heard the argument and with Plum Stephens at Hugo's."

Jones was pleased this slightly inaccurate version of events was sliding off her tongue with ease.

"Plum?"

"My mum's friend. She's my godmother. She's come back for the week."

"And would anyone remember seeing you at Hugo's?"

"Oh well, Hugo I suppose. He served us. But I don't recall talking to anyone else."

Christopher nodded. Not an ounce of expression showed on his face. The police training coming to the fore.

"And was there anything else I should know? Did anything happen at The Progress Association?"

"Nothing I would think was related to Lorne's death." Jones felt comfortable now that they were moving into the portion of the timeline where she didn't need to fudge her responses.

"But something of note happened?"

"The main thing was we received a few letters of complaint. About the Christmas Lights."

"Oh really? Who were they from?"

"One was anonymous and one was from Molly Shepherd," Jones said. She couldn't think how this would relate to Christopher's murder investigation, but I guess he couldn't leave any stone unturned.

"Molly Shepherd," said Christopher, taking notes. "And was there anything else? Was everyone at the meeting? Anyone missing?"

"No, no one missing," said Jones. "Flick was running late like I mentioned. Otherwise, everyone was there and perfectly normal."

"And how late was Flick?"

"Not too late," said Jones. "But she definitely arrived after the start of the meeting. I imagine it was recorded in the minutes if you need to check?"

"I will," said Christopher, matter-of-factly. This surprised Jones, but also got her thinking. Flick. Was she someone they should be considering as a suspect? She glanced at Autumn, willing her to make a note of this information so they could discuss it later.

"Did she say why she was late?"

"Not that I can remember," said Jones. She found herself frantically recalling Flick's arrival. She did seem a little flustered. It had never crossed Jones's mind to think this had something to do with her father's death. And why would it? The way Flick was when she saw her dad's lifeless body on the floor. There's no way she could have had anything to do with it. Could she?

"Ok, and do you remember what time the meeting closed?" asked Christopher.

"No, sorry," said Jones. "It wasn't very long. Maybe eight. You could ask Tara, though. Tara Galati. She took the minutes."

"Yes, I have arranged to speak with her," he said. "And how about Rex? How did he appear?"

"Rex? He seemed perfectly normal. Why?"

Cogs were whirring in Jones's brain. She realised she had completely overlooked the idea that Flick or Rex, or anyone else at the Progress Association Meeting, for that matter, could have had anything to do with Lorne's death. Wren had mentioned Rex had been questioned, but was that really because he could be a suspect?

"Oh nothing," said Christopher. "We're just investigating anyone that was associated with Lorne in the weeks before his death."

"And Rex was associated with him?

"Lorne had been helping him with some of the setting up of the Christmas lights and decorations down the Main Street," said Christopher. "And they worked together fairly regularly on gardening projects. Not that I should be talking about this with you." Christopher raised his eyebrows and showed a hint of a smile. Maybe he wasn't as good at remaining professional as she'd thought.

It was nice to have Christopher as a friend. Although Autumn and Wren did like to hint at Christopher being interested in being more than just friends, Jones ignored them. She was interested in Hugo, and Christopher would know that. But it didn't hurt to have another friend in Lilly Pilly Creek, and his being a police sergeant was certainly a bonus. At least it had been over the past few months.

"Do you think you're any closer to working this out?" Jones thought she might test the waters to see how much Christopher would divulge.

"We've certainly got a few leads we're investigating," said Christopher. "I will say, there are probably a few more leads than normal to work through." He didn't raise his head from his notebook, but Jones did notice him pause for a moment. It seemed he was trying to share something with her without being too unprofessional.

"Poor Lorne," said Jones. "No one deserves to die like that."

"They certainly do not," said Christopher. "No matter how this town feels about him."

"What does that mean?" Autumn piped up.

"Well, I'd better continue on my way. I've still got quite a few people to talk to." Christopher nodded goodbye and made his way out.

"What was all that about?" asked Autumn at full volume. Fortunately, Atlas was still outside in the garden, so Jones felt she could talk normally.

"It seems pretty clear that Rex and Flick are at the top of the suspects' list!" said Jones. "Flick! Can you believe that?"

"It's very surprising," said Autumn. "I can't possibly imagine Flick could kill her father. But Rex Keegan, well, who knows?"

"I'm flabbergasted that Christopher asked about Flick, but I guess she is one of the closest people to him. They work together and she's his daughter. But honestly." Jones just shook her head in disbelief.

"It *was* a woman's voice I heard when they were arguing, remember," said Autumn.

"But Flick? Really?"

"I have no idea," said Autumn. "It could have been. I wasn't close enough to see or hear properly."

"The thought just makes me feel sick," said Jones. "But she was there. She was the one who found him. She couldn't fake the reaction I saw, could she?"

"How exactly did she react?" asked Autumn.

"It was awful," said Jones. "The noise she made. It was gut-wrenching. Harrowing. If she killed him, well, she gave an Oscar-worthy performance."

"Let's for a moment assume she is the killer," said Autumn. "Why would she invite you to the nursery to choose the water feature? Knowing her father was lying dead in a pool of his own blood?"

"That just doesn't seem plausible."

"Or does it?" said Autumn, floating down right in front of Jones. "It could be a perfect plan. Ensuring someone was on site when she discovered the body. Pointing the police away from her deliberately."

Jones gasped. "You're right!" The logic of what Autumn was saying struck her. If you had killed someone, the best way to point the police to someone else, would be to discover the body, with a witness. Jones's mind began to race.

Was Flick a killer?

CHAPTER 12

As Jones went through the remainder of the day, serving customers and working behind the counter, she couldn't stop thinking about Flick. Unfortunately, the more and more Jones considered the possibility that she was the culprit, the more it made sense. Flick had access to the nursery, she could lock the front door, and Autumn was convinced that Lorne was arguing with a woman. The only thing Jones was questioning was why Flick was so surprised the roller door to the warehouse was unlocked. Was it because she thought she had locked it? Or was it genuine?

Autumn was floating around The Memory Bank throwing ideas around throughout the afternoon.

"It sounds like not a lot of people liked Lorne," said Autumn. "So I imagine working with a father like that may not have been very enjoyable."

Jones nodded as she rang up a customer who had asked her to gift wrap a bundle of art supplies for her nephew's birthday.

"But what made her snap this week?" Autumn asked. "Enough to whack him over the head?"

Under her breath, Jones said, "And what weapon did she use? Where is it now?"

"Well, that's something we need to find out," said Autumn. "I think that will be a big clue. Was it something they brought with them, or was it something they grabbed in a fit of rage?"

Atlas left early after planting out all the remaining herbs.

"Thanks so much, Atlas," said Jones. "I'm so glad to have that done. It's a weight off my mind."

Of course, Atlas was happy to help, as he always was. "But I'm very much in need of a shower!"

Eventually, it was five o'clock and Jones could lock the front door with relief.

"Come on Jones! Let's get into the escape room and find these papers!"

"I thought you would have already found them?" said Jones, as she started lugging books off the shelf so she could slide the furniture back and reveal the hidden door.

"I think I know where it might be, but I haven't been able to unlock it." Autumn was leaning gracefully on the wall whilst Jones was working away.

"I guess that's a good start," said Jones, puffing as she lifted a pile of books off the top shelf. "I think I might stack these differently next time."

Eventually, Jones had the bookshelf clear, and with her hip, pushed it aside to reveal the door. It had been a while since Jones had last been in the hidden room, or as it now was, Autumn's escape room.

"In the metal locker," said Autumn. "I think it must be in there. It was too dark for me to see"

"But it's locked?" said Jones. "Any idea about keys?"

"Back of the door," said Autumn. Jones spun around and yes, there was a large ring of keys hanging, covered in dust. "Good luck with that!"

Jones rolled her eyes, but was desperate to take a look at these newspapers, so sucked it up and started trying every key. It took a while but there was a cheer when the metal door finally swung open.

Autumn was spot on. Inside was shelf after shelf of newspapers.

"How exactly are we going to do this?" Jones stood staring for a moment, attempting to work out the best way to approach all the yellowing pages before them.

Autumn was peering at the piles, assessing what they had in front of them.

"It appears it may be sorted by year. Most recent on the very top I think," she said.

"Any idea where the ones from exactly thirty years ago might be?"

"It looks like they might be at the back of the third shelf from the top."

At first, Jones attempted to lug one large pile from the shelf but was quickly made aware of how heavy and awkward newspapers were. So she resigned herself to pulling two or three down at a time. Autumn was glancing at the dates as she went.

"It's the right year, but we need December," said Autumn. "Unfortunately, I think it's going to be at the bottom of the shelf."

Finally, she found the papers for the weeks of December. They started with the last week and found a brief update from a previous article about the violent robbery at The Memory Bank.

"Police have provided an update on last week's incident at The Memory Bank's Christmas Party. Molly Shepherd has regained consciousness and has been discharged from the hospital. Doctors say there should be no long-term

effects. Police have stated several suspects in the assault are being questioned, but if you have any information or noticed anything unusual on the night of the Christmas Party, please contact them urgently."

"We need the previous article," said Jones.

It wasn't hard to find. There it was right on the front page of the next newspaper. A photo of their grandparents standing out the front of the Bank, obviously told to ensure they were looking very forlorn.

LIGHTS OUT AT THE MEMORY BANK - Local assaulted and left unconscious in the old Bank

Jones flipped to the second page and there was a full-page article alongside many photos, detailing the events. She read one paragraph aloud.

"This year's Lilly Pilly Creek Christmas Lights Awards evening took a dramatic turn when Molly Shepherd was found injured and unconscious inside The Memory Bank, the venue for the evening's events. It was later discovered Molly had been assaulted. It is not known who assaulted Miss Shepherd or why."

"It doesn't say that anything was taken from the bank," said Autumn. "That's strange, right?"

"It is strange," said Jones. "Why wouldn't they report on that?"

"Maybe they didn't know?" suggested Autumn.

Jones furrowed her brow. "You mean Granny didn't tell anyone that her opals were stolen?"

"Well, perhaps no one official."

"But why?"

Jones sat on the couch that took up much of one wall in the room and stared at the ceiling, thinking.

Autumn perched herself on top of one of the filing cabinets, her legs crossed, chin in her hand. "Put yourself in their shoes," she said.

"I'm trying to," said Jones.

"What would you think if someone stole something from *us*? From the lockbox room. What would that do to our business?"

"Well it wouldn't be great," said Jones. "No one would feel their items were safe with us anymore."

"Exactly," said Autumn. "So I bet that's why no one told the reporter about the missing jewellery."

"Yep, I think you're right." Jones nodded but then pursed her lips. "So, they didn't tell the reporter. Does that mean they didn't tell the police either?"

"Good question," said Autumn. "Possibly not. If the police were told I imagine it was only a matter of time before the rest of Lilly Pilly Creek found out."

"But Plum knew," said Jones. "Do you think Mum told her?"

"I guess so," said Autumn. "They were best friends. Can you recall anyone else mentioning the jewellery?"

Jones paused, trying to remember if anyone had mentioned the theft. "No, I can't. Not that I've specifically spoken to anyone about it."

"Ok well, perhaps we need to keep the fact that the jewellery was stolen under wraps too."

"What, you think people will start doubting our security, all these years later?"

Autumn shrugged. "Who knows? For now, let's keep it to

ourselves."

Jones picked up the previous paper and started flicking, not looking at what was on each page, as she considered what they'd discovered.

"Stop!" Autumn cried out.

"What?" Jones looked at her sister, startled.

"Go back a couple of pages," Autumn said.

Jones did what she said.

"There! Look at that photo."

It was a photo of their parents. They were standing together on one side of the photo. A larger group stood opposite them. In between was a giant red button which their dad Kitt and another man had their hand on. Everyone was beaming.

LILLY PILLY CREEK PROGRESS ASSOCIATION PRESS THE START BUTTON FOR THIS YEAR'S LIGHTS

Today the Lilly Pilly Creek Progress Association presented The Memory Bank with a giant red button which will be used each year to mark the start of the Christmas Lights. The funds raised from the town's recent car boot sale have enabled the association to make this generous donation in support of the annual Christmas Lights competition. Once again, the Awards night will be hosted by the Eldershaw family at The Memory Bank.

"A giant red button?" said Autumn. "I've never heard of it!"

"Or seen it," said Jones. "I wonder what happened to it?"

"Absolutely no idea! But I wish we still had it. How cool would that be!"

Autumn leaned over Jones's shoulder to take a closer look at the photo.

"Is that you?"

"What?" Jones didn't understand what her sister was talking about. Autumn pointed. There in their mother's arms was a tiny baby. Glancing at the newspaper's date, just to check, she realised Autumn was right. It could only be her.

Jones hadn't often seen photos of her mum holding her, and she got quite emotional. Her vision clouded, and she wiped her eyes.

"Is that Molly Shepherd? And look, it's Rex and Lorne." Autumn was reviewing the rest of the photograph. "But who is that next to Rex?"

Jones moved her arm to reveal the list of names underneath the photograph.

"Astrid Kelly," said Jones. "Do you know who that is?"

"Nope," said Jones. "And look, there's Plum, behind Colin!"

So it was. There, partially obscured by Colin Fletcher was Jones's godmother.

"They were all part of the Progress Association? Gee Rex and Colin have been on it a long time," said Autumn.

"Well, we've found the newspapers," said Jones. "And I think that in itself is pretty cool. But what have we learnt?"

"I think the main thing is that no one knew about the jewellery being stolen. Maybe even now they don't know. No wonder it was never found," said Autumn.

"That's true," said Jones. "Those opal earrings are probably lost forever. Which is sad, but I guess it doesn't compare to Molly getting whacked over the head. They did say they were interviewing suspects. Do you think anyone was charged?"

"I think you'll have to ask Molly that when you see her," said Autumn. "Oh, and we have learned one other thing."

"We have?"

"Yes," Autumn was grinning. "We've learnt that you've been destined to be in newspapers since you were a baby."

Jones laughed. "I think you're right!"

"But now you'd better go and get ready."

"Oh, I almost forgot!"

"There is no chance you almost forgot about your first date with Hugo," said Autumn. "Quickly. You'll need to restock the bookshelf before you go."

Jones groaned.

CHAPTER 13

Hugo parked his dual cab ute out the front of the Haunted Cellar winery.

"I have to say, it's the strangest name for a winery," said Jones, staring at the glowing cellar door sign.

"Tell me about it!" said Hugo. "I know nothing about it, so hopefully they share the story with us."

"Don't worry, if they don't, I'll put my journalist skills to work and ask them myself."

Hugo laughed, and they got out of the ute. There were a few cars parked nearby, but it looked like the exclusive wine tasting might be a small affair.

A well-lit pathway led them to a gazebo where a group of people were standing. At the centre of the circle was a young man wearing a striped shirt, jeans, and brown RM Williams boots. He was holding a clipboard and greeting people as they arrived.

"Welcome to Haunted Cellar," he said. "My name is Jed, and I'll be your host this evening. Can I take your names?"

"I'm Hugo, and this is Jones."

"Ah, Hugo of Hugo's Wine Bar?"

"Yes," Hugo smiled. "And this is Jones of The Memory Bank."

Jones looked sideways at Hugo. She was sure Jed would have no idea what he was talking about, and assume she too ran a bar of some sort. Jones was wrong.

"Oh wow! The Memory Bank with the lockboxes. I've heard about you. I keep meaning to visit."

"Well, you're welcome anytime." Jones smiled at Jed and then at Hugo.

"We're just waiting for a few more people and then we will begin," said Jed.

Hugo and Jones moved off to the side of the gazebo. The night was still very warm. Jones had chosen a sundress with a light cardigan over the top and sandals. Hugo looked gorgeous as always, wearing navy corduroy pants, brown boat shoes, and a short-sleeved shirt. He leant against the timber and glanced around before bringing his attention back to Jones.

"Do you do a lot of these wine tastings?" Jones asked him.

"I've done a few in my time," said Hugo. "Although I have to say this one does have a different feel to it."

"It's probably because the place is haunted," Jones said, raising her eyebrows with a smile. Fortunately, Hugo laughed at her joke.

"Yes, you're probably right," he said. "Do you believe in ghosts?"

Jones was taken aback by his question and didn't quite know what to say. "Oh, um, do you?"

"I sure do," said Hugo. "In fact, I think I may have seen one once."

"You do?" Jones felt her heart thump. Had he seen Autumn?

"Yes," said Hugo. "I'm not exactly sure. It was almost like it was in my peripheral vision, although it was right in front of me."

"It? What do you think you saw?"

"A figure of some sort," said Hugo. He closed his eyes as though trying to remember.

"Where were you?"

"Well, it was a long time ago."

Jones let out a small sigh of relief. "Were you a kid?"

"I was a teenager," said Hugo. "I'd gone to visit my Grandparents on their farm on the west coast, near Cummins. I'd been there a few times, but I got to wander around a bit more on this visit. I went to one of the old houses on the property. No one lived there. It was falling apart."

"What did you see?"

"I walked into one of the bedrooms and it looked like someone was sitting in the wooden chair that was there. It was almost the only furniture in the entire place. The only furniture still in one piece at least."

"Did it last long? What you saw?"

"Long enough for me to question what exactly I was looking at," Hugo said. "I blinked my eyes a few times and the figure was still there. But it was blurry, like an imprint of something from long ago. Except it moved."

"It moved!"

"Yes," said Hugo. "It stood up and started walking towards me. Scared the shit out of me actually." Hugo laughed as he said this, but it did appear to have affected him.

"I bet it did," said Jones. "What did you do?"

"I turned and got the hell out of there," said Hugo. "I finally had enough nerve to look back when I was about a hundred metres away and it was gone."

"Did you ever go back in?"

Hugo shook his head. "God no! But I did mention it to my dad once."

"Oh really? What did he say?"

"He just nodded as though he knew exactly what I was talking about and told me not to mention it to my grandma."

"Do you have any idea who it was?"

"Nope," Hugo said. "You know, I've never told anyone that story, other than my Dad."

Jones smiled and felt her cheeks turn pink. "Thank you," she said. "Thank you for telling me."

Hugo smiled.

"Ok, everyone!" Jed was calling the troops to order. "If you'll all just follow me, we'll make our way down into........," he paused for a moment before loudly pronouncing, "The Haunted Cellar!"

The group burst out into laughter. Hugo and Jones looked at each other and couldn't help but join in the laughter. Hugo put his hand out in front, indicating for Jones to walk ahead, and off they went.

Jed held a torch leading the way. Jones wasn't quite sure if this was for dramatic effect, but it certainly added to a now rather spooky atmosphere. She hoped Hugo hadn't brought her to one of those role-playing events where all the staff would be dressed up, and the guests would be forced to play along. That was not the type of first date she had envisioned.

They were asked to halt outside a small stone building. Jed pulled out a large key, and with a flourish, unlocked the wooden door in front of him. Inside, Jones was surprised to see flame torches flickering on the wall.

She glanced at Hugo who raised his eyebrows.

"Please be careful as we descend into the cellar," said Jed. "Not because it's haunted, although that is the case, but because the staircase is quite steep and worn. There is a rail on the left-hand side. Please keep clear of the flames. Yes, that is real fire."

Obviously, Jed had been asked that question before. Jones and Hugo followed the crowd, all now deathly quiet navigating the stairs. As everyone entered the room, they gasped. The sight before them was stunning.

The room was small, cosy and cool, lit by candles, and lined with dusty bottles of wine. They were directed to take a seat at one of the black bentwood chairs that surrounded a long timber table. Each place was set with a selection of wine glasses, and underneath them, a piece of brown parchment identifying the wine they would be tasting. Down the centre of the table, black candles flickered amongst branches of pink blossoming gum. On the walls, more flame torches flared. Staring at them from the farthest wall, opposite the staircase, was a large portrait of a very stern-looking woman, her hair pulled back tightly, wearing a black dress with a high lace collar and holding a ring of keys.

"It's like she's staring right through you," whispered Hugo to Jones.

"I know!" He was right. The woman's piercing eyes were a very pale icy blue and seemed to be focused on everyone in the room.

"This is Miss Harriet Treasure," explained Jed. "It is her ghost that haunts this cellar."

A few people around the room began to laugh.

"You may think I'm joking," said Jed, a stern tone to his voice. "But you would be wrong. I have seen her. I have heard her. And I can tell you, she is not impressed that she is trapped in this cellar, the place where she was pushed to her death."

CHAPTER 14

Jones felt Hugo's hand grip her knee. He turned to her. "Are you ok?" he whispered.

Jones nodded, but couldn't speak. The similarities to Autumn's death were startling, and it wasn't only the manner of the woman's death that shocked Jones. The fact that Jed truly believed Harriet was haunting this cellar, for the first time, Jones realised there may be someone else out there who sees ghosts.

Looking down, Jones took a deep breath and attempted to regain her composure.

"We can leave if you like," said Hugo.

"No," Jones whispered. "I want to hear more. And I'm now very much in need of wine." She looked up at him with a smile. He grinned back and squeezed her knee again. It felt nice, and she was pleased he took a few moments before he removed his hand.

"What will she think of us being in her cellar?" one of the guests asked.

"I know she likes company," said Jed. "But only in small doses. I can't guarantee she won't try to run us out of here before the night ends."

The room started murmuring and looking about, expecting a woman in black to walk through the wall at any moment.

"Let me pour you our first wine," said Jed. "And then I'll tell you the story of Miss Harriet Treasure."

They started with a Sauvignon Blanc called The Screaming Queen.

"Every one of our wines is named after a famous ghost," Jed explained. "Our first wine is named after the fifth wife of Henry VIII, Catherine Howard, who is said to haunt Hampton Court Palace."

Jed gave them a rundown of the delicate green apple and passionfruit flavours in the white wine.

Hugo nodded appreciatively. "Very nice," he said.

Jones agreed. "Although I don't think I will ever be able to pick the flavours of the wine like they talk about," she whispered.

"It's usually just a lot of waffle," Hugo said quietly, with a wink.

"Now, back to Miss Treasure," said Jed. "She ran a small boarding house for girls who attended the local school. Her boarding house was a few paddocks away from where we stand. I'm told the building no longer exists, except for some stones that are hidden amongst blackberry bushes."

"When was this?" a woman asked. "What year are we talking about?"

"Good question," said Jed, and he reached behind to pick up a large piece of paper. It was a very enlarged news article.

FATAL FALL DOWN A CELLAR

Gumeracha, March 5

Miss Harriet Treasure of Gumeracha was found dead in the cellar at the orchard of Mr. W. A. Lee. It is believed she lost her way and went into the cellar by accident. The coroner has been informed.

"Oh, how sad," Jones said aloud to the room.

"Very sad," said Jed.

"But why was she there?" a man asked.

"Why was she here? Why was she here in the exact spot?" Jed asked, not taking his eyes off the man.

Jones glanced at Hugo, hoping he shared her appreciation for Jed's sense of the dramatic. He smiled back at her.

"Let's try our next wine before I reveal that."

The crowd laughed, and the few who had yet to finish their first sample quickly downed the last drops.

The next wine was a Pinot Gris which, they were told, had notes of honeysuckle and pear. It was called The Caretaker.

"Named after the ghost of Francis Cluney who haunts the Adelaide Arcade, one of Australia's oldest shopping arcades," Jed said. "His body was found mangled in the machinery that powered the arcade's electric lights."

The crowd groaned.

"But back to Harriet. So why was she here, you ask?"

The crowd murmured and looked expectantly at Jed as they sipped the Pinot Gris.

"Well, what we're told is that one of the girls from the boarding house had run away. The girl had a habit of doing this and was usually found in a nearby barn or shed." Jed stopped to take a sip of his wine before continuing. "This night was particularly dark and stormy and Harriet couldn't bear the thought of her out there alone. She left the Head Girl in charge of the boarders, whilst she went out in pursuit of the girl."

"What happened to the girl? Was she ever found?" Hugo asked.

"Ah," said Jed. "Yet another good question. But first, let's turn our attention to our Pinot Noir Rose."

The crowd laughed and one man even humorously called out, "Oh come on!"

"Now this one is called The Bell Witch, so named for a ghost that was said to haunt a family named Bell from Tennessee," Jed told them.

"I'm tasting strawberries and cream," Jones said quietly to Hugo, grinning.

"Very good! Strawberries and cream. Spot on," said Jed.

Jones burst out laughing.

"See, you're a natural!" said Hugo.

"Some also say a hint of almond," said Jed.

Jones shook her head. She wasn't going to admit that the strawberries and cream comment had been completely made up to begin with.

"So, was the girl found or not?" a woman asked.

"Oh, so impatient!" But Jed smiled as he continued the story. "Yes, the girl was found. She returned to the Boarding House the next morning, shivering and soaking wet, but fine. But she was barely noticed, because everyone was still out searching. For Harriet."

"And how do you know this?" one astute listener pointed out.

"Ah-" but Jed was cut off before he could finish.

"Don't tell me. We need to try the next wine!"

"Spot on!"

Jed poured everyone a glass of Pinot Noir. This one was called The Headless Nun.

"Gosh, they get more and more morbid as we go on!" a woman

said.

"Well, she was from New Brunswick in Canada, and they say she was beheaded but there are conflicting versions. My favourite is that two sailors cut off her head when she refused to reveal the location of pirate treasure."

"How ridiculous!" said the woman.

"But a great story," said Jed. He then proceeded to describe the wine as being big in personality which seemed to fit the name. "With aromas of rose and cherry."

"Totally," whispered Hugo, leaning into Jones.

Everyone sat silently this time, savouring the pinot noir, but also, it seemed, not wanting to be the next one to demand Jed continue the story. He stood at the head of the table, swirling his glass, and watching all of them.

Finally, it was too much and Hugo asked "Well, are you gonna tell us?"

Jed looked at him in mock surprise. "Oh, right Harriet."

Everyone laughed, but turned their eyes to him, eager to hear the rest of the story.

"Well, one of those boarders kept a diary, and many years later, it was found in the homestead right here on this property."

"Yeah, right," one man said.

"It's true," said Jed, as he again turned to the table behind him, and held up a very faded and frayed book. "It is this exact book I have in my hands. That boarder married the son of the orchard owner, and it was those two that slowly turned this property into the winery it is today."

Jed took a sip of his wine before continuing. "In it, she describes searchers discovering Harriet's body. They believed she had become disorientated in the rain, not realising she was opening the door to the cellar. She must have tumbled down, not expecting the staircase."

"But didn't you say she was pushed?" a woman asked.

Jed nodded and winked. "That I did," he said, taking another sip. "Despite official records, the rumours persisted. No one believed Harriet could make a mistake like that. They were all convinced she had been pushed. But no one could ever work out by whom."

There was much murmuring around the table.

"So, who was the first person to see the ghost of Harriet?" another man asked.

Instead of responding, Jed picked up the final bottle of wine. The label was clear to all of them. The Harriet Treasure. In silence, he poured them all a glass, and let each of them savour it.

"We've been told the missing girl came to visit her boarding house friend many years later and asked to see the cellar," Jed explained. "She had been consumed with guilt and believed that seeing the scene of Harriet's death might provide her with some closure."

"Oh, bad idea!" one man called out.

"I think you could be right," said Jed. "The story goes that she walked down into this very cellar, sobbing and begging for forgiveness. As she was down on her knees on the cold floor, she looked up and there, looming over her was the figure of Miss Harriet Treasure. The girl was so shocked she ran screaming from the cellar. It is said she was admitted to a mental institution to live out the rest of her days."

"How awful!" said Jones. Without realising it, Jones had grabbed Hugo's hand during Jed's description and was gripping it tightly. Hugo patted her hand and squeezed back.

"Have *you* ever seen Harriet?" Jed was asked.

Jed slowly turned to face Harriet's portrait, his back to them.

"Once, as a young boy, I saw Harriet standing on the threshold of the cellar, her hand over her eyes, searching for something."

"For the missing girl," someone said.

The group murmured, all eyes on the portrait, not one person sipping their wine.

As Jones stared at the portrait, Harriet blinked.

CHAPTER 15

"Are you telling me Hugo didn't see it?" asked Autumn early the next morning.

Jones shook her head. "No, he said he didn't see a thing. I told him I must have been dreaming."

"But it is strange, right," said Autumn. "How it was so similar to...."

"Very strange," said Jones.

"And was it all real or just a story?"

"I googled it on the drive home. Hang on, I'll find the article." Jones pulled out her phone and tapped away.

"Yep," said Jones. "Here it is on Trove. The same article Jed showed us, and quite a few more. It was a big story back in 1906." Autumn stood behind Jones and read the article.

"Wow," said Autumn. "I wonder who the girl was who married the farmer? The one who lived on the property?"

"Oh, I didn't think to ask that," said Jones.

"And did Hugo have any idea this wine tasting was going to be so, ah, theatrical?"

"Ha, that's one way of putting it!" Jones laughed. "Hugo had no idea. He told me he thought it was just going to be a run-of-the-mill wine tasting. But let me tell you, there was nothing run-of-the-mill about Haunted Cellars."

Autumn floated closer towards her sister and looked her in the eyes. "But did you like it?"

"The wine tasting? Oh, it was brilliant! If I was still a journalist, I would write the most amazing review."

"You should absolutely do that," said Autumn.

"For who?" asked Jones. "I mean, I guess I could submit it to The Advertiser and see what they thought?"

"At the very least write it," said Autumn. "You never know when it may come in useful."

Jones nodded. Autumn had a point. When she had the urge to write, she really should just write, and not worry about who it was for.

"But that's not what I meant," said Autumn. "Did you like your date with Hugo?"

Jones dropped her eyes, not wanting to reveal too much to Autumn. She remembered the drive home.

They had sat together in Hugo's ute, quietly, enjoying their time together.

"Thank you, Hugo," Jones said. "I had a lovely time. It was not at all what I expected. But I really enjoyed it. Thank you for asking me."

"You are very welcome," said Hugo. "It was great."

"We should do it more often, don't you think?" Jones had kept her eyes directly ahead as she asked this question, worried she may have been too forward.

"Yes, we should," said Hugo, and he'd reached out and took her hand. She'd squeezed it, breaking out into a huge grin, which she hoped was somewhat hidden in the darkness.

"I know that look!" cried Autumn, bringing Jones back to the present. "Oh, this is so exciting! Hugo and Jones. Jones and Hugo.

What's his last name again?"

Jones frowned. What was Hugo's surname again? He'd always just been Hugo. But she knew he'd told her.

"Oh well," said Autumn. "He'd probably just take your name, anyway."

"What!" Jones burst out. "Autumn, let's not get too carried away."

"What else am I supposed to do with my time other than dreaming about your wedding to Hugo?"

"Oh Autumn, I'm sure there's plenty of things you can do," said Jones. "Gilbertson! Hugo Gilbertson."

"Well done," said Autumn. "And I have something I wanted to show you." Autumn floated over to one of the gift tables, waving at her sister.

Jones followed, wondering if there was something broken or out of place. Instead, Autumn stopped in front of a pile of art paper. She floated there, hovering her hand over the top, not taking her eyes off the pages. Jones looked between Autumn's face and the papers, waiting. And then she heard a noise. Quickly looking back to the papers, she saw the corners were fluttering.

"Oh, Autumn! Are you doing that?"

Autumn didn't reply. She concentrated until finally, she was able to lift one page above the rest, move it to the side, and then place it down on the table.

"Ooof," Autumn sighed, before floating down to sit on the floor. "That's hard work."

"I can't believe it! You can move things!"

Autumn nodded but frowned. "That has taken me weeks and weeks. And all I can move is one measly piece of paper."

"Autumn! It is amazing. You can move things with your mind, with your energy. Who knows? If you can do that after only a few weeks, imagine what else you'll be able to do!"

Autumn looked up and smiled at her sister. Her disappointment had changed to happiness.

"I'm so proud of you, Autumn!"

Autumn slowly rose from her spot on the ground, but then wobbled and went back down. "The problem is how much energy it uses."

Jones crouched down, staring intently at her sister. "Are you ok?"

"I'm fine," said Autumn. "I think I just need to build up my strength. I'm sure it's like running. You have to train for long distances."

"I hope so," said Jones, glancing up at the clock. "I need to head to Molly Shepherd's house, so I'm back in time to open up. Or shall I cancel?"

"I'll be fine. I think I'll make my way to the escape room for the morning."

"That sounds like a plan," said Jones. She stood and watched until she saw Autumn float through the wall into the hidden room before she made her way out of The Memory Bank.

The morning light was bright as Jones drove to Molly's farm. She could already tell the day was going to be a hot one. Driving through the streets and then past paddocks, she spotted Christmas decorations everywhere. One farming family had turned bales of hay into a giant teddy bear wearing a Christmas hat. There was a shearing shed with a shining star on the top of it. And as she turned down the laneway to Molly's house, she saw a row of corrugated iron alpacas tied to a sleigh.

Slowly, Jones drove down the bumpy track looking to her left and right. She was surprised to see how many alpacas Molly had. This wasn't a small operation. There were alpacas in every paddock as far as the eye could see. In the distance, Jones spotted a very old, mustard-yellow Land Rover and headed that way. It wasn't long before she recognised Molly, wearing a wide-brimmed hat, a short-sleeved navy shirt, jeans, and Rossi boots, loading rectangular bales of hay onto the back of the vehicle.

"You made it," Molly said by way of a greeting.

"Absolutely," said Jones, striding towards her. "I wanted to talk to you, about your letter."

"Go on then," Molly nodded, not pausing between bales.

Jones stopped for a moment, watching Molly, and considering the best place to start. She decided to start at the very beginning.

"Do you mind telling me what happened? That night at the Christmas Party. I know it was very traumatic for you. But we," Jones hesitated. "I mean, I've never heard about it until this year. When I agreed to host the Christmas Party again, I didn't know anything about the attack. I wondered if you would tell me?"

Molly turned away, lifted a bale of hay and slammed it on the back of the ute. She grabbed another one, and then another. Jones began to wonder if she had been dismissed. Should she just leave?

Molly finally spoke. "Yes, it was very traumatic." She didn't stop stacking the bales, and she didn't look at Jones. "And although I don't remember much, waking up in that lockbox room of yours, on the ground, covered in blood. Well, it's something I will never get over."

Jones nodded.

"I understand the lights are good for the town, but I don't know why you had to have the party at The Memory Bank? Even if you didn't know about it, Rex and Colin sure did."

"Rex and Colin. They were there that night."

"Of course they bloody were. The whole town was," said Molly. "But you said there were two letters. Who else complained?"

"Well, I just assumed both were from you. It wasn't signed. So, it wasn't you?"

Molly shook her head. "I've already told you. I only wrote one letter!"

"You were all on The Progress Association back then, weren't you? You, Rex, Colin?"

"Yep. We all worked hard to get that year's Christmas Lights competition happening. It was the biggest one they'd had yet."

"I saw a photo of you all. In the paper," said Jones. "You were handing my parents some big button."

"Oh yes," Molly smiled in recollection. "The giant light switch! Oh, we were so proud of that! We pressed that button and the front of The Memory Bank lit up. It was the beginning of the Awards. Then everyone went into the Bank. The crowd cheered! Everyone was so happy. It was supposed to be the best Awards event we'd ever had. But we didn't get that far."

"Hadn't the awards been presented when....." Words failed Jones. She didn't know what to say.

"When I was conked on the head with a brick, you mean?"

"Yes," said Jones. "Yes. Wait, a brick?"

"Oh, I don't know," said Molly. "They never found out what it was. I'm just guessing."

"And they never found out *who* it was?"

Molly's face stiffened. She turned back to her bales of hay. "Nup," said Molly.

"Did they ever charge anyone?" Jones asked.

"Not that I know of, but I was in hospital, so they might have."

"Did you have any suspicions?"

"None whatsoever," Molly declared.

So, Molly didn't have Colin on her list of suspects like their Granny.

"And, just one more question, if you don't mind," said Jones.

"Go on then, you may as well finish," said Molly, turning to face Jones, hands on her hips.

"Well, do you know why? Why someone would do such a thing?"

"I always assumed it was because they were trying to get into the lockboxes," said Molly. "But I know nothing more than that. Now, I need to get this hay out before it heats up. Is that everything?"

"That's everything," said Jones. "And can I presume you're ok for us to continue the Awards at The Memory Bank? I'm planning to lock the area where the lockboxes are so no one can get there. We're going to hold most of the main festivities in our new garden, anyway."

"Oh yes," said Molly. "The new garden."

"It's amazing. Lorne and Flick have done an amazing job. Oh-" Jones realised what she'd said. "Lorne *did* an amazing job. You heard about Lorne?"

Molly nodded as she lifted the tailgate and slammed it shut.

"Sounds like there were quite a few people he'd rubbed the wrong way over the years," said Jones, fishing slightly to see what Molly might know. She may as well investigate both mysteries while she was at it.

"Ha! That's putting it mildly. Well, I've gotta go." She opened the driver's door and then turned back to Jones. "I do hope the party goes well. It wasn't your fault. What happened to me. Lilly Pilly Creek should shine again. I appreciate you coming to speak to me." Molly smiled and then got into the ute. The door closed. Jones walked away as Molly started the ute and drove off.

For a moment, Jones leant on a fence post overlooking a paddock full of alpacas. A curious black and white one walked up and sniffed at her hand. Jones lifted it to pat the animal, but in revolt at her having no treats, the alpaca violently spat in Jones's face and trotted away.

CHAPTER 16

Jones's run-in with the alpaca, more so than her visit with Molly, had shaken her. She rushed into The Memory Bank a little after nine and rapidly turned on the lights, glad no customers were hovering outside, wondering why she was late.

"Oh, I haven't even grabbed a coffee from Sybil yet!" Jones moaned out loud, apparently to herself, as Autumn hadn't appeared.

"Never fear, coffee is here!" Atlas strode in, brandishing a tray of coffees, grinning as he attempted to walk like an English butler.

"Atlas, I have never been so glad to see you!" Jones exclaimed.

"Don't act like it's me you're pleased to see," Atlas said, a cheeky grin on his face. "I know you only use me for my coffee."

"That is entirely untrue," said Jones. "At least, every other day. Today I must admit the coffee in your hand is a winner!

Atlas handed her the flat white. Jones took a long sip, savouring the hot drink.

"I've already had quite the morning," Jones explained. "For one, I've had an alpaca spit at me!"

Atlas burst out laughing. "What are you talking about?"

"I went and visited Molly Shepherd. The lady who wrote the letters, or at least one of them."

"And she has alpacas?"

"Acres of them! Apparently, she's a leading alpaca farmer. All I can say is she works jolly hard. You should have seen her hefting the bales of hay onto the back of the ute."

"How old is she?"

"I think maybe early sixties."

"Jeepers, very impressive."

"And she said she was okay for us to have the awards here," said Jones.

"Oh, that's good," said Atlas. "What changed her mind?"

Jones shook her head. "I don't know. It was like she just needed to talk it through, to have someone listen and empathise, and then she felt comfortable for the town to resume the tradition. The way she spoke of the giant light switch, the smile on her face, I think she realised there were some good memories."

"Giant light switch?"

But before Jones could share this with Atlas, Flick emerged from the back garden.

Flick looked gaunt, as though she hadn't eaten or slept in days, which she likely hadn't. Jones recalled Christopher's questions, leading her to understand that Flick was on his list of suspects. Jones studied Flick, pondering whether guilt had a part to play in her current state.

"Flick!" said Jones. "I didn't expect to see you today. You don't need to work. You should be home."

"Doing what?" sighed Flick. "I have no idea what to do. Mum and Aunty Jessica are sorting out the funeral. I'm no help with that. And I've got to keep the business running. It's what Dad would want."

Jones guided Flick to sit down at one of the tables with her.

"Maybe you should be at the nursery, getting things in order there."

"I can't go back there. Not after….." Flick sobbed.

Jones sucked in her breath. She'd said the wrong thing. Of course, Flick couldn't go back there. It was the scene of her dad's death. His murder. Although Jones couldn't bring herself to believe Flick really could have done it, if she were the killer, it would seem unlikely she'd want to spend any time there.

"Well, Atlas had a go at planting the herbs yesterday, so there isn't a huge amount to do."

Flick rubbed her hands across her face and clasped her hands together. "I need to do something. I need to work. I've brought the water feature."

"You have?" This surprised Jones. The water feature had been in the warehouse where Lorne's body was found.

"Yep," said Flick. "I asked one of the guys who works for us to get it out and load it up onto the ute. I guessed which one you'd like. Do you want to come and take a look?"

At that moment, Jones saw movement out of the corner of her eye. It was Autumn.

"Be careful," her sister whispered in her ear. "She might whack *you* over the head next."

Jones waved her sister away, ignoring her warnings. Together, they followed Flick through the garden and out to where she had parked her ute. Loaded up on the back was something large and heavy, wrapped in black plastic.

"Hang on," said Flick. "I'll just get this off." She pulled out a pocketknife and slid it through plastic and tape. She then slid back the black layer back to reveal the contents.

The water feature was a large, copper half-sphere, but the centre curved down to form a hole in the middle. The water flowed down the centre and was then pumped back up into the main area. Inside it was golden coloured, but the outside was a tarnished green. It was sleek and modern, but also rustic.

"Oh, I love it!" said Jones.

"It's perfect," said Autumn.

Flick turned to Jones, tears in her eyes, clearly pleased with Jones's reaction.

"But how are we going to get it off the ute?" Jones asked.

"Well, I've got the sack truck and a ramp," said Flick. "I thought the three of us might just be able to do it ourselves."

"The three of us?" asked Autumn. "Surely she can't mean me."

"I'm sure Atlas will be happy to help. I'll go get him." Jones turned back to the Bank and rolled her eyes at Autumn.

Autumn slapped her forehead. "Of course, she meant Atlas. Oh well. Maybe one day I'll be able to move something as heavy as a water feature."

"One day," Jones muttered as she walked through the doorway and over to Atlas's office.

"Just don't let her accidentally push it on top of you," Autumn said helpfully.

"Honestly, you don't really think she killed her own dad?" said Jones.

"She's as likely as anyone else at this stage in the case."

Jones knocked on Atlas's door. "Do you think you might be up for a bit of manual labour?"

As always, Atlas jumped at the chance to help.

Once they had positioned themselves around the ute, Flick carefully pulled the ramp into place before walking up with the sack truck.

"Atlas, if you could come up and hold the sack truck whilst I wiggle the water feature into position," Flick said.

Atlas thumped his way up and held the blue sack truck firmly against the edge of the water feature. Flick's years of gardening had earned her muscles unseen. With a bit of grunting she managed to get the edge of the feature onto the sack truck's footplate.

"Ok, now, together we'll carefully tilt it back, then we can slowly move backwards," Flick instructed. "Jones, could you please make sure the ramp doesn't wobble too much and just be ready to hold the water feature at the end."

Jones and Atlas nodded. It took some effort and a few attempts for the water feature to tilt appropriately and sit securely on the sack truck. Atlas took a few tentative steps backwards, guiding the sack truck whilst also resting the weight of it against his hip. Flick pulled back on the water feature to counter some of the weight and help steady its descent.

"Slowly, slowly," said Flick. "That's it, careful. Ok. Jones, are you ready?"

Jones stepped right up to the side of the ramp and put her hands firmly on the water feature. Flick jumped down and held onto the other side.

"We just need to get it over that last bump," said Flick.

It wasn't pretty, and there was a moment where Jones was sure the water feature would topple over, but they managed to get it on the ground.

"Phew!" said Jones.

"Good work, team." Flick smiled.

Autumn was clapping. Jones wished she wasn't the only one who could hear her.

Together, Jones, Atlas and Flick manoeuvred the water feature into position in the garden.

"Your Dad would be proud of you," said Jones.

"Ha, he never was before," Flick said, glancing at Jones before averting her eyes, ashamed of her words.

Jones smiled sadly at her. "I'm sure he was proud of you, even if he couldn't express it."

"Of course he was," said Atlas. "You're amazing with garden design."

"I'm not so sure," said Flick. "The day before he died, he told me he wasn't going to retire at Christmas time after all. He didn't think I was ready to take over."

"Oh, Flick," said Jones, and she put her arm around the woman standing next to her.

"I've never been quite good enough for him, no matter how hard I tried." Flick burst into tears, gulping as she cried.

Autumn whispered in Jones's ear. "That sounds like a motive for murder."

CHAPTER 17

Jones jumped at the sound of Autumn's voice.

"Are you ok?" Flick sobbed, startled by Jones's sudden movement.

"Yes, just a cramp in my leg." Jones turned to glare at Autumn. But she had to admit, her sister was right. In the heat of the moment, angry at her father, Lorne's change of heart could have been enough for Flick to lose her temper and do the unthinkable. The woman crying in her arms could very well be emotional as a result of guilt rather than grief alone.

"You know I'm right," said Autumn, hovering around the pair. "I'm not sure how I feel about potentially having a killer working for us in the Bank."

Jones raised her eyebrows and nodded slightly. She couldn't say anything, but she agreed with Autumn. Not that she thought she was in harm's way. At least, as long as she didn't get on Flick's bad side. However, tipping off the police would be one way to achieve that. Jones felt her heart beat a little faster, recognising a rising panic. She needed to move away from Flick so she could think logically.

"Look Flick, do you think you should go home?" Jones took her arm from Flick's shoulder and walked to the front of her, looking her in the face.

Sniffling, Flick nodded. "That's probably a good idea. Hopefully, my aunty has left by now. I might do some of *my* gardening. God knows I never get time to do that."

"Great idea," said Jones. "Let's get your ute packed up so you can head home. Did you say Rex would be hooking up the fountain at some stage?"

"Yes," said Flick. "I can't remember when. But he was going to make sure it was done before the party."

Jones put her hand on Flick's back, guiding her through the garden. "That's fine. I'll contact Rex if he doesn't show up. You don't need to worry about a thing."

Flick had tears still streaming down her cheeks. Atlas helped her get the sack truck, ropes and plastic back into the ute, and she finally drove away.

"Poor thing," said Jones to Atlas.

"Seems like Lorne was as nice to his daughter as he was to everyone else," said Atlas, rolling his eyes.

"I wonder why he changed his mind?" asked Jones.

"And I wonder if the police know about this," said Autumn.

"I imagine he started panicking about what he was going to do after retiring," said Atlas. "I remember my Grandpa being like that when Dad took over the farm."

"What did your dad do?"

"He just let Grandpa look around the sheep and gave him some odd jobs. He was happy."

Jones nodded thoughtfully. She could understand how Lorne would feel. She glanced at Autumn. If their dad were still alive, her sister would have eventually had to go through this. Jones wondered how they might have handled it.

"I suppose we'd better get back to work," said Atlas, pointing towards an old man who had just walked in.

"Mr Manowski!" said Jones. "Lovely to see you."

"And you too, Miss Eldershaw," he responded. Mr Manowski, the tailor, was with Jones a few months ago when they witnessed Iris Wainwright collapse at her final dress fitting. Her brother had been poisoning her with death cap mushrooms by putting them into her muesli.

"How can I help you?"

Mr Manowski lifted a brown paper bag he was holding. "Some more things to add to my lockbox, if I may?"

"For sure!" said Jones. "Follow me!"

Jones led Mr Manowski into the lockbox room and, taking his key, she unlocked the small door that opened the slot containing his box. Sliding it out, she held it under her two forearms and brought it to one of their private rooms, where Mr Manowski could take his time.

"Shall I leave you to it?" she asked.

"Thank you, yes. Although," he sat down and then turned to look at Jones. "I hear you were witness to an unfortunate turn of events at the nursery the other day. Are you ok?"

"Yes, thank you, Mr Manowsi," said Jones. "I'm fine. It was Flick who found her dad. Fortunately, I only needed to have a glance. It was awful."

"Indeed," said Mr Manowski, nodding and frowning. "Does anyone know what happened to him?"

Jones shook her head. "No, but Christopher, ah, Sergeant Schmidt is investigating."

"An awful business. I was never particularly fond of the man myself," said Mr Manowski. "But I didn't think he would ever have done something worth killing over."

"It is rather shocking," said Jones. "Had you heard if he had any serious run-ins with anyone?"

"Well, the only person I recall is Rex. They worked together a lot. When we had a beer at the pub, he'd complain about Lorne all the time."

"Did he? But he kept working with him?"

"Seems like they had a lot of contracts together," he said. "I imagine getting too riled up would risk his income. Not that Rex ever said that. It's just the impression he gave me."

"I wonder what happens to those contracts now?" said Jones.

"Who knows?" Mr Manowski turned back to the table and opened his lockbox. Jones closed the door and left him to it.

"What did he say?" asked Autumn, whizzing up to Jones's side.

Jones looked around, and noticing what appeared to be a mother and young daughter looking at the scrapbooking paper, walked into the stacks to quietly respond to her sister.

"He mentioned that Rex and Lorne worked together a lot, and Rex would always complain about him at the pub."

"So why did he keep working with him?"

"Well, that's the interesting thing," said Jones. "They worked on a lot of contracts together. I guess Lorne did all the garden design and Rex did the related electrical work. Like he's doing with our water feature."

"That makes sense, I suppose," said Autumn.

"What I'm wondering is, what happens to those contracts now? Does he keep working on them with Flick? Is his life easier now that Lorne is out of the way?"

"You think he would kill Lorne just to make his life easier?"

"I don't know," said Jones. "But it does seem Lorne was killed in the heat of the moment. What if Rex decided he'd just had enough?"

"It's certainly possible. But more possible than Flick?"

Jones sighed. "I just hate to think that Flick would kill her father. Do you believe she could have?"

"Yes, I do," said Autumn.

"Autumn!"

"No, I don't mean I think she's a killer. But I can understand when you've been desperately waiting for something and it's taken away from you. I suppose I can understand doing something unforgivable in a split second."

"What about Flick's mum? It seems some people think one of his ex-wives might have done it."

Autumn casually waved her hand through the bookshelves, thinking.

"Was she even in town? I don't know much about them. I wonder if Plum does?"

"Plum?" Jones looked up to see Autumn had shoved her head through the shelf.

"Well, she's just walked in," said Autumn, as she pulled back. "Maybe we can ask her?"

CHAPTER 18

"Jones! Jones! Tell me all about it!" Plum was rather loud as she hurried across the main bank floor. The mother and daughter looked up, as did an older lady who had come in whilst Jones was talking to Autumn.

"Tell you what?" so much had gone on so far today, Jones couldn't for the life of her think what Plum was talking about. Her outfit was quite distracting as well.

Today, Plum wore a dark purple beret, a green silk singlet, and wide purple culottes with white slides.

"Your date with Hugo, of course!" Plum hooked her arm in Jones's and they strolled through the Bank.

"Gosh, I almost forgot about that."

Plum's eyes widened. "That bad, was it?"

Jones laughed. "No, not at all!"

"The best night of her life, in fact," Autumn called out playfully as she gracefully came up beside them. Jones felt her cheeks turn pink, but ignored Autumn.

"So it was good?"

"Yes," said Jones. "It was very good. And very bizarre."

"Bizarre isn't the usual way to describe a first date," said Plum. "At least not a good first date."

Jones went on to explain all about the Haunted Cellar, Miss Harriet Treasure, and even went so far as to tell her about the blinking portrait.

"Oh, my goodness!" said Plum. "This sounds like the best first date ever!"

"Told you," said Autumn, grinning at Jones.

"It was certainly memorable," said Jones.

"And so romantic. A bit of a fright never hurts. I hope you took the opportunity to dramatically grab his hand?"

"Plum! That's enough!" Jones laughed.

Jones walked to the counter and sat on one of the stools. Plum placed her handbag on the counter and leaned her hip against it.

"Plum," said Jones. "I did want to pick your brain."

"About men?" Plum winked.

Jones shook her head, smiling. "No, about Lorne Fox."

"Oh?"

"Well, you knew him, didn't you?"

"What do you mean?"

"I found a photo of you with him and The Progress Association. With my parents."

Plum nodded. "Yes, I guess you're right. We *were* on The Progress Association. Although I don't think I was on it for long. What did you want to know?"

"Well, who was his first wife?"

"Ah, that would have been Astrid," said Plum. "Although I'd left Lilly Pilly Creek by the time they were married."

"You left?"

"Yes," said Plum. "I'd only come back for about a year or so after university. I was having trouble finding work. I lived with my parents in Lilly Pilly Creek. But then I got a job in Melbourne."

"Astrid Kelly was in the photo," said Autumn, hinting at what Jones should say next.

"Yes, I think Astrid was in the photo I saw. Were they a couple then?"

"No, I don't think so," said Plum. "I think Astrid and Rex were a thing back then."

"Rex!" Jones was genuinely surprised by this.

"I think so," said Plum. "I don't think Lorne was with anyone in particular. He was a bit of a ladies' man. Didn't like to be tied down."

Jones nodded. "Do you know why Astrid and Lorne's marriage ended?"

"No idea," said Plum. "That was long after your mum died. She was the one who would always share the Lilly Pilly Creek gossip with me. After that, I was pretty much out of the loop."

"Neha didn't tell you?"

"Well, Neha and I weren't that close back then," said Plum. "It's only been since we had one of our school reunions where we reconnected."

Jones sat still, thinking. It seemed there may have been a bit of a love triangle, between Rex, Lorne and Astrid. Could that have any bearing on the end of their marriage? Or Lorne's death for that matter?

"Why are you asking?" said Plum. "Have you found something out?"

"Don't tell her about Flick," said Autumn. Jones was confused but listened to her sister for now.

"No, nothing," said Jones. "Just easy to get caught up with the town speculation. That's all."

"I understand. What about the letters? Have you found out any more about that?"

"I went and visited Molly Shepherd, actually," said Jones.

"You did! I bet that was an interesting conversation."

"She's a bit abrupt," said Jones. "But she did say she only wrote the one letter. Not the anonymous one that came to us. And she's happy for us to have the Christmas Party here. She said it brought back some memories for her, but she's over it now."

"Yes, I imagine it did bring back some terrible memories. Did you ask her anything about that?"

"Well, the thing is Plum," said Jones. "I don't think anyone except my grandparents, my parents, and you knew anything about the stolen opals. I don't think Granny ever went to the police or told anyone about it. Molly certainly didn't say anything."

Plum furrowed her brow. It seemed this was news to her. "Now that I think about it, I can't recall your mum ever talking about the police. I left for Melbourne not long after the whole debacle, so I probably didn't know what was going on. But you could be right."

"If that's the case," said Jones. "I don't think we'll ever know about the opals. I doubt the culprit is going to come forward. Why would they now? Molly remembers nothing, and if there was no investigation, well, I imagine that's the end of it."

Plum nodded. "Yes, I suppose you're right. I guess your granny thought so too. She just resigned herself to the fact they were gone forever. Would be nice to know what happened to them though, wouldn't it?"

"It sure would," said Autumn.

"So, you said you're staying for the Christmas Party, is that right?" Jones asked Plum.

"Yes I am," she said. "Do you need any help tomorrow or Saturday? With the setup?"

"That would be amazing. Perhaps, if you don't mind, you could pop in sometime tomorrow afternoon and just touch base with me. I haven't got my head on straight today, but I'll try to map out a plan this evening."

"Sure can," said Plum. "I'd love to help in any way I can!"

"What are you doing for the rest of the day?" Jones asked. Jones glanced at the clock and realised it was already past noon. No wonder she was feeling hungry.

"I'm going to head into Hahndorf," said Plum. "Thought it would be a good place for lunch and to do some Christmas shopping. I've got lots of nieces and nephews who are counting on a present from Aunty Plum. I don't want to disappoint!"

"And it's a perfect day to stroll down the Main Street there," said Jones. "Sounds lovely. I'm sure you'll find some interesting bits and pieces."

"I'll see you tomorrow afternoon!" Plum said, and off she went.

"What about some presents from The Memory Bank?" asked Autumn, as they watched Plum walk away.

"Don't be silly Autumn," said Jones. "Of course, Plum would buy anything she liked. Perhaps she just has some particular items in mind."

Autumn shrugged. She genuinely seemed put out that Plum hadn't even looked at The Memory Bank stock for options.

"Meanwhile, how are we going to find out more about Astrid?" asked Jones.

"And Rex!" said Autumn, bringing her attention back to the matter at hand. "That was a bit of a bombshell, wasn't it?"

"It certainly was," said Jones. "Maybe it was Rex after all? Maybe he finally got one back on Lorne for stealing Astrid from him?"

"Do we think he stole her, though? We don't know anything about it."

"And how on earth are we going to find out? Should we talk to Flick?"

"No," said Jones. "But I do think it's time we speak with Rex."

Jones nodded her head towards the garden. There, walking between the plants, was Rex Keegan, carrying his toolbox.

CHAPTER 19

"Jones! Stop!" said Autumn as Jones was sliding off her stool.

"What is it?"

"That's it!" said Autumn. "Look at what he's carrying! Can you guess what might be in it?"

Jones looked at the toolbox and back at her sister. What did she mean? Of course, the toolbox was full of tools. Spanners, wrenches, hammers.

"What?"

Autumn raised her eyebrows. "Well, couldn't it possibly carry the murder weapon?"

Jones felt her eyes bulge. She turned to see Rex opening the glass door and stride into The Memory Bank.

"I don't think you should say anything to him," said Autumn. "He could be dangerous."

"Well, I have to say something," Jones said under her breath as Rex moved closer.

"Only about the water feature," said Autumn. "Not another word. Not a single word about Lorne."

Jones couldn't reply because Rex was now at the counter.

"Afternoon Jones," said Rex. "How's things?"

Jones smiled at him, attempting to appear relaxed.

"Good thanks, Rex. Busy, as you can see." Jones gestured to the shop floor, which was now quite full of customers.

"Excellent," he said. "A good time of year to be busy. Stocking up on Christmas presents, I imagine."

"I think so," said Jones as the man and a young girl came over with a wire basket full of items.

"Well, I'll leave you to it," said Rex. "I'm just here to install the water feature. Is it all in place?"

"Ah, yes, I think so," said Jones. "But I might just grab Atlas. He helped with the design so he can point you in the right direction."

"Atlas!" Jones called out, hoping she wasn't being too loud. Fortunately, he heard her and looked up. Jones signalled she needed him, and he made his way over.

Atlas nodded at Rex as he reached the counter.

"Atlas, do you mind helping Rex with the water feature? You know where it's being situated, don't you? The right positioning?"

"I sure do," said Atlas. "Flick and I spoke about it last week. Happy to help."

Jones and Autumn weren't able to continue their conversation, as Jones served a steady stream of customers. Her mind was racing, but she attempted to ignore all thoughts about Rex and focus on serving their customers. Jones put the items through the online system Atlas had set up and sent each customer off with their purchase in one of The Memory Bank calico bags. Jones had introduced a few new features into The Memory Bank, and one of them was the addition of the branded bags. She often saw people walking around with them, and many customers brought them back to reuse with their future purchases. It always made her smile.

After a busy moment at the counter, Mr Manowski came out to let

Jones know he was all finished.

"You can lock my box back up," he said with a smile.

"Perfect," said Jones. "I'll do that immediately."

"Was that Rex I saw arrive a little while ago?" he asked.

"Yes, he's come to wire up the water feature. Get it pumping."

Mr Manowski nodded but said no more. He smiled at Jones and left.

As Jones was sliding the lockbox back into place, Autumn whooshed up next to her.

"So? What do you think?"

"What do I think about what?"

"You know! Rex!"

Jones turned to face Autumn. "Honestly, I don't know. I mean, it is just speculation."

"Ok, so Lorne steals his girlfriend. They work together for years and years, constantly driving each other bonkers, and then it all just becomes too much for Rex and he snaps. He has his toolbox with him, he whacks Lorne over the head with his hammer, puts it back in and walks out."

"Yes, I mean when you say it like that," Jones raised her eyebrows. It was a valid motive.

"Plus, he would have access to the nursery, I would have thought. Do you think he might have had keys to lock up?"

"Maybe," said Jones. "But did he need them? The warehouse door was open, and couldn't someone just pull the front door shut and it would lock?"

"I don't know. That's something we would need to investigate," said Autumn. "You know, The Eldershaw Detective Agency need to investigate."

"What exactly did you have in mind?" Jones asked.

Autumn floated up slightly, her fingers to her temples. "It hasn't come to me yet," she said. "But when it does, I'll let you know."

"Anyway," said Jones. "Is it knockoff time yet?"

Autumn floated through the lockbox room wall and quickly returned.

"Nope, sorry, it's still ten to four. You've got a while yet. Got something you need to get to? Or someone?"

Jones rolled her eyes. "No. I'm just ready for today to end."

"Sure, sure," said Autumn. "And it wouldn't hurt if it ended at Hugo's bar, would it?"

"If it goes that way, then so be it." Jones strode out of the lockbox room, a grin on her face.

Autumn flew up beside her. "Okay, I'll let you work. For now. But while you are, I want you to think about our key suspects. At the moment, we have Rex, Flick, and Flick's mother. But we haven't even met Astrid. Is she in town? We need to find out about this. And also, is there anyone else we should be considering?"

"Ok," Jones whispered. "I'll ponder it. We can talk about it when we close."

And ponder it, she did. Now that she had resigned herself to the fact that they were never going to find out what happened to her Granny's opal earrings, the Lights as she'd called them, Jones found herself more focused on Lorne Fox. Maybe it *was* a job for The Eldershaw Detective Agency. At least they could attempt to help Christopher's investigation in some way. But how?

Jones knew she could try to have more of a chat with Flick. But how much would she even reveal? Then there was Rex. Should she ignore the possible danger and see what he thought about Lorne's death? If she did it when other people were around, surely she would be ok. But Astrid, the ex-wife, was a challenge. A few people had mentioned her, but where was she? What did they even know about her? Jones realised the best person to speak to was Sybil. She would make a point of chatting to her in the morning on her usual coffee run.

However, there was another person in Lilly Pilly Creek who was known to be privy to town gossip, and that was a person she certainly planned to run into before tomorrow.

Hugo.

Jones couldn't help but smile as she went and straightened the journals. She had enjoyed the previous night. And she most certainly wanted to spend more time with him, preferably away from the bar. Only so he wasn't distracted by customers, and she would have his full attention.

Time and time again, he had shown himself to be caring and thoughtful, not to mention brave and willing to put himself on the line to help her. This was, of course, not required at the Haunted Cellar, but it hadn't gone unnoticed that he'd been immediately aware of the similarity between Autumn's death and the story Jed had told them. As she thought about it now, she realised how much this had meant to her. She was on his radar, and he was looking out for her.

Jones also realised that she wasn't thinking so much about where her future was. She knew she had held herself back a bit with Hugo, knew she wasn't sure how long she would stay in Lilly Pilly Creek. But it was becoming home again. She felt like she belonged to this town again, that it had brought her back into its fold. The city and her journalism career seemed far away. Not that she ever wanted to give up her journalistic endeavours, but it did seem her future wasn't as black and white as newspapers.

She had to admit, despite the circumstances, Jones did enjoy investigating these mysteries with her sister. They worked well as a team, and Autumn's ghost skills no doubt had their advantages. She did wonder how they were going to use them this time, however. Hopefully, there might be an eavesdropping opportunity. Or perhaps Autumn needed to sneak into the nursery and take a look around.

"Come on! Let's go see Hugo!"

Autumn twirled down from the ceiling directly in front of Jones. Jones couldn't help but smile. Glancing around, The Memory Bank was empty of customers, and Atlas was just locking up the garden doors.

"Atlas, coming to Hugo's for a drink?"

"I don't mind if I do!"

Jones and Atlas, with Autumn gliding behind them, locked up and made a beeline for the wine bar.

CHAPTER 20

When Atlas and Jones pushed the door open to Hugo's, she was pleased to see both Wren and Plum sitting up at the bar. They were chatting with Hugo, along with another familiar face, Jed from The Haunted Cellar. She knew her cheeks were pink, but she was excited to see Hugo, despite knowing both Wren and Plum were watching her every move.

"Hi," she said quietly to Hugo, before sitting down and greeting the two women. Jones felt an overwhelming desire to plant a kiss on his cheek. But they weren't at the stage of public affection, so fortunately she refrained from embarrassing herself.

Hugo lifted a bottle of the Haunted Cellar's Rosè, asking Jones if she'd like a glass. She nodded enthusiastically.

"Jones, you remember Jed?" Hugo said.

"Of course," said Jones. "Thank you for a fun evening."

"I'm glad you enjoyed it," Jed smiled.

"It was wonderful," said Jones. "I was thinking of writing a review."

"Really?" Jed cocked his head.

"Yes. I'm a journalist, but I'm currently on sabbatical," she explained. "Well, running The Memory Bank, so it may have to wait for now."

"Well, I would welcome that any time," Jed lifted his glass and Jones clinked hers against it.

Jed and Hugo resumed chatting whilst Jones turned to Wren and

Plum.

"I didn't realise you two knew each other?" said Jones to the women.

"We don't!" said Plum.

"I knew she was your godmother, so I just introduced myself," said Wren.

"Of course you did," Jones laughed. "And Plum, have I introduced you properly to Atlas yet?" Atlas had already found a seat next to the women and was also holding a glass of the Rosè.

"Hi Atlas," said Plum, extending her arm. "I hear you are the key to ensuring The Memory Bank runs smoothly."

Atlas smiled at this lovely compliment. "Oh no, not at all. I just help where I can."

"He's being modest, of course," said Jones. "There's no way we could be where we are without Atlas."

"Or me!" said Autumn. "Don't forget me." Autumn was grinning from the other side of the bar, perched up on the rear bench.

"Another one, ladies?" Hugo asked Plum and Wren, holding up the Rosè bottle. Jones looked up and saw that Jed had left, so hopefully Hugo might linger.

Jones smiled at him. "This was one of our favourites last night," she explained to Wren and Plum.

"Oh, the big date!" said Wren. "How did it go?"

"Tell Wren all about it!" said Plum enthusiastically.

"Well, where do we start, Jones?" said Hugo, ready to regale his audience with the story of the Haunted Cellar.

Jones let Hugo take the lead as he described the descent into the cellar, the imposing portrait, and the dramatic way Jed told them the story of Harriet Treasure. Wren gasped, clapped and laughed at all the appropriate moments. He didn't mention the blinking portrait, and Jones didn't add this to his story, although she quickly glanced at Plum, who nodded slightly. Jones wasn't quite sure why she was comfortable revealing this to Plum and not to Wren.

"This is amazing!" said Wren. "I am totally getting a seat at their next wine tasting. You can organise that, right Hugo?"

"I'll see what I can do," Hugo said with a wink.

"Of course you can!" said Jones and then explained. "That was the owner Hugo was just speaking to," said Jones.

"Well, that's sorted!" said Wren. "But now, what I want to know is, has anyone heard anything about what happened to Lorne Fox?"

"I haven't heard a lot at all," said Jones. "I didn't even visit Sybil this morning."

"You didn't? This is shocking information," Wren said with mock surprise.

"Don't worry, I did," said Atlas. "But Sybil doesn't share any of the gossip with me. Just made us amazing coffee."

"That is true," said Plum. "I finally ordered one today. They are divine. But what has visiting Sybil got to do with Lorne Fox?"

"Tell her Jones!" Autumn piped in.

Jones smiled. "Sybil is the font of all knowledge," she explained. "At least when it comes to Lilly Pilly Creek. If you need to know something, you go to Sybil."

"And you think she knows who killed Lorne?" Plum's eyes widened.

"No, not necessarily, but she hears things," said Jones. "A lot of things. If anyone's going to hear a clue no one else does, it will be Sybil."

"Except for the local ghost," said Autumn. "She can hear more than most."

Jones took a drink to hide her grin. Autumn was right. She could hear more than even Sybil could.

"Gosh, it's Colin!" said Wren, turning to see who had loudly entered the bar.

"He never drinks here, does he Hugo?"

"Can't say I've ever seen him before." Hugo shook his head. "Who is he?"

Wren explained. "He's a bit rough around the edges, old Colin. Always got a beer in his hand, and doesn't do much these days."

"Except he is on the Progress Association committee," Jones commented.

"Mostly so he can get a free beer!" Wren laughed.

"Probably true," said Jones. "But he has his uses. Doesn't mind getting his hands dirty if he knows there's a beer or two waiting at the end. And he does know a little about a lot of stuff."

"Jones! Fancy seeing you here!" It was Colin, a wobble in his step as he came up next to Jones and leant against the bar.

"Hi Colin," said Jones. "What brings you in here?"

"Too many memories," said Colin.

"Too many memories? What do you mean?"

"At the pub. Too many memories of poor Foxy. I thought a few beers would help." Colin shook his head and didn't say another word.

"So you thought you'd try Hugo's?"

"Uh-huh. Doesn't look too bad either," Colin said, turning to take a glance at the place. "Not really my cuppa tea, but they do serve beer. Don't they?"

Hugo stuck his hand out in front of Colin. "Howdy Colin, I'm Hugo."

"Hugo? As in Hugo Hugo?"

"Yep, I'm Hugo Hugo. And yes, we do sell beer."

"Just all the fancy stuff, or have you got some Pale Ale here?"

"Coopers? Sure do! Let me grab you a schooner."

"Appreciate it," said Colin, and he shuffled around, pulling up a stool next to them.

"Jones, ask him questions. He might know some stuff," Autumn piped up, coming to stand closer to their group.

"So Colin, were you and Lorne good friends?"

"Me and Foxy? Well, I don't s'pose you'd call us good friends. But we'd known each other since we were kids. He was just always there. And I have to say, he helped me out a few times when I needed it."

"Did he really?" said Wren.

"I know everyone says he was a bit of a jerk," said Colin, gratefully accepting his beer from Hugo and taking a gulp. "And he was. But that was just Foxy. If you were selling him a shirt, he'd bargain you down to nothin', but then he'd give it right back to you if you needed it. I don't know what kind of man that makes him, but what I know is I'm gonna miss him." Colin turned, picked up his glass, and, amazingly, finished the rest of the beer.

"So Colin," said Jones. "If he wasn't as bad as everyone is saying, then who would want to hurt him?"

Colin slid his glass towards Hugo, nodding for another one, and then turned to Jones. "I don't bloody know," he said. "I've been wracking my brain about that one. It could have been almost anyone. Foxy must have just gone too far this time, didn't know when to let things lie, pushed the wrong person." Colin shrugged. "But if you ask me," Colin grabbed the second beer and took another, smaller sip this time, wiping the foam off his top lip with the back of his hand.

"Yes?" asked Plum, who had leaned in, clearly enjoying the conversation.

"If you ask me, I reckon it could have been Astrid."

"His ex-wife?" said Wren.

"Yep," said Colin. "I think Lorne still owed her a lot of money, and she was trying to get him to sell the house to pay it. But that home had been in Colin's family for years. He would have only sold it over his dead body. Sorry. Didn't mean it like that. But you get what I'm sayin'."

Everyone nodded. They knew exactly what he was saying. And with money and emotions combined, it could be enough to make someone snap.

"We need to find this Astrid woman," said Autumn.

CHAPTER 21

"How did he get home?" Sybil asked the next morning, as Jones described the previous evening to her.

"He just strolled out of the bar about twenty minutes later," said Jones. "I think Colin can hold his alcohol a lot better than the average person."

"Well, he has had plenty of practice!" said Sybil as she pulled a ham, pineapple and cheese toastie out of the sandwich press and slid it into a paper bag.

Jones had to laugh and gratefully took the hot sandwich.

"But he seems to think Astrid has something to do with it. Do you know her?"

"You don't see her around Lilly Pilly Creek much anymore. She moved to the city years ago, after she and Lorne got divorced. But I think she may be staying with Flick. I'm sure I saw her head into the Lilly Pilly Pantry yesterday."

"Surely you could visit Flick, you know, pretend you just want to check on her after yesterday?" It was Autumn, whispering in her ear. Jones had found her floating at Sybil's van when she arrived, knowing full well where Jones's first port of call was going to be that morning.

"What about you, Sybil? Any ideas on what could have happened to Lorne?" Jones took a bite of her toastie and leaned forward to prevent the pineapple juice from spilling on her shirt. A pineapple juice stain would not look good across today's quote.

'Christmas Spirit is not something you can turn off like a faucet on

December 26th!' A classic from Lorelai Gilmore.

"Well, I don't know. But I have heard rumours that the police have questioned both Rex and Flick."

"Questioned? As suspects?"

Sybil frowned. "That's what I heard. But wouldn't you have better information?"

"What do you mean?"

"Well, aren't you a friend of Sergeant Schmidt?" Sybil kept her eyes on the milk she was frothing, not daring to make eye contact with Jones.

"Not really," said Jones. "I mean, friendly, I guess. But not friends."

"Mmmm," said Sybil. She didn't give the impression she believed Jones. Maybe she hadn't heard about Jones's date with Hugo. But surely not! Jones couldn't imagine that hadn't already become common Lilly Pilly Creek knowledge.

"I haven't heard anything more than you. And I didn't know he had questioned them both," Jones said. "But Christopher did ask me questions about both Rex and Flick because they were at The Progress Association meeting with me the night before."

"Interesting," said Sybil, handing Jones her coffee.

"Anything else?" asked Jones.

"Not that I can think of. Most people think it's either his ex-wife or someone he's annoyed through the nursery. It could be almost anyone."

Jones sighed. "That's the impression I'm getting, too."

"Well, enjoy the sandwich!" said Sybil. "I'll let you know if I hear anything else."

Jones turned, and Autumn floated next to her.

"Well, that wasn't any help at all," said Jones.

"Except now we know where his ex-wife might be," said Autumn. "I think we're going to have to pay Flick a visit."

Jones took another bite of the cheesy ham and pineapple sandwich, and then a long sip of her coffee. She was going to need more caffeine this morning before she would be an effective private detective.

It just seemed that this case (and Jones still felt weird even thinking about working on a case) didn't seem to have any clear leads. The only thing they knew, that others didn't, was that Lorne had been overheard arguing with a female. So did that eliminate Rex from the suspect list, or was the argument completely unrelated?

"Do you think the argument you overheard could have been Lorne telling Flick he wasn't retiring?"

"I was thinking about that," said Autumn. "It makes sense, and also places Flick away from the nursery when the argument happened."

"Does that make her more or less likely to be the killer?" asked Jones, sipping even more coffee.

"I guess it makes her less likely. If she was going to whack Lorne, it probably would have been then. Don't you think?"

Jones nodded as she put the last piece of hot sandwich in her mouth. "I do actually," she said. "Although, I guess it is likely she could have started up again back at the nursery. That isn't out of the question."

"The other possibility is that the argument wasn't with Flick at all. It could have been with Astrid," said Autumn.

"If she was even in town at that point," said Jones. "I mean, it makes sense that she's in town *now*, helping Flick. But if she was in town on the day of Lorne's death, why? Was there something that caused her to come and confront Lorne?"

"This is what we're going to have to find out," said Autumn. "I imagine Christopher already knows the answer to that. Do you think you might wheedle some information out of him?"

"Wheedle?"

"Good word huh!" Autumn grinned.

"That's debatable," said Jones. "But it seems like we have two options. Visit Flick in the hope Astrid might be there. Or try to chat with Christopher."

"If only everyone didn't already know about your romantic date with Hugo," Autumn sighed, closing her eyes as she floated in front of her sister.

"Everyone?" said Jones. "And what does that have to do with it?"

"You know exactly what," said Autumn. "Christopher will be more suspicious of you now if you try to charm him. He'll know you're just trying to get something out of him."

Jones rolled her eyes, and instead of responding, sipped her coffee, resisting the urge to look through the windows as they walked past Hugo's.

Autumn floated directly through the front door as Jones unlocked it and then turned off the alarm.

It was the day before the big Christmas party. They had a lot to do and had decided to close at lunchtime. They would need the afternoon to move tables to make a clear area for the stage that was being set up the following day.

The Progress Association was coming along to help, as well as Hugo, who had agreed to set up a bar in the garden for the event. He was leaving the wine bar open on the night of the party but knew most people would be at The Memory Bank, so he was happy to manage the bar with some of his staff in return for the takings. Jones thought it was a brilliant idea and was also happy Hugo would be there to be a part of the festivities.

"Do you know what I think I've found in the escape room?" said Autumn, as Jones placed her handbag behind the counter and started getting ready for the day.

"What? More newspapers?"

"No, I think I've found the old Christmas decorations?"

"Really? How old?" Jones looked at her sister, intrigued.

"Quite old I think," said Autumn. "I don't want to get too excited, but it kind of looks like it might be Granny's handwriting on the outside of the box."

"Really! Oh, how cool would it be to have some of Granny's decorations? That would just bring things full circle."

"You might want to take a look before everyone gets here. How quickly do you think you could be in and out?"

Jones glanced at the clock. Twenty minutes until opening.

"I think I can do it," said Jones. "I only put a few things back on the top shelves this time."

Jones worked as quickly as she could. Autumn apologised profusely as she couldn't help and eventually, Jones had to get stern with her.

"Autumn! It's fine! You're dead. Of course, I don't expect you to help."

Autumn gasped. Jones had never spoken to her quite like that.

"Autumn, I'm sorry," said Jones.

"No, it's totally fine," said Autumn. "You put it perfectly. You're right. I am dead. You know that. I know that. I'll just shut up and focus on what I *can* do to help."

Jones nodded, managing a small smile, as she leaned her back against the bookshelf and pushed. The door appeared, and she quickly unlocked it.

"So, where do you think these decorations are?"

"Up on the top of that cupboard. Behind the cane basket." Autumn had floated up and was craning her neck over the top of a box. "Yep, it definitely says Christmas decorations."

Looking around the room, Jones searched for something she could stand on. There she found an old plastic orange drinks crate. She flipped it over in front of the cupboard and stepped up. Jones pulled the cane basket down and bent to drop it lightly on the floor. She then reached for the box.

"It's not heavy at all!" Jones said, surprised.

"That seems like a good sign," said Autumn. "It's probably filled with tinsel."

Jones lifted it down and decided to leave the basket where it was so she could leave quickly and get everything back in order before opening time.

With the shelf back in front hiding the door, and the decorations box plonked on the counter, Jones rushed over to unlock the Bank's front door. As she pushed it open, she found something had been slid underneath.

"I'm sure that wasn't there when I arrived?" said Jones, picking up the blue envelope.

"What is it?" asked Autumn, who had noticed Jones bending down. Jones held it up for her to see. "Another blue envelope?"

Jones raised her eyebrows and nodded. What would it say? And who had managed to slip it under the door at the perfect time? "Do you think they watched me?" asked Jones

"What do you mean?"

"Well, it wasn't here when I arrived, I'm sure of that. And I bet you would have noticed?"

Autumn nodded.

Jones continued. "So I wonder, do you think they watched me go into The Memory Bank, knowing we don't open until nine, and then slid it under?"

"Possible," shrugged Autumn. "But why? Why would it matter?"

"I don't know," said Jones. "Maybe they just wanted to make sure I was the one who got it."

"But it could very easily have been Atlas," said Autumn. "He has a key too."

"Yes, you're right. Maybe they just wanted to make sure it was one of us and not a customer?"

"Or that it wasn't anyone who's been coming to the library lately. Like Flick."

This made Jones stop and think.

"Well, open it up already!"

Jones shook her head, realising she had forgotten she was holding an envelope for a reason.

"Until they find who caused the attack at The Memory Bank all those years ago, the Christmas Party should not resume. The police should do their job, and as the owners of The Memory Bank, you should be insisting they investigate. I will do everything in my power to stop this."

"Everything in their power?" repeated Autumn.

"That does sound ominous," said Jones, looking up at her sister. "I think we need to report this."

"Jones! Thank goodness!" It was Atlas, almost stumbling into the Bank, coffee wobbling in the tray he was carrying.

"What is it, Atlas?"

"This!" Atlas hurriedly placed the coffees on one of the product tables near the door, and rushed over to Jones, waving-

"Another blue envelope!" Jones cried out.

"Another?" Atlas's eyebrows narrowed.

Jones held up hers. "This was just slid under the door."

"You're joking! I found mine poking out of my car door this morning."

"Your car door! Oh, that is not good," said Jones.

"We have to call the police," said Autumn. Jones nodded, daring to take a glance at Atlas, as he was opening his envelope.

"Read this." He shoved the piece of paper at Jones.

"As an employee of The Memory Bank, I would be refusing to work whilst they are still planning to host The Christmas Party. The culprit of the attack all those years ago has never been found, and I, for one, would not want to put myself at risk of the same thing happening. You must take a stand with your employer and insist the police reopen the   investigation before it's too late."

"Well, if that's a *thinly* veiled threat," said Jones, handing Atlas her letter, "Then this is laid on thick."

Atlas frowned as he read and then looked up with anger all over his face. "We have to do something!"

"Yes, we do," said Jones. "*I* need to go to the police. *You* may need to go home."

"Go home! Why?"

"Atlas, it's not safe here. These are two letters that are clearly threatening us, and just as the letter says, I can't risk you getting hurt. Or worse." Jones was shaking her head sadly.

"You think the person who attacked Molly Shepherd years ago is going to rock up here and attack me?"

"No, not them. At least that does seem rather unlikely." Jones paused for a moment. "But I think this letter writer might."

"And what if the letter writer and the attacker are the same person?" said Autumn.

"Oh, I didn't think of that!" said Jones, unable to ignore Autumn's declaration.

"What?"

"The letter writer. What if the letter writer and Molly's attacker are the same person?"

"Surely not!" said Atlas. "Look, of course, you should go to the police, but I think this is just someone bored and looking for attention."

"Really?" said Jones. "Do you think?"

"Who else would be so invested?" asked Atlas. "Unless it's Molly Shepherd who's sending these letters."

"And she has made it pretty clear she only sent the one to the Progress Association," replied Jones.

"Exactly. So who else would even care? What does it even matter if we host the event here? I mean, I understand Molly being upset. And maybe if anyone from your family was still here."

Jones shrugged, ignoring Autumn, who decided to take this moment to dance wildly behind Atlas to make her presence known.

"Yes, I know what you mean," said Jones. "It doesn't make sense, other than as someone who's trying to cause trouble."

"And I, for one, am not going to let them," said Atlas.

"Ok, ok. You're right," said Jones, picking up the coffee cups and handing one to Atlas. "But I've still got to tell Christopher."

Atlas sipped his coffee. "Of course you do. At the very least, they're a menace who should be stopped."

The two of them stood there quietly for a moment, sipping their coffee and pondering the morning's events. Jones was feeling unsettled by the letters. She was surprised there was someone out there who felt so strongly about the Christmas Party they would go to all the trouble to hand deliver these letters. It seemed like such a waste of time. Did they think they would cancel the party? And if they felt so strongly about it, why didn't they just come and speak to her?

"Forget about it and let's look at the Christmas decorations!" called Autumn, who was currently walking sideways along the bookshelves.

Jones had completely forgotten about the box of Christmas Decorations.

CHAPTER 22

"Atlas," Jones said. "Come and look at what I found."

"We! What we found!" Autumn joked, and she glided over to the box they had brought out.

"What is it?" Atlas asked, sipping his coffee as he followed Jones around to the rear of the circular counter.

"I'm hoping it's Christmas decorations," said Jones. "Really old ones from my Granny."

"Cool," said Atlas. "Well, hurry up. Open it!"

Jones looked at the brown tape that was beginning to lift from the cardboard box. Did she need scissors, or should she just rip it? She decided on scissors. She wanted to honour whatever her granny had put inside this box. Sliding them down the top and flicking the scissors along the ends, the cardboard flaps popped open.

"Seems to be packed full." Atlas peered down but didn't touch it. He left that to Jones.

"Oh, come on Jones! I can't wait," said Autumn.

Carefully, Jones folded back first the side flaps and then the ends. Layers of pink tissue paper covered the top of the box. She lifted each piece gently and even went to the effort of attempting to flatten each one neatly before moving on to the next. Autumn sighed but kept her mouth shut.

Underneath the layers of tissue paper, there was more tissue paper. But this time it appeared to be protecting individual items. Delicately, Jones lifted the first item and unwrapped it.

"Oh, it's lovely," breathed Autumn.

"Very nice," said Atlas.

Jones was holding a clear glass bauble containing dried red bottlebrush flowers.

She unwrapped the next one. This time, the bauble contained dried wattle flowers, their colour still bright and golden. There were six in total, each containing a different flower. Kangaroo paw, red gum blossom, pink Geraldton wax, and some Australian daisies finished the collection.

"These are amazing," said Jones. "I've never seen anything like them."

"They're unique," said Atlas. "Will you put them on the tree? Or do something else?"

"I'm not sure actually," said Jones. "I don't think they fit with the key theme. I wonder, could I put a eucalyptus branch in something and hang them on that?"

"That's a great idea!" said Atlas.

"Agreed!" called out Autumn.

"Maybe it would look good up here, on the counter?"

Jones had placed the baubles carefully on the piles of tissue paper and was now reaching in to see what else might be inside.

"I think this might be a wreath," Jones guessed as she lifted it out. Pulling the layers of tissue paper back, she was proven correct. Made of twisted branches, the wreath was decorated with a variety of gum leaves and banksia flowers. Unusual seed pods had also been slid in amongst the foliage.

"We need this on the Bank door immediately!" said Atlas. He took it carefully from Jones's hands, and without hesitating, headed directly to the front door. Using the hanging wire already attached, he hooked the wreath onto a metal notch on the door and twisted it tight.

Jones followed to view his handiwork. "Yes, you're right, Atlas. That is perfect."

Atlas smiled, rubbing his hands together. "Is there anything else left in the box?"

"Yes, I think there was something on the bottom," said Jones, and they both swiftly headed back to the counter.

Jones lifted the final mystery parcel from the box.

"Guess!" said Atlas, encouraging Jones's game.

"It feels like a picture frame," said Jones. "But is that even a Christmas decoration?"

"Hurry up!" said Autumn.

Jones placed the final parcel carefully face down on the wooden countertop. The back was taped up so Jones took the scissors again and carefully slid them underneath the paper. Gently she folded it back and then, after a moment's hesitation, she lifted the frame and turned it over.

Autumn gasped.

"Oh my goodness," said Jones.

Atlas didn't say a word. He looked at the picture and then back at Jones. "Is this your family?"

Jones nodded. She felt her eyes prickle and her nose tingle. If she spoke, she knew she would burst into tears. Atlas was correct. It was her family. In the picture were her Granny Matilda, Pa Baxter, Dad Kitt and Mum Margot. There was also a baby in her dad's arms and a little girl holding her mum's hand. Baby Autumn and young Jones.

"I've never seen this before," said Autumn.

"No," said Jones. "I've never seen it, ever."

"Really?" said Atlas. "You've never seen this before? I wonder why it was packed away?"

Jones knew. She didn't tell Atlas, but she knew it was because after their mum died, it would have been too painful. It wouldn't have been too long after they took this picture that she had died of cancer. Possibly this was the last family photo taken.

"Are you ok Jones?"

"Yes," said Jones. "I'm okay, thanks Atlas. But do you know what? I don't think we should hide this away any more. I think we need to find a place to hang this, permanently. It is the legacy of The Memory Bank."

Jones took the chance to glance up at Autumn and she saw glittering tears flowing down her cheeks. Jones couldn't recall if she had seen Autumn cry in her ghost form. Certainly nothing like this. Her sister looked up and smiled despite her tears.

Looking back at the picture, Jones was suddenly struck because the only person alive in that entire picture was that one little girl. No longer a little girl, she would give anything to hold her mum's hand again.

"Good morning!" a loud voice called out. Before even looking up, the sound of heels on timber signalled who was striding across the

Bank floor.

"Good morning, Prue," said Jones. "Is everything okay?" Then she saw the blue envelope in Prue's hand and realised no, everything was not okay.

"Have a read of this," said Prue.

Jones took the letter from Prue and read a letter very similar to the one she and Atlas had received. Jones nodded and then turned to pick up their envelopes. "We got one too. Atlas and I."

"You're joking!" said Prue. "So she is serious then."

"She?" asked Jones.

"Molly Shepherd of course," said Prue.

"Perhaps," said Jones. "But when I spoke to Molly the other day, she was adamant it wasn't her. She also gave me her blessing to host the party here. And I am inclined to believe her."

Prue's mouth was open wide. "You mean *someone else* is threatening us!" She looked personally affronted, as if it were her business they were writing about. Jones supposed it was the Christmas Party, not just The Memory Bank the letter writer was angry about.

"Yes, and I think we need to take these to the police," said Jones, holding up the blue envelopes. "Do you know if anyone else has received any?"

"Good question," said Prue. "Let's get on the phone with all the Progress Association Committee members first, and then we may need to go to the police together. A united front."

Jones nodded. Prue was always overly professional, sometimes to extremes. But in this case, Jones certainly thought it warranted.

Prue pulled her phone out of her black leather handbag but then paused. Jones watched her, wondering what was going through her head.

"Emergency meeting," said Prue.

"What?" Jones frowned.

"We need to call an emergency meeting," Prue explained. "Yes, we need to go to the police, but we also need to talk this through and do a risk assessment for tomorrow's event."

"Well, I'm happy to hold it here when we close at twelve," said Jones. "Maybe an emergency lunch meeting. So, should *I* go to the police, or you?"

"You need to go to the police station, obviously," said Prue.

"Obviously?"

Prue rolled her eyes. "Come on, everyone knows Christopher Schmidt has a thing for you."

Autumn burst out laughing, and Jones was sure she heard Atlas snort.

"Prue, don't be ridiculous," said Jones.

"Oh, you think just because you're dating Hugo that Chris is over you?"

"Christopher," Jones corrected Prue without thinking.

"Sorry, *Christopher*," said Prue. "Proving my point."

"Ok, that's enough, Prue," said Jones. "But I am happy to go to the police station and talk to whoever is there.

"Right," said Prue. "You go to the police station. I'll round up the troops. We'll meet you back here. I'll get some food brought in." Prue immediately started tapping on her phone as her heels cracked across the floor and she left the building.

"The cyclone has gone," muttered Autumn.

"Atlas," said Jones. "I presume you got all of that. Are you right to man the place?"

"Absolutely," he said.

"And you will be careful won't you," said Jones. "I doubt the letter writer is brave enough to set foot in the Bank, but just in case."

"I know," said Atlas. "If I feel any sort of threat, I'll call you. Or the police."

"Yes, me or the police. Your safety is more important than anything else."

Jones tried to sound calm, but with blue envelopes coming in thick and fast, she couldn't deny she was starting to panic.

It seemed someone really did want to harm The Memory Bank.

CHAPTER 23

"Of course, I'm coming to the police station!" said Autumn. "You know I work my magic there. Who knows what I might see?"

Autumn and Jones were in the Bank bathroom. Autumn was perched on a basin after she had been scolded for leaning over Jones's stall to continue their conversation.

"But Autumn, there's nothing to see," said Jones. "Christopher doesn't know about these envelopes. It's the first time he'll have heard about it. There won't be any sort of case file to look over. I need you to watch out for Atlas."

"Atlas will be fine," said Autumn. "And there's nothing I could do to help him, even if I wanted to."

"You might be able to move something, do something, to scare them?" Jones was feeling guilty about leaving Atlas alone at The Memory Bank. Even if Autumn couldn't do anything, having her there would make her feel better.

"Jones, I'm coming to the police station," said Autumn. "I want to hear what Christopher says, and to be honest, I need to get out of here. If Atlas needs you, he said he'd call."

Jones sighed and flushed the toilet.

"Alright, alright," said Jones. "I know there's nothing I could do to stop you, anyway."

Autumn grinned and folded her arms.

"No need to look so smug," said Jones, but she smiled back at her sister as she washed and dried her hands.

Collecting the envelopes on the way, including Prue's which she had left, Jones waved to Atlas and walked to the Police Station. Glancing into the bar as she passed, she saw Prue talking to Hugo.

"What's she doing?" asked Autumn.

"No idea," said Jones. She didn't let Autumn know, but it surprised Jones how quickly a tinge of jealousy crept up on her. Of course, she knew there was nothing between Prue and Hugo, but Jones was not quite prepared for the intensity of her feelings towards Hugo at that moment.

Rolling back her shoulders, Jones focused on the current mission. The sisters crossed at the pedestrian lights and continued up Main Street to the red brick station. Autumn floated through as Jones turned the handle and walked in. The desk was empty and, as Jones went to press the bell on the counter, Autumn stopped her.

"Can I try? Please?"

Jones waved her hand and stepped aside to give Autumn a go.

Extending one finger, she held it over the button and closed her eyes. Jones's eyes darted between her sister's face and her finger. She was willing Autumn to press the button. She knew how much it would mean to her sister.

As Autumn concentrated on pressing the button, it was almost as though Jones could see a ripple of energy around her sister. The air between her finger and the button seemed to blur.

"Brzzzz!"

"Oh, you did it!" Jones cried out, before clamping her hand over her mouth.

Autumn flew backwards, as though the force of the bell had pushed her away. She was grinning, staring at her hands in amazement.

"I can't believe it!" said Autumn. "Yesss!" She twirled up into the air and back down just as a police officer pushed the rear door open and walked through.

She was an officer Jones had met before when they had arrested Jamie Royce, Autumn's ex-boyfriend, and the person who pushed her down the staircase.

"Jones Eldershaw," she greeted her. "How can I help you?"

"Hello, sorry I've forgotten your name," Jones felt a little flustered, surprised that the officer would remember her so clearly.

"Constable Partridge," she said, nodding with a small smile on her face.

"Yes, of course," said Jones. "Look, I'm here on behalf of myself, Atlas and also The Progress Association. We have been receiving some threatening letters, and everything seems to have escalated this morning."

"Threatening letters? About what?"

"The Christmas Party," said Jones.

Constable Partridge couldn't help but laugh at this.

"I'm serious," said Jones. "Although I know on the surface it sounds ridiculous. Here." And Jones laid out the four letters on the counter.

The Constable raised her eyebrows and picked up the first letter. As she began to read, Jones watched Autumn filter through the rear wall into the back of the police station.

Jones watched the Constable closely. She clearly thought Jones was dramatising the situation, and that a few letters in pretty blue envelopes couldn't be considered threatening. However, as she read, it appeared the Constable's understanding of the situation was changing.

"Hmmm," she said, laying the first letter to one side before picking up the next.

Constable Partridge continued reading. "Hmmm," she murmured again, quickly picking up the third letter. She read the last letter at speed and then looked at Jones. "Yes, these would appear to be credible threats."

"Exactly," said Jones. "So what should we do? What *can* we do?"

"The problem is we don't know who these are from," said Constable. "Or do we?"

Jones shook her head. "No, we don't. Although some had thought it was Molly Shepherd."

"Molly Shepherd, the alpaca lady?"

"The very one," said Jones.

"Christopher is coming," said Autumn rather loudly as she whizzed back into the front room of the Police Station.

Jones looked at the rear door before she heard a sound. She hoped Constable Partridge didn't notice her obvious expectation that Sergeant Schmidt was about to walk into the room.

"Jones! What brings you to the station?" Christopher smiled, a vast change from the first time Jones had walked into this very station.

"Look at these," Constable Partridge pointed the Sergeant to the letters.

"Hi Christopher," said Jones. "I've just been letting Constable Partridge know about some threats we've been receiving."

"Threats!" Christopher's face immediately turned to one of concern. "Are you ok?"

Jones smiled, appreciating his concern. "Yes, I'm perfectly alright. But I am a bit worried about tomorrow's Christmas Party."

"The Christmas Party?" Christopher was confused and picked up the letters. He skimmed them and turned to the Constable. "We need to open a case and we're going to need to speak to each of the recipients of these letters." He turned back to Jones. "Has anyone else received these?"

"Prue is currently phoning all the members of the Progress Association Committee," she replied. "And we are having an emergency meeting at twelve when The Memory Bank closes."

He nodded. "Ok, that is probably prudent. I may ask one of my officers to pop in. And we should probably think about some extra security tomorrow."

"So you are taking this seriously?" said Jones.

"Of course we are," said Christopher. "This is a big community event. These are multiple credible threats. We need to take that very seriously."

"Thank you," said Jones.

Christopher reached down and pulled out a form, which he began to fill in. Jones saw Autumn hover behind him, reading his words. After a few moments, he looked up. "Are you able to stay for a few minutes just to answer some questions?"

"Yes, sure," said Jones.

"I won't be long," said Christopher before returning to his writing.

Jones took this opportunity to glance up at Autumn. She was making some unusual faces, which made Jones wonder if Christopher knew something that perhaps they didn't. Were these the first threats the police had seen? It seemed the Constable knew nothing more than what Jones had shared with her. Did the Sergeant perhaps have information no one else had?

As it appeared Christopher had a lot to document, Jones took the opportunity to take a seat. Yes, she had been concerned about the letters, but now that Christopher appeared to be quite disturbed, she felt her gumption start to wobble. Did they have a reason to be worried about the security of tomorrow's Christmas party? What would they need to address in the emergency meeting?

Christopher began speaking to her, asking Jones questions, which she promptly answered. But her mind was a whirl. Would they need to cancel the event? Would they need to restrict it to just award winners and finalists and quickly present the awards before ending the evening? Would the police have a strong presence? This all sounded ludicrous, but the more questions she was asked, and the more she thought about it, the more worried she became.

"Also Jones, could I ask you a question on another matter?"

"Another matter?" Jones couldn't for the life of her think what else Christopher would need to speak to her about.

"Well, obviously, I am busy investigating the unfortunate Lorne

Fox case," he explained.

Oh yes, of course. She felt silly to have let that slip her mind.

"Yes, yes, how can I help?"

"Have you spoken to Flick in the last few days?" He tilted his head slightly, ready for her answer.

"She did come into The Memory Bank yesterday," said Jones. "To deliver our water feature."

"Oh? She's back to work?"

"It surprised me too," said Jones. "I told her to go home, to take some time. But she said someone needed to keep the business going. Although, after a bit of an emotional breakdown, I think she did end up going home for the rest of the day. At least that was my impression."

"Emotional breakdown?"

"Yes, we were talking about her father, and it got a bit too much."

"What specifically were you talking about?"

Jones knew she should answer. Knew she had to answer. But she also knew her response was going to put the spotlight firmly on Flick, and she still couldn't believe that she could have killed her father.

"Ah, well, she mentioned that her dad had decided not to retire."

"Not to retire? Was he planning on retiring?"

"That's what Flick told us," said Jones. "She said her dad was planning to retire at Christmas time, and he was handing the reins over to her. Only he changed his mind."

"When exactly did he change his mind?"

Jones shrugged. "I'm not sure when *he* changed his mind. But he told Flick the day-" Jones paused. "The day before his death."

CHAPTER 24

"What did he write?" Jones asked Autumn immediately after they stepped out of the police station.

"Oh, so you noticed," said Autumn.

"Gosh yes. Your face was contorting like you were in pain!"

"Well, he was noting that Molly Shepherd had a history of *violence,* as well as Colin."

"What, he thinks Colin wrote the letters?"

"I think he does," said Autumn. "At least he was one possibility."

"Do you know why?"

"Because he was the prime suspect in the attack on Molly!"

"No! Really?"

Autumn was nodding. "Yes! That's what he wrote down."

"But why would Colin not want the Christmas Party to go ahead? Even if he was the main suspect? He's on the Progress Committee. I don't think he's ever expressed any negativity towards the event."

Autumn raised her eyebrows. "But could he?"

Jones stopped talking as they walked, pondering this. Could Colin secretly wish the Christmas Party wasn't going ahead? Was he concerned that the party might bring attention back to the attack?

"If he was the attacker, wouldn't he want to fly under the radar?" Jones asked.

"I would have thought so," said Autumn. "I mean, if I were the attacker, I would remain as inconspicuous as possible. I'd possibly even go overboard with my enthusiasm for the event."

"Yes, that makes sense," said Jones. "I think the letters would draw more attention to you than the other way around."

"But they're anonymous," said Autumn. "Perhaps they're meant as a diversion tactic. Make people so concerned about the present Christmas Party they won't have time to think about the one from long ago."

Jones nodded. "Meanwhile, do you think they're really considering Flick to be the murderer? Of her own Father?"

"It sure sounds like it," said Autumn. "It's awful, but maybe it is that simple?"

"I think I'm going to visit her tonight. See how she's going, but also to see if we can meet Astrid. It seems she's also in Christopher's sights, at least from what we've heard. I'd like to get a better understanding of her, too."

"Should we be investigating Lorne Fox's murder, when we have so much to worry about with the Christmas Party?" asked Autumn.

"Probably not," said Jones. "But do you think Flick could have killed her father? The way she reacted to his dead body. I just can't believe it. I'm worried the police are laser-focused on her and may miss the real culprit."

"And you think the real culprit could be Flick's mother?"

"Well, think about it. She probably hates Lorne. We've been told he owed her money. And if Flick told her that Lorne had reneged on their deal, then maybe all the bile spewed out and she could no longer contain her hatred towards her ex-husband."

"It sounds just as plausible as it being Flick," Autumn agreed.

"At the very least, they should be seriously considering other suspects, and if we can help that, then shouldn't we make it a priority?'

They were walking past Hugo's again, and Jones couldn't help but glance in. She didn't see the bar's owner anywhere. At least he was no longer chatting with Prue. Jones knew she was being ridiculous, so she turned towards The Memory Bank and focused on the task at hand. The emergency meeting.

Twisting the doorknob, it surprised her to see someone standing on the other side of the door.

"Hugo!"

No wonder he wasn't in the bar. He was right there inside the Memory Bank.

"Hi Jones," he grinned. "I've just delivered lunch."

"You have?" Jones smiled back, still thrilled by the sight of him.

"For the meeting. Prue arranged it."

"Of course!" said Autumn, as she floated away, leaving Hugo and Jones alone.

Jones felt embarrassed by her sense of relief. Not that she thought Hugo had any interest in Prue. But Prue had a way of manipulating situations to get what she wanted, especially situations that involved Jones. If she had her eye on Hugo, Jones would not put it past Prue to go to any lengths. Fortunately, it appeared in this case, she was way off base.

"Oh lovely," said Jones. "That's a great idea."

"I heard what's going on." Hugo's voice took a serious tone. "Are you ok?'

"Yes," said Jones. "I'm fine. I've just been to the police."

"You have? Oh, is it that bad?"

"I think it's all ok," said Jones. "I mean, I have no idea what's going to come out of our meeting. I sure hope we don't have to cancel. Someone from the police station is going to pop in. Christopher was certainly taking the whole thing seriously. Honestly, I don't know what to think!"

"Well, you know I'll help with anything at all," said Hugo. "Just ask."

"Thank you," said Jones. "I might pop in after the meeting if that's okay. I'll let you know what we've decided, in case I need your help with any changes."

"Absolutely!" said Hugo. "It will be quieter then, anyway. Sounds good." He smiled and then reached down and kissed Jones on the cheek. Her legs wobbled, and she couldn't help but grin from ear to ear. It was only her cheek, but she melted at the touch of his lips just the same. Plus, she was relieved her first proper kiss with Hugo wasn't in front of Autumn and Atlas, who she could see hovering around in the background. That was not how she imagined it.

"See you later," Jones said quietly, and Hugo made his way out of the Bank.

Autumn let out a wolf whistle that made Jones jump.

"What was that?" asked Atlas.

Jones turned and stared at him. Surely not!

"What was what?" Jones asked.

"Oh, I'm sure it was nothing," said Atlas. "Just before you jumped, I'm sure I heard a train whistle or something in the distance."

"You did?"

"Holy crap!" Autumn called out.

"Yep," said Atlas, shaking his head. "I'm sure I'm imagining things. But what made you jump?"

"I just thought I saw a spider on my arm," said Jones. "Maybe we both need a break, if we're imagining things. Letting things get to us."

"Nice cover," said Autumn.

"Yes, you're probably right," said Atlas. He walked out from behind the counter. "Now, I got Hugo to set up the lunch on one of the outside tables. All the food's covered, and it's not too hot just yet. I hope that's ok?"

"Yes, sounds great," said Jones. "It will be nice to show everyone the new garden."

"And here they come," said Atlas, as Prue and Tara walked in, closely followed by Rex and Colin. They had obviously all met up out the front before walking in.

"Hi everyone!" Jones called. "Lunch is served in the garden."

"Lovely!" said Prue. "Now we're just waiting on Flick and Iris. Iris was picking her up."

"Oh, is Flick coming? I thought it might be too hard for her," said Jones.

"She insisted," said Prue. "Said there was no way she was going to let anyone ruin The Christmas Party as it was the only thing she had to look forward to."

"Poor Flick," said Tara. "What a rough couple of days she's had."

"She's a tough kid," said Rex. "She'll be right."

Jones nodded at Rex but eyed him up and down. She hadn't forgotten that he'd been mentioned as a potential suspect in Lorne's murder. She was going to keep an eye on him. And she hoped Autumn would, too.

"Yes, she sure is," said Prue. "Let's head to the garden. I'm sure they won't be long."

Colin just nodded at Jones as he walked across the room. She noted he was carrying a plastic bag. A couple of tinnies inside, no doubt.

Jones followed the group, asking Atlas if he could keep an eye out for Iris and Flick. "Oh, and we are technically closed, so please send any customers away if they poke their heads in. Probably better if we keep things private this afternoon."

Atlas nodded and leaned against a table near the front door, ready to assist.

What Hugo had done blew Jones away as she arrived at the table outside. Although simple, he had laid out a white linen tablecloth, and set each place just as he would in the Bar. He'd provided platters of food, salads, and even a selection of cool drinks.

No alcohol was on the table, just water and soft drink, and Jones guessed that was Prue's doing. She needed a professional meeting. At the top of the table sat Prue, with Tara by her side.

Rex and Colin had sat opposite each other, and Jones chose to take a seat at the other end opposite Prue. She wanted to keep her eyes on both Colin and Rex. One a possible violent attacker, and one a potential murderer.

Jones almost laughed out loud at the absurdity of the whole thing. Instead, she reached across and started pouring drinks for everyone.

"I think we have soda water, lemon lime and bitters, and coke. As well as water."

Everyone put their orders in, with Colin just asking for water. Jones narrowly avoided raising her eyebrows.

"Ah, Flick, Iris!" Prue greeted the last two committee members. Iris had her hand resting gently on Flick's back. Flick's eyes were looking puffy, and she couldn't even bring herself to smile. She took her seat and kept her eyes on her hands, which rested on the table.

"Now, everyone help yourself to lunch and I'll bring the meeting to order," said Prue.

No one spoke as they loaded their plates, except to ask to have items passed along the table. When everyone had started to devour the delicious pomegranate and chicken salad, marinated squid and grilled eggplant, or the cured meats and cheeses on offer, Prue officially opened the emergency meeting.

"As you are now well aware, almost all of us have received a threatening letter today, or in days prior," announced Prue.

"Almost all?" asked Jones.

"Yes, everyone except Colin," said Prue.

"Well, that's a red flag," Autumn said. The woman in red was sitting at one of the garden benches off to the side. Jones didn't dare look in her direction, but she fully agreed with her sister's sentiments.

What did it mean? Was he the attacker? Had he sent the threatening notes?

"Probably just missed it," Colin said, his mouth full of mortadella.

"I think that is highly likely," said Prue, looking down her nose at Colin. He proceeded to pull one of his beers from the plastic bag, take a long sip, and return it to the bag. As if no one was aware of what he was doing.

"We'll need to let Christopher know," said Jones. "About the other letters."

"Indeed," said Prue. "And did you speak to Christopher this morning?"

"Yes," Jones nodded. "And Constable Partridge. One of them is going to pop into the meeting. They want to speak with everyone. Did you bring your letters?" Jones looked at Rex, Iris, Tara and Flick.

"I have them here," said Prue. Of course, she did.

"But what are the police even going to do about it?" Rex asked. "Are they going to shut us down? I mean, it's probably just someone having a lend."

"You think they'd go to all this trouble for a joke?" asked Tara.

"Who knows?" said Rex. "What are they even trying to achieve?"

"At this stage, I think that is somewhat irrelevant," said Prue.

"Irrelevant! Why?" Rex banged his fork down on his plate rather forcefully, and everyone was a little taken aback.

"Of course it is important," said Prue, a firm tone in her voice. "But right now, we have to decide what we are going to do about the Christmas Party. Are we going ahead?"

"We *have* to go ahead," said Iris. Everyone was a little surprised at the passion in her voice. Iris was usually quiet at these meetings, putting her hand up for jobs, and happy to work hard in the background. This was unlike her.

"And why is that, Iris?" asked Prue.

"Because it's so important to everyone," Iris said. "Not just to us here, but everyone in this town. There has been so much sadness recently," Iris glanced at Flick. "It's important for everyone to have the opportunity to enjoy themselves. We need to bring the town together. If we cancel the Christmas Party, then they've won. The letter writer will have won."

"Here, here!" said Colin. Despite not being the preferred leader, everyone at the table agreed with him and applauded spontaneously.

Iris smiled, turning a little red, and then looked down at the table.

Jones knew exactly what she meant. And it wasn't only Flick who had suffered in recent months. It was Iris too, and of course, Jones couldn't forget herself. They couldn't let the bad outweigh the good. By meeting the demands of the anonymous letter, they would be acknowledging the sadness, especially during Christmas. They needed to act accordingly.

"Are we ready to take a vote?" asked Prue. "Or does anyone else want to say something?"

"I'm ready to take a vote," said Rex. "But I just wanted to reinforce everything Iris has said. We can't let these people push us around. We can't let them scare us. And it's up to us as the committee to show a united front. We want to demonstrate the importance of these events to

Lilly Pilly Creek and assure them we will make the Christmas Party and Awards Ceremony a success."

"All those in favour of continuing with The Christmas Party, say aye," said Prue.

Every person around the table, as well as Autumn, loudly called out, "Aye!"

"I believe that is unanimous," said Prue. "Tara, please ensure that is clear in the minutes."

Tara was typing away on her laptop and nodded in Prue's direction.

"Excuse me." The group looked up to see Sergeant Christopher Schmidt standing there.

"Sergeant Schmidt," said Prue. "How can we help you?"

"Well, I am hoping I can help you," he said. "Do you mind if I take a seat?"

Christopher took a seat adjacent to Jones and placed his clasped hands on the table. Making eye contact with everyone, he said, "I hear you've been receiving some threatening letters."

The group nodded and mumbled their agreement.

"Have you decided what to do about the Christmas Party?" he asked, looking at Jones and then at Prue.

"We had just finished voting as you arrived," said Prue. "It was unanimous. We will be proceeding."

Christopher nodded, a serious look on his face. "In that case, I think we need to talk about security."

"What were you thinking?" asked Prue.

"Well, for starters, there will be a police presence."

The group nodded in agreement.

"And I am wondering if we need to do any sort of checks on the way in?"

"Whatcha gonna check for? Blue envelopes!" Colin laughed loudly at his joke. The others stared at him, frowning, and then turned back to Christopher.

"I think it would be prudent to do a general bag check," Christopher suggested.

"Won't that cause a lot of hassle?" asked Jones. "It would take time and mean everyone was lining up to get in."

"Is this a ticketed event?" he asked.

Prue said no. "The finalists and their guests, plus some VIPs do have formal invitations which they can show at the door. But for the rest, it was going to be first come first serve."

"So you were going to have someone at the door counting?"

"Roughly," said Rex. "I think the CFS said the capacity for the Library was a maximum of 200 people. We could have a bit extra if the weather holds so people can use the garden."

"We were going to be surprised if that number turned up," said Prue.

"I think you might find your event proves to be a bit more popular than you expect," said Christopher.

"Really?" said Tara.

"That's the word on the street, anyway," he said.

Jones noticed that Prue couldn't resist a smile. Seeing her pleasure, the rest of the group joined in, Rex leaning back, nodding to himself.

"Well then," said Prue. "It sounds like we would be needing your help anyway, with or without the troublesome letter writer. So we will gratefully accept any assistance you can offer."

"Leave it with me," Christopher said. "We had already allocated a couple of constables for the evening, but I'm wondering if a few more wouldn't hurt." Christopher stood and pushed his chair back from the table. "And I promised not to mention that we may or may not have Christmas-themed uniforms." He winked at Jones and walked away.

Jones and Autumn laughed, but it appeared the others had missed the last comment as they turned to stare at Jones, confused.

She waved them away. "Nothing, nothing. Sorry. Keep going Prue."

"Right, well, it sounds like we need to have people manning doors to keep track of numbers. I will draw up a roster so that we all know what we're doing. But we might need a few more helpers. Any suggestions?"

"I'm sure Atlas would be happy to help," said Jones.

Prue glanced at Tara to ensure she was writing names down.

"I can ask Drew," said Iris.

"What about Hugo?" Prue turned to Jones.

Jones was a little taken aback but said, "Well, he's running the bar with his staff, remember?"

"Oh yes, yes, of course." Jones could tell that Prue felt a little silly for asking.

"Ha ha, good try Prue. One point, Jones," Autumn said, clapping her hands and laughing.

"Unless there is any more business," Prue glanced at everyone around the table, who all shook their head. "I will declare this meeting closed. Let's head into The Memory Bank and get to work."

CHAPTER 25

"Surely it's knockoff time!" called out Rex at about four o'clock. The Committee and Atlas, but without Colin who had slunk off hours ago, had worked hard all afternoon getting The Memory Bank ready for tomorrow's Christmas Party.

Tables were moved, decorations hung, windows washed, and a small area had been cleared ready for the stage to set up on the edge of the main room. Rex had hung a disco ball and had a pleasant white light reflecting off of it.

At that moment, he was just climbing down from a ladder next to the Christmas tree.

"I certainly think it's knockoff time," said Jones, who was standing there, hands on her hip, staring up at the star Rex had just installed atop the key tree. "But first, aren't you going to turn it on? Check it works?"

"You just want to see what it looks like," Rex chuckled, as he stepped off the last rung.

"Of course I do!" Jones laughed.

"Yes, turn it on! Turn it on!" Autumn cheered from her floating position near the top of the tree.

"Everyone! Come and check this out!" Rex bellowed. The committee members stumbled over to where Jones was standing, each one looking rather hot, dishevelled and exhausted.

"We'll inspect Rex's handiwork," said Jones. "And then I think it's time to head next door for a drink."

"Absolutely!" Iris shouted, and the group laughed.

"Alrighty then," said Rex, walking over to the box that was to turn the light on. "Here...we....go!"

The switch was turned and after a moment's hesitation, the light flickered into life. It was beautiful. The star's beams lit up in all directions, causing the keys on the tree to glow.

"Rex, it really does finish off the tree," Jones said appreciatively.

"It sure does," Tara said. "You've done a brilliant job, Rex."

"Right well, you can thank me with a pint!" Rex turned the star off again and started packing up his tools.

Within ten minutes, the group was entering Hugo's Bar.

Prue found a large table inside and promptly waved Hugo across.

"I'll pay for drinks for the table," she generously offered. "And I think some food to share would be good, too."

Smirking slightly at Jones, Hugo nodded, memorising each person's order and indicating he'd bring out a selection of food for everyone.

"Rex," Jones heard a quiet voice calling.

Looking around, Jones saw someone was signalling for Rex to come over and speak with them. It was none other than Molly Shepherd.

Molly looked like she'd attempted to tidy herself up for her visit to Hugo's. She was wearing a long floral skirt, a flouncy blue blouse, and some thick brown sandals. Yet she was clutching a woollen beanie in her hand, despite the fact it was still very warm outside. It almost looked like a security blanket. No doubt it was alpaca wool.

"That's interesting," said Autumn, who was sitting on top of the table in front of Jones. "I don't recall seeing Molly in the bar."

"Go and listen," Jones hissed under her breath. Autumn immediately whizzed away.

Jones did her best not to stare and was glad when Flick tapped her on the arm.

"Jones," she said. "I'd like you to meet my mum."

Jones glanced up to see a woman standing next to them. She was the spitting image of Flick. Tall, with a slightly weathered face but beautiful all the same, and a pleasant smile.

"Lovely to meet you finally, Jones," the woman said, her hand resting on Flick's shoulder. "I'm Astrid."

The Astrid. Finally! She wouldn't have to make a fake visit to Flick's after all.

"Oh hi," said Jones. "I had heard you might be in town. It's nice to meet you too."

"You'd heard I was in town?" she asked, a quizzical expression on her face.

"It's nothing," said Jones, immediately feeling awkward. "Just obviously, considering the situation, your name had been mentioned."

Now Astrid was looking seriously at Jones, cocking her hip to one side. "In connection to what exactly?"

It surprised Jones how defensive this woman was. Alarm bells started ringing, and she wished Autumn was here to witness this conversation.

Kicking into journalist mode, Jones responded. "Well, you are the mother of Flick, the ex-wife of Lorne. It is expected you would be brought up in conversation."

"Oh, it's expected, is it?"

"Mum," whispered Flick. "That's enough."

"I'm confused," said Jones. "You appear to be agitated. You've only ever been mentioned in passing. Is there something more to it?"

Astrid let out a flowery laugh. "Of course not! Of course, they would bring me up. My apologies Jones. I'm a little tense. It seems some think I'm rather more connected to the nasty events than simply being here to support Flick."

"Yes, I thought you had probably only arrived in town to support your daughter," Jones said.

"Well, I have been here for a week, helping Flick with the big plans-"

"Mum!" Flick hissed, cutting off Astrid.

"Well, that's irrelevant. But you're right, I'm here to support Flick in any way I can." Astrid extended her hand towards Jones. "Lovely to meet you, Jones. I'll pop into The Memory Bank one day."

Astrid patted her daughter's shoulder and walked away.

"Sorry about that, Jones," said Flick. "She's been very on edge since Dad died. I think she's more upset about it than she wants to let on."

"Did they get on ok?"

Flick squashed a laugh. "Get on? Oh, no, not at all. Thank goodness they were divorced. Still bickering until the last days. No, they did not get on at all." Flick took a sip of the coke Hugo had just placed in front of her. "But I still think she had some feelings for him. Just the way she spoke. I could be imagining it, I suppose."

"They got married for a reason," said Jones. "Maybe those feelings don't ever go away, but you're just not meant to live together."

Flick nodded and then looked up. Iris was pulling up a seat next to Jones.

"Nice to see your mum out and about," said Iris.

"Oh yes, causing a scene as always," Flick shook her head and finished her coke. "I think I'm gonna need something stronger than this." She got up and headed to the bar.

"Had you met Astrid before?" asked Iris.

Jones picked up her glass of red wine and sipped it before responding. "No. She's, well, I'm not quite sure how to explain her."

"A whirlwind on legs is how I've heard my mum describe her."

Jones laughed! "Gosh, that is pretty good. She just switched so quickly between pleasant, to foreboding, and then back again."

"You seemed to handle her pretty well," said Iris.

"Ha, well, that was my journalist's training. I think she thought I was interrogating her."

"Were you?"

Jones cocked her head and looked at Iris. She could trust her. "It didn't start that way. But I have to admit, by the end of it, I couldn't help but push her buttons. The way she was reacting," Jones shrugged. She didn't want to be the one to say it out loud.

But Iris didn't have the same qualms. She leant forward and whispered her question to Jones.

"You think she could be the murderer?"

CHAPTER 26

Jones spent a few moments chatting with Iris about Astrid, speculating about whether she could be involved. Tara soon came over to join them, drinking a glass of her own Casa Galati wine, where she was the head winemaker.

"Well, from what I hear, the police are narrowing in on two key people."

"Oh?" said Jones, eager to find out exactly what Tara knew.

"Who?" said Iris.

Tara leaned in, and Iris and Jones followed suit. "The ex-wife, of course, isn't it always? And," Tara glanced around to see who was nearby. Seeing the coast was relatively clear, she whispered, "Rex!"

"No!" said Iris, genuinely surprised. Jones did her best to appear shocked by the information, but of course, Rex and Astrid, along with Flick, were already on her suspect list.

"Rex? But why?" asked Jones.

"Well," said Tara. "I'm told even though they've worked together a lot, they've been feuding on and off for years. Like since they were in their twenties."

"Any idea why?" asked Jones. She felt her journalist instincts returning and did her best to rein them in.

"A love triangle," said Tara matter-of-factly, before leaning back in her chair and taking a sip of wine.

"No!' gasped Iris. "What, with Astrid?"

"Well, that's the thing," said Tara. "The person I was speaking to, and I can't name names, of course."

Jones and Iris nodded in agreement, but Jones would have put money on the trusted source being none other than Davina Anderson, Iris's future mother-in-law. Tara had gone out with Drew before he met Iris, and Tara and Davina were still chummy.

"They hinted it wasn't Astrid, but another woman involved."

"Really? And this is from years ago?" Jones felt her mind racing. She knew she had considered the love triangle before, but the news that there could be another woman put another spin on things. The image of the old photograph of The Progress Association flickered in her mind.

"Yep," nodded Tara.

"And you have no idea who the other woman might be?" asked Jones.

"None at all, unfortunately," said Tara. "They didn't know themselves. Just heard rumours about some mysterious woman."

The three women went silent, sipping their drinks, pondering this new information.

"Well, that was interesting," Autumn said quietly, as she slid next to Jones to update her on her eavesdropping. It seemed she was learning to speak quietly in a crowd, to avoid Jones jumping out of her skin.

"Mmmm?" Jones mumbled under a veiled sip of wine.

"Molly was not happy," said Autumn. "She was talking at a million miles an hour. Not letting Rex get a word in. And she seemed all over the place. Talking about the Christmas Party, and a wrong done to her, and Lorne's murder, and how all the stress was putting the farm under pressure."

Jones shifted in her seat, dying to ask questions, but unable to. Ideally, she would have asked Autumn to wait until they were alone before she continued. But of course, Jones couldn't say anything with Iris and Tara right next to her.

"Something about her feelings being taken for granted, and over the years she'd been ignored, and that she couldn't believe the Christmas Party was still going ahead."

Jones abruptly stood. "Just need the loo," she explained to Tara and Iris.

She strode across the room, pushing her way into the Bar's toilets, and then snuck into the accessible toilet, Autumn following closely behind.

"Autumn! So much information when I can't say a word."

"Sorry, sorry, I know. But I just wanted to download before I forgot everything," Autumn explained.

"Ok, so do we think she actually is the letter writer?"

"No idea," said Autumn. "But despite what she told you, I don't think she's happy about the Christmas Party going ahead."

"Oh, I'm so confused," said Jones. "I've also heard about some sort of love triangle between Rex, Lorne and some mysterious woman."

"Love triangle! But isn't Rex married? Oooh, that is juicy."

"No, no," said Jones. "I don't think it was a present-day love triangle. I'm told it was when they were younger, in their twenties."

"Now I'm getting confused. Isn't that around the time of the theft at The Memory Bank?"

"Possibly," said Jones. "I don't know the exact time. But I'm told that the mysterious woman is not Lorne's ex-wife Astrid, who I just met, by the way."

"Did you! Gosh, a lot has happened in a short space of time. What's she like?"

"If I had to describe her in one word, I would say defensive."

"Defensive? You mean, about Lorne's death?"

Jones nodded. Reflecting on the conversation, it seemed more and more obvious that Astrid was feeling emotional about Lorne's death.

"She gave the impression she was sick of people pointing the finger at her. But, I'm not so sure."

"I think we need to get back to The Memory Bank so we can talk about this properly," said Autumn.

"Yes, you're right. The accessible toilets are not the best spot!" Jones laughed, and then flushed the toilet and turned on the tap.

Autumn stared at her.

"What? I needed to look like I used the toilet!" Jones explained before opening the door.

Jones rushed out of the toilet and slammed straight into Rex Keegan.

"Oh, sorry Rex!"

"That's ok. Are you alright?"

"I'm fine," said Jones. "But I did see you talking to Molly. Is everything okay? Does she know we're continuing with the Party?"

"A bit loopy, truth be told," said Rex. "Couldn't understand much of what she was saying. I think she's gotten herself all worked up and can't think straight. But I don't think she's anything to worry about. I imagine when it comes time for the Christmas Party tomorrow, she'll be tucked up in bed after a few rums. That's the type of thing Molly would do."

"Do you know her well?"

"Just as well as you know someone you've known your whole life," said Rex. "But I haven't had much to do with her in recent years. She's become a bit of a hermit on that farm of hers. First time I've seen her out in ages, come to think of it."

"Was she friends with Lorne too?" Jones dared to ask.

"Oh, we all went around in the same group in our younger days," said Rex. "Not sure they were friends, at least not anymore."

"It seems Lorne got most people in his life offside, eventually." Jones made sure to catch Rex's eye when she said this.

"Lorne did know how to get under people's skin, that's for sure." Rex didn't lose eye contact with Jones and eventually, she was the one to glance away.

"Well, I'd better let you go," said Jones.

Rex nodded and continued on his way.

"Oh gosh, now Astrid and Flick are talking to Molly," groaned Jones, looking out into the room.

"Is that Astrid? She certainly looks imposing," said Autumn.

"Poor Molly looks like she doesn't know what hit her," said Jones. "I can only imagine what Astrid's saying to her."

"Probably yacking about everyone accusing her of her ex-husband's murder," said Autumn.

They stood and stared at the room for a moment. Tara and Iris were still in conversation. Prue had moved away to talk with an older couple in one of the booths. As they watched, Molly managed to extricate herself from Astrid and Flick and walked out into the rear garden.

"What are you doing, skulking in the corner?" It was Hugo.

"Oh nothing," said Jones with a smile. "A bit of people watching. A bit of pondering."

"Ah, a bit of pondering?" Hugo said, crossing his arms and turning to look out over the room, over his bar.

"You know me," said Jones. "Just pondering murder."

"Murder, of course, of course," said Hugo. "And have you come to any conclusions?"

She glanced up at Hugo before looking back out at the crowd.

"Nope, this one has me stumped."

"But you have a shortlist. Right?"

"Ha!" said Jones. "You *do* know me!"

"Well, I'm trying my hardest," said Hugo, lightly putting his hand on the small of her back. Shaking slightly, Jones reached around and put her hand on his back, as well. They didn't move any closer, just rested their hands there, very comfortably.

"Well, my shortlist, for what it's worth, is, are you ready for it?" asked Jones.

"Yep!"

Jones glanced around, and then leant in, whispering. "Rex, Astrid and, unfortunately, Flick."

"Really," he said, looking down at her, nodding. "Well, I will say there are no surprises there, although it pains me to think that Flick could do such a thing."

"'S'cuse me."

Jones nearly jumped out of her skin at Rex's voice. Jones and Hugo pulled their arms away and let him walk through.

"Bloody hell," whispered Hugo. "Do you think he heard us?"

"Surely not!" said Jones. "I wasn't that loud. Right?"

"Yep, I'm sure he couldn't have heard a thing." Despite Hugo's smile, Jones wasn't convinced.

"Gosh, I hope not," said Jones. "That would not be good." Jones rubbed her hands over her face.

"I wouldn't dwell on it," said Hugo. "But I'd better get back to it. Are you gonna stay a bit longer?"

"No, I need to pop into The Bank to finish up a couple of things, and then I want a good night's sleep before tomorrow."

"Good plan," Hugo said. "I'm looking forward to getting my bar area set up."

"I can't wait to see what you have planned."

Hugo winked. "You'll love it." He bent down and kissed her on the cheek, and then, squeezing her hand quickly, headed back to the bar.

Jones knew she was beaming. It was almost feeling normal.

As Jones went to pick up her handbag, she wondered if she could slip out without having to say goodbye to everyone. She was sure they'd understand. And she'd see them all soon enough tomorrow.

Bending down, she felt someone grasp her upper arm. Rising, it shocked Jones to see it was Molly Shepherd.

"Molly," said Jones. "How are you?"

"Good, good," she said. "I just wanted to say I'm happy you're going ahead with the party."

"You heard," said Jones. "Well, I'm glad about that."

"I'm going to come," said Molly. "I'm going to come to the Party."

"Really? Well, that is good news. You will be very welcome."

"Thank you," she said. "I won't stay long. But I think it's time to put the past behind me."

Jones nodded and smiled. She didn't know what else she could say to the woman standing in front of her.

Molly took the beanie she had been clutching all evening, slid it onto her head and walked out into the night.

CHAPTER 27

"Getting serious, isn't it?" Autumn said as they walked into The Memory Bank.

"What's getting serious? The party? The potential that we just spoke with Lorne's murderer?"

"No!" Autumn laughed. "You and Hugo!"

"Oh, Autumn!"

"I saw you two," said Autumn. "I may have floated away to give you some privacy, but I was watching you. Hugo has it bad."

Jones swatted her sister and didn't even mind that her hand went straight through Autumn's arm.

"Meanwhile, back to more important things," said Jones. "What are we thinking about Astrid?"

"Well, I didn't speak to her," said Autumn.

"Obviously." Jones playfully rolled her eyes.

"Ok, what I meant was, I didn't overhear your conversation," said Autumn. "But I did overhear another conversation she was having with Flick."

"Oh really," said Jones, swinging herself up to sit on the counter.

"Uh-huh," said Autumn. "And if she was my mum, I'd be a nervous wreck. She was very cutting to Flick, telling her she had to pull herself together. That they hadn't worked so hard all these years to have her run the business for her to fall in a heap now."

"No! She didn't say that!" Jones's mouth was gaping.

"She did," said Autumn, swinging from side to side. "And if that doesn't sound like a confession, then I don't know what does."

"So you think Astrid did it," said Jones. "Astrid is the killer?"

"Well, she has a strong motive, and the way she was speaking tonight, it all just seems to point to her." Autumn spun in front of Jones and then came back down to the floor. "Plus, why else haven't we seen her around? She's been in hiding."

Jones raised her eyebrows, considering the plausibility of this idea. "But why come out tonight?"

"Maybe she realised she was looking too suspicious," said Autumn. "Maybe she wanted to appear normal and casual."

"Well, she did *not* succeed at that!" Jones shook her head, still unsure about her interaction with Flick's mum.

Crack!

"What was that?" Jones cried out, but Autumn was already zooming off toward the sound. Not until that moment had Jones truly appreciated how fast Autumn was in ghost form. It also helped that she could fly directly through the garden windows. However, Jones wasn't sure if she had improved eyesight in the dark, so she ran over to turn on the newly installed outdoor lighting.

Jones then went back to her handbag, digging out her keys so she could unlock the door. As she was doing so, Autumn rushed in.

"Something's been thrown into the garden!" Autumn said. "It hit the water feature. That was the crash."

"Is it broken?"

"The water feature? No, I don't think so, although I didn't inspect it."

Jones had finally clicked open the doors and was rushing over to the newest area of the garden.

Reaching down, Jones picked up something heavy. Wrapped around the item and secured with a rubber band, was a piece of blue paper.

"What is it?"

Jones carefully pulled off the piece of paper and took a look at what she was holding in her hands. "It looks like some sort of gardening shears."

"Weird," said Autumn. "Read the note."

LOOK NO FURTHER

"Look no further?" said Autumn. "What does that mean?"

Jones glanced around, suddenly aware that whoever had thrown this over the garden fence may still be nearby.

She rushed inside the Bank, hurriedly locking the doors.

"Are you ok?"

"Lorne," said Jones. "This is referring to Lorne!"

"Oh gosh," said Autumn. "I think you may be right. Look no further into his murder."

"I think the killer threw that over the fence," said Jones. "And this-" She lifted the shears in front of her face.

"The murder weapon!" Autumn cried.

"What does 'Look No Further' mean?" Asked Jones. "Look no further for the weapon? Here it is! Or, look no further or you'll regret it?"

"Oh, you're right. It could mean almost anything!"

"I think I'd better put this down. Hopefully, I haven't already ruined any fingerprints that might be on it."

"Yes, and I think you need to call the police," said Autumn.

"What, now?"

"Yep," said Autumn. "The sooner the better. What if the perpetrator is still lurking around?"

"The perpetrator," said Jones, raising her eyebrows.

"I'm in investigator mode. Give me a break!"

Jones knew Autumn was right. She pulled out her phone and dialled the non-emergency number. It surprised her when they said they would connect her directly to the Lilly Pilly Creek Station's night number. Constable Partridge answered the phone.

"Shears? Over your garden fence?"

"The Memory Bank's garden fence, yes," Jones explained. "And it had a note attached. I think it may have something to do with Lorne's murder."

"And what gave you that idea?"

"Let's just say I have a hunch," said Jones.

"Tell her you feel scared for your safety and need someone to come around straight away," prompted Autumn.

Jones rolled her eyes but had to agree Autumn's strategy was solid. The Constable said she would head directly there.

"Who do you think it was?" asked Jones.

"It has to be someone from the bar, don't you think?" said Autumn.

"What makes you say that?" said Jones, pacing back and forth in front of the Christmas tree.

"It's the only time we've let anyone know that we're investigating Lorne's murder," said Autumn. "We've stirred the pot and now they're angry."

"Well, we're not really, are we? Investigating."

"Technically, probably not," said Autumn. "But you know the Eldershaw Sisters Detective Agency. We can't help but gather clues."

"Remind me, what clues do we have so far?"

"Well, a woman arguing with Lorne," said Autumn.

"Which could very well have been just an argument and not an argument with his future killer."

"The gardening shears," continued Autumn.

"Ok, that's not looking good for Flick," said Jones. "But they could be anyone's."

"And, well, ah...." Autumn tried to think of more clues but came up short.

"See, it's not much to go on, is it?" said Jones.

They both stood there, pondering the information they had. Most of it was just speculation from friends or acquaintances of Lorne. Many people seemed to have some sort of grudge against him, so it was hard to pin anything down. But what sort of grudge would be strong enough to kill for it? Jones could only think of two things: money, or love.

"The love triangle!" said Jones.

"What? Between Rex, Astrid and Lorne?

"Yes," said Jones. "But apparently there was another woman."

"Another woman?"

"Yes! Tara told us tonight," said Jones. "She said Davina had told her there was another woman involved."

"So not a love triangle, but a love square?"

"The photo," said Jones, striding over to the Bank's counter. She had just picked up her phone when there was a loud banging on the front door.

"Jeepers!" said Jones, juggling her phone before placing it back on the counter.

"The Constable, I presume?" said Autumn, whizzing over to the door and poking her head through it. "I stand corrected. Guess who it is? How surprising."

Jones was rushing over, keys rattling. "Who? Should I open it? Is it safe?"

"Oh, it's safe alright," said Autumn, leaning casually against the wall opposite.

"Who is it?"

"You'll see," said Autumn, grinning.

Jones pulled the door open and there was Sergeant Christopher Schmidt, a satchel over his shoulder.

"Told you," said Autumn, gliding away.

"Christopher," said Jones. "We, I was expecting Constable Partridge."

"Yes, she called me as I was driving back from an incident, and I told her I'd pop in. We needed someone to man the station."

"Sure you did," said Autumn, the sarcastic tone in her voice obvious.

"They may still be here," said Jones. "Do you want me to unlock the garden?"

"It's okay. I circled the building and did a quick scan of the streets. Aside from a few stragglers coming out of Hugo's, the streets are empty."

Jones let out a breath, not realising quite how worried she had been that the culprit may have still been nearby.

"So, what's happened? Constable Partridge mentioned something about gardening shears?"

Jones took Christopher over to where she had placed the shears, all the while explaining how they had ended up in The Memory Bank's garden.

"I may have gotten my fingerprints on them," said Jones. "I'd already picked them up before I realised they were probably the murder weapon."

"Murder weapon?" Christopher looked at Jones, frowning.

"Yes," said Jones. "Take a look at the note."

Christopher read it before looking back at Jones. "And you think this has to do with...."

"Lorne's murder? Yes!" Jones folded her arms across her chest as if it should have been obvious why these shears were delivered to her.

"And why is Lorne's murderer sending *you* a message like this?"

Jones glanced down at her feet. "Ah, well, I may have possibly asked one too many questions tonight."

Christopher tilted his head, a smirk on his face. "Jones, asking questions amid the police's murder investigation? No! Never!"

"Ha ha," said Jones. "It wasn't intentional. It was almost handed to me on a platter. That Astrid Kelly is, how do I put it?"

"Intense? Dramatic?" said Christopher.

"Ruthless? Devious?" Autumn piped in.

"Guilty?" Jones suggested.

Christopher looked Jones in the eyes and nodded. "Perhaps," he said. "But what makes *you* draw that conclusion?"

Jones explained her interaction with Astrid and what she'd observed when Astrid was talking to Molly. She also indicated she may have overheard a conversation between Astrid and Flick. Jones didn't share that her ghost sister was the one eavesdropping. That wouldn't have helped the current situation at all.

"Probably didn't hurt that I spent a couple of hours interrogating her today," said Christopher.

"You did?"

"Yes, but I really shouldn't have said that," said Christopher.

"So you *do* think she's guilty!" Jones exclaimed.

"No, no, not necessarily," said Christopher. "That's not the only reason I was questioning her."

Jones narrowed her eyebrows, trying to guess what Christopher meant.

"You think she's covering for someone," said Jones. "You think she's covering for Flick."

"Now, those are your words, not mine," said Christopher. "I can't talk to you about what we do or don't think."

"I understand," said Jones, nodding. "But you think it's Flick. Don't you?"

"Ask him about Rex!" Autumn called.

"So, there's Astrid and Flick. Is there anyone else on your suspect list?"

Christopher laughed. "You think I can tell you that?"

"Well, let me just throw another name out then," said Jones.

"Go on then," Christopher crossed his arms, smiling.

"Rex," said Jones. "Rex Keegan."

His forehead creased, and he walked back and forth. "Look, I can't say we haven't considered Rex. What I will say is, I don't think he is an immediate threat. To your safety, I mean."

"Oh, I'm not worried about my safety," said Jones.

"You should be!" said Autumn. At the same time, Christopher said, "Well, I am!"

He stopped and stared at Jones, not saying another word. They locked eyes for a moment before Jones shook her head and said, "Well, you needn't be. I'm not the mysterious woman mixed up in their love triangle. Or love square."

"Love square?" asked Christopher. "What are you talking about?"

"I presume you know that years ago, Rex and Astrid were a thing before Lorne?"

Christopher nodded.

"Well, I've heard through the grapevine that there was a fourth person involved, another woman."

"Another woman? Who?"

"That's the thing," said Jones. "I have no idea. But I have a feeling discovering the identity of the mystery woman will crack the case."

"Crack the case, hey?" Christopher's smile had returned to his face.

Jones rolled her eyes, aware of how cliche she sounded. "You know what I mean," said Jones.

"Well, I don't think we're going to crack the case tonight," said Christopher. "Let me bag this up, and we can talk more tomorrow."

Jones nodded and watched as Christopher pulled out gloves and an evidence bag from his satchel.

"Do you need me to drop you home?" he asked as he stood in the doorway to leave.

"We need to look at the photograph," said Autumn.

"No thanks," said Jones. "I drove today, so I'm fine to get home."

"Well, keep safe," said Christopher. "I don't think you've got anything to worry about but, well."

"Someone did throw a pair of gardening shears over the back fence."

Christopher nodded. "Exactly. I'm going to have a closer look around the back of the garden, just in case you hear any noises."

Jones nodded.

"Ok, goodnight then," said Christopher.

"Goodnight."

Jones pulled the door shut and locked it.

"Ugh, the romantic tension between you two is ridiculous!"

"Stop saying those things," said Jones. "I have absolutely no interest in Christopher."

"I know, I know. You're with Hugo. But honestly, if he wasn't such a gentleman, I don't think it would take much for Christopher to push you up against a wall and-"

"Enough!" Jones said, marching back into the room. "We have to focus."

Jones grabbed her phone and flipped through the photos to find the one she had taken of the newspaper article. There it was, the photo of the Progress Association presenting their parents with the giant red button.

Autumn floated next to Jones, peering over her shoulder at the photo on the phone. "And why are we looking at this photo?"

"I don't know why, but I just feel the answer is in the photo," said Jones.

"The other woman, you mean?

Jones shrugged. "Honestly, I don't know. But maybe that's a good place to start."

"So aside from Mum, which I'm assuming we can safely say is not the mystery woman, as she was happily married with a toddler, and presumably a baby on the way."

"I would have to agree with that," said Jones.

"So then, the only other women in the photo are Astrid, Molly and Plum. "

"Plum! Oh no, you don't think? Could it? No." Jones's voice took a deep tone as she ended her exclamation.

"Well, perhaps? Is there any reason it couldn't be?"

"I mean, I suppose not," said Jones. "She *could* be mixed up in all of this. She arrived in town and the next day Lorne is found dead."

"We don't think she killed him, though? Right?"

"No way!" said Jones. "No, I just mean, maybe her return stirred some things up. Some long past emotions."

"Okay, well, I guess the only thing to do is to ask Plum," said Autumn.

"Ask her what, exactly?"

"I don't know! Maybe 'Hi Plum, did you have a relationship with Lorne or Rex back in the day?'"

"Just like that?" Jones rolled her eyes a little.

"No, not just like that," said Autumn. "I'm sure you'll work something out. You always manage to find the right thing to say."

"Usually because you're whispering in my ear."

"Exactly!" said Autumn, unable to resist a grin and a wink.

"But if she is the other woman," said Jones. "Then it seems more and more likely that Astrid is the killer, don't you think?"

"Astrid, or someone avenging her," said Autumn.

"Avenging her? Hmmm, I hadn't thought of that. Do you mean like Rex? Her old flame heroically swooping in to deal with her troublesome ex-husband and the man who stole her from him?"

"Sounds as good as any other theory we've had," said Autumn. "But how are we going to work out the truth?"

"Honestly, after the night we've had," said Jones, letting out a yawn. "I'm going to have to sleep on it."

"Good plan," said Autumn. "You sleep, and I'll brainstorm ideas on how to corner our killer."

"So, you don't need to sleep?"

Autumn shook her head. "No, not really. Muscle memory does mean I can lie down and sort of tune out for hours at a time, but I don't think it's required."

"Interesting," said Jones. "Ok, well, when I return in the morning, I expect some solid plans on how we are going to unmask the murderer."

Autumn saluted, and then made a dramatic exit, launching herself through the escape room wall like Superman.

"Good night!" Jones called after her.

"Night, night!"

CHAPTER 28

"I've remembered something important!"

Jones sat bolt upright in bed.

"Autumn! What are you doing here?" Jones shook her head and glanced at the window. It still looked dark outside. "And what time is it?"

"It's just after five o'clock, but I couldn't wait any longer."

"Five o'clock! What is so important at five o'clock?"

"I just told you. I've remembered something!"

"Oh yes," said Jones, pushing herself back so she could lean on the bedhead. She rubbed her eyes and let out a sigh.

"Do you remember what I told you Christopher had written in his notes when we were at the police station?"

Jones paused, arching her eyebrows, trying to get her brain to start working. "Um, something about Colin?"

"Something about Colin *and* Molly."

"Oh yes, Christopher thought Colin was the one that attacked Molly," said Jones.

"Not only that," said Autumn. "He wrote that both Colin *and* Molly had a history of violence. Now what if he meant Colin and Molly had a history of *domestic* violence?"

"What, you think Molly is the other woman?"

"Yes! And I'm wondering if it wasn't Rex, Astrid, and Lorne who were in a love triangle. I'm wondering if it was Molly, Colin and Lorne?"

"So, you think it was Colin that attacked Molly, and it didn't have anything to do with the theft, or at least, not directly?"

"Exactly," said Autumn. "But, and I know I'm taking a bit of a leap here. What if Lorne and Molly were having a fling all those years ago? What if the Christmas Party has brought up too many memories for Colin? I mean, he does seem to have amped up his drinking of late, even for Colin. What if he just snapped, still angry at Lorne after all these years?"

"And whacked him on the head with some gardening shears?"

Autumn splayed her hands out to her side, offering this option up to Jones.

"Look, there are a lot of guesses in this," said Jones. But, if you are right, and Colin and Molly were in a relationship all those years ago, and she *did* have an affair with Lorne, then I suppose the rest of the story is possible. At least as likely as any other scenario we've come up with."

Jones closed her eyes, attempting to process all of this information.

"I don't think I can function until I've had a shower and a cup of coffee. Two cups. Two cups with double shots."

"Ok," said Autumn. "Sorry to wake you up. But was it worth it?"

Jones looked up at her sister, a serious expression on her face. "Yes Autumn, I do think it was worth it. Well done."

"I'll head back to The Memory Bank. I don't want to get too low on energy before the big day begins. I'll see you there?"

"Yes," said Jones. "But don't expect me to rush."

"No rush at all!" Autumn stepped backwards through the window, slowly disappearing, leaving only her right hand poking through, waving.

Jones did take her time that morning. She knew with all the set-up they had planned that day, as well as the party no doubt extending to the early hours of the morning, she didn't need to exert herself. She managed to doze for another hour before getting herself into the shower.

Today's outfit was chosen with care. She wore emerald green shorts and a black singlet with cream sandals. Across the singlet, today's quote read, *"Having a perfectly decorated tree is not what Christmas is about. It's about being with the people that you love."* Monica Geller, Friends.

She decided to go wild and pop on a pair of galah earrings, each wearing a Santa hat. They were made by a local and new stock for The Memory Bank. The last item was her blue sunglasses, and with her handbag, she was ready to head out into Lilly Pilly Creek.

There was no doubt today would be hot. Jones had checked the weather on her phone, but as soon as she stepped outside, she could feel the heat in the air already. The flowers in her front garden were still open and vibrant, but she knew it wouldn't take long for them to droop. Ants were out, collecting food before marching back into their cool tunnels.

Jones jumped in her Mini and headed towards Sybil's coffee van.

Numerous people were out walking their dogs, beating the heat. Before long, the animals, along with their owners, would be back inside, no doubt lazing in front of an air conditioner.

Despite all of that, Jones was still looking forward to her strong, hot coffee from Sybil, and thought she might add a muffin to her breakfast order this morning.

Sybil was alone, aside from Frank the ginger cat, who today was curled up in the shade underneath the van. Jones was relieved there were no other customers. She wanted to pick Sybil's brain about Colin and Molly.

"Morning, Sybil!"

"The usual?"

"A double shot today please," said Jones. "And I was thinking I'd have a muffin. What do you have today?"

"I'm so glad you asked! Today we have Apple and Lavender, Chai Crumble, Orange and Cardamon, or Pineapple and Coconut."

"What a selection! Who makes them?"

"Neha is the muffin expert," said Sybil.

"I should have guessed from the ingredients that Neha might have something to do with it," said Jones. "I think I'll take one Apple and Lavender, and one Orange and Cardamon."

Sybil cranked the coffee machine, and as the mahogany liquid flowed into the cup, she packaged the muffins into two brown paper bags.

"Sybil, I need to pick your brain, as usual," said Jones.

"Of course!"

"Well, do you know if Molly ever had a boyfriend, you know, years ago? When she was in her twenties? Did she ever perhaps go out with Colin?"

"Colin? Oh no, Molly never went out with Colin," said Sybil. "No, the only person I can remember Molly going out with when she was younger was Lorne."

Jones gasped. "Lorne? Lorne Fox?"

"Yes," said Sybil. "They were a bit of an item for a while, but everyone knew Lorne had his sights set on Astrid."

"Ah, so they were the love triangle?"

"Love triangle? I think that may be going too far. I just know that Molly and Lorne broke up, and not long after Astrid and Rex broke up. Then at some point, probably not too long afterwards, Lorne and Astrid got together, and that was that."

Sybil handed Jones the paper bags, and Jones absentmindedly pulled a piece off the orange and cardamon muffin and popped it into her mouth.

"Oh my gosh, that is delicious!"

Sybil smiled. "Wait until you try it with coffee!" She went back to preparing the milk for Jones's double-shot flat white.

"But Molly and *Lorne*? I just can't picture it?"

"Well, Molly was quite the looker in her day," said Sybil. "And lots of blokes had their eyes on her. She was fun and outgoing and bubbly."

"That sounds nothing like Molly," said Jones.

"Well, she's not like that now," said Sybil. "After the bump on the head, she was never really the same again. No one ever mentioned brain damage, but no doubt there was some."

"But by all accounts, she's an amazing farmer and businesswoman," said Jones.

"That she is," said Sybil. "No, that part of her brain wasn't affected. Maybe it was enhanced. She became a lot more straightforward, focused, and driven. Always got what she wanted. It's why her alpacas are so renowned. She worked hard to develop her stock so they'd have high-quality fleece. She's known for it."

Jones nodded and reached out to take her coffee cup from Sybil. Pulling off another piece of the muffin, she popped it in her mouth before sipping the coffee. "Oh, you were right. This is amazing."

"Enjoy it!" said Sybil. "And all the best for today. What time do you want me to park the van out the front?"

Jones was thrilled Sybil had agreed to cater the coffee for the evening. She wasn't entirely sure how popular it would be. But she knew there would be at least a few people who would enjoy an iced coffee, and she bet the kids would be partial to a hot chocolate, even in this weather. It was Christmas, after all.

"I think any time from four. All the trucks bringing in the equipment should be done by then," said Jones. "That reminds me, I need to put the witches' hats out as soon as I get to The Bank. I'd better go. Thanks, Sybil!"

Jones savoured her muffin and coffee as she walked to the Bank. She knew today was a big day, and now might be the only moment of peace.

But she couldn't shake the nagging feeling that there was something she was missing.

CHAPTER 29

"There is no way Lorne Fox and Molly Shepherd were an item!" exclaimed Autumn as Jones updated her.

Rex had left a pile of witches' hats with her yesterday. Jones had lugged them out to the front of the bank and was now using them to ensure the parking area in front remained clear for the various deliveries they were expecting.

"Look, that's what Sybil said. Oof these are heavy." She dropped them unceremoniously on the asphalt and then began picking up one at a time and spacing them out on the side of the road.

"I'd help if I could," said Autumn.

"Surely you've worked out how to lift something heavier than a piece of paper by now," Jones joked, moving back to the pile of orange cones and grabbing the next one.

"I'm sorry to say I have not," said Autumn. "But I did lift the front cover of a hardback book yesterday."

"Well, that is progress!"

"I thought so," said Autumn. "Anyway, back to the love triangle."

"Yes, so it appears the love triangle wasn't so much a love triangle as a series of failed relationships, culminating in a successful one," said Jones.

"Until that also failed," said Autumn.

"But there is something I just can't put my finger on," said Jones. "I'm sure there's something I'm missing. Any ideas?"

"Aside from the fact that we appear to be no closer to discovering the identity of Lorne's murderer? In fact, I would say we are even further away."

"Well, if the simplest solution is the answer, then it would seem likely that Rex is the murderer. In retaliation for stealing Astrid away," said Jones.

Autumn had to nod. "Yes, I agree. And yet, I just don't get that vibe from Rex. Do you?"

"No, I have to say I don't," said Jones. "But I wouldn't be relying on my senses if we were to base it on past events."

Jones was referring to the fact that she had no idea Autumn's ex-boyfriend Jamie Royce was the one who had killed her. They had even become quite close in the days after Autumn's death. Or so Jones had thought.

"You can't blame yourself for that," said Autumn. "You were grieving. Your radar was all off."

"Ok, done!" Jones proclaimed as she placed the last witches' hat on the road. "What's next?"

"Maybe put up the sign you made, letting everyone know we're closed today," suggested Autumn.

Jones headed back into The Memory Bank and found the page she had printed yesterday. Rifling through a drawer, she found some blue tac and went to post it outside, next to the front door.

"Morning Jones." Jones spun around to see Atlas standing there, holding the beloved tray of coffees. He handed one to Jones. "Sybil said you were on double shots today. I hope that's ok?"

"Absolutely! Amazing. Thank you Atlas," said Jones.

"So, where do you want me to start?"

Jones smiled as she followed Atlas in. His enthusiasm for his work at The Memory Bank always amazed her. Having an office inside helped, but ever since he first started working there, he had been nothing but loyal to Jones and the Bank.

They spent the morning dusting and wiping down shelves and windowsills. With the ladders in the building, they could reach places that had not seen a feather duster in years.

Gradually, each member of the Progress Association arrived and got to work. At around eleven, Plum walked in. She was a sight! She had a purple floral scarf wrapped around her head and was wearing denim overalls, a purple t-shirt underneath, and sparkly purple sneakers.

"I come ready to pitch in!" she declared, plonking a small cooler bag on the counter.

"What's that?" asked Jones.

"Snacks and refreshments," she replied, winking. Jones wondered what on earth it held.

Jones and Plum walked out into the garden. "Unfortunately, there are already weeds popping up, so I thought you and I might get down and dirty and get rid of as many as we can."

Plum rubbed her hands together. "Weeding is one of my many specialities." Jones grinned, and together they found a patch of garden, chatting as they pulled. Jones's shorts weren't ideal for kneeling, but she made it work by grabbing one of the seat cushions and kneeling on that. Plum did the same.

"You have to ask her about Molly and Lorne," Autumn said as she floated past. Jones couldn't help but stare at her. Since Plum had arrived, Autumn had changed her outfit, and she looked like a poster girl for a female mechanic during World War Two. Her hair was done up in victory rolls, a red scarf tied around them. She wore a red shirt with the sleeves rolled up high, and denim capri pants.

"So Plum," said Jones. "I found out something surprising today"

"Oh yes," said Plum, not taking her eyes off the weeds she was clutching.

"Were Molly Shepherd and Lorne Fox a couple once upon a time?"

"Hmmm," she paused for a moment, looking up, thinking. "Yes, I think they were. I don't think it was a serious thing, though. Who told you that?"

"Sybil," said Jones.

"And why did that come up in conversation?" Plum resumed her weeding, tossing the greenery into a pile at her hip.

"Well, last night, someone mentioned a love triangle involving Astrid, Rex, and Lorne. But they mentioned a mystery woman," Jones glanced at Plum. "So obviously I asked Sybil about it."

"Obviously," Plum said, a slight grin on her face.

"So you think Molly might be the mystery woman?" Jones made sure to keep her eyes directly ahead.

"I don't think there was any mystery woman at all," said Plum. "I think it was common knowledge that Lorne was with Molly, but he had a thing for Astrid."

"What about Molly?

"Did Molly know? Oh, well, I suppose not. I can't remember."

"And you don't think there could be another mystery woman?" Jones kept her eyes on the weeds she was pulling.

Plum paused, sat back, and looked at Jones. "What are you trying to ask, Jones?"

"Well, I'm not sure," said Jones. She glanced at Plum but then kept pulling the weeds. "I mean, did you have any boyfriends back then?"

"Do you mean was I secretly with Rex or Lorne?"

"No, not secretly," said Jones. "I mean, I wasn't around then. I just don't know who was with whom."

"Let me assure you, I was most certainly not the mystery woman," said Plum. "I wasn't particularly appealing to the boys in this town." Plum went back to her weeding and this time it was Jones who sat up.

"Why on earth not?" Jones couldn't imagine why all the guys wouldn't want Plum.

"Oh, I was too wild for them. And in too much of a hurry to get out of Lilly Pilly Creek," said Plum. "I didn't want to be tied down, and they didn't want someone who didn't love this town the way they did."

"What, don't you love Lilly Pilly Creek?"

"I do now," said Plum. "I love visiting. But back then. Oh my goodness, it was suffocating. Well, maybe it was more so my parents than the town, but it felt like the same thing to me. I couldn't wait to leave."

Jones and Plum went quiet and continued their weeding.

"Howdy Jones!" She turned to see Rex standing there, hands on his hips, an unusual look on his face.

"Hi Rex," she said. "What's up?"

"Well, it's time for you to skedaddle?"

"What do you mean? There's so much work to do!" Jones stood up, brushing her hands on her shorts.

"Remember, I mentioned a surprise?"

"Yes," said Jones, tipping her head, and then spotting Prue and Iris walking up behind Rex.

"I need to get it in position," said Rex. "And I need you to leave so I can."

"Leave? Where am I meant to go?"

"To Hugo's," said Iris. "He's expecting you for lunch." Prue and Iris stood with very smug looks on their faces, obviously entirely pleased with their plan.

"Well, I won't say no to lunch," said Jones. "Plum, do you want to join me?"

Plum waved her hand. "No, I only just got here. Plus, I've brought my lunch. Off you go. Enjoy the break."

Jones frowned a little at everyone and then shrugged. "Fine, if you want me to stop working. I won't argue!" She walked into The Bank and everyone smiled at her. She felt very awkward and a little nervous. What exactly did Rex have planned?

"Do you want me to stay?" said Autumn, sidling up to Jones.

"No," said Jones. "If I'm getting surprised, then so are you!"

"Fair enough," said Autumn.

Jones and Autumn made their exit, and as they walked to Hugo's,

Jones said. "What is with that outfit?"

"Don't you love it!" Autumn twirled. "Plum inspired me. That woman is a fashion icon!"

"You two are peas in a pod. Maybe she was supposed to be your godmother rather than mine. You're all about red, she's all about purple. I don't get it?"

"It's all about making a statement," said Autumn. "Although I wish I was brave enough to wear as much red when I was alive as I do now. But what are you talking about? You wear quote T-shirts every single day. If that's not making a statement, then I don't know what is."

Jones couldn't argue with that and was smiling as she walked into Hugo's.

"Welcome, welcome!" Jones was startled to find Hugo just inside the doorway, waiting for her. She was also surprised to see the room was empty, aside from a young girl behind the bar and a chef in the kitchen who were both watching on.

"What is going on?" asked Jones.

"I am glad you asked!" Hugo led Jones over to a booth. On the table were cutlery, white napkins, a vase of flowers, and even a lit candle. "Voila!"

Jones looked at Hugo. "And yet I'm still very confused."

"This," said Hugo, waving somewhat dramatically. "Is our second date!"

"Oooooh! How romantic!" Autumn's sing-song voice reverberated in Jones's ears.

"Oh, wow!" Jones knew she was grinning from ear to ear, and she was happy about it. "But why? Shouldn't you be flat out at Saturday lunchtime?"

"No, we've closed for lunch today. I wanted the team to have a break before a hectic night. They'll be busy over here, not to mention at the Christmas Party. So, when Iris popped in wondering if you could come in here for lunch, well, I just whipped this up. Take a seat."

Jones slid into the booth seat, smiling. "I love it."

Hugo slid in opposite her, clearly very pleased with himself. Jones saw Autumn float away, through the glass and into the rear garden.

The girl behind the bar walked over and showed Jones a bottle of the Haunted Cellar Pinot Gris. When Jones nodded, she poured Jones and Hugo a glass each.

Next, the chef walked out, carrying two plates, which he placed in front of the couple.

"I've taken the liberty of arranging a few of your favourite items from the menu," said Hugo. "Starting with a small serving of crunchy Thai salad."

"I can't say no to that!"

Hugo lifted his glass and held it out towards Jones. She lifted hers, and they clinked. "Thank you, Hugo. This is wonderful. I was wondering when we might squeeze in another date."

"A pleasure, of course," said Hugo. "Apologies, it's not quite as intriguing as our first date."

Jones laughed. "Oh, I'm not sorry at all. A more low-key date is well in order."

They tucked into the salad, Jones as always savouring the crisp noodles along with the sweet tang of the dressing covering the cabbage.

"Mmm," she said, her mouth full. "So good."

"Can you guess what the main course might be?"

Jones thought for a moment, and then said, "Salt and pepper squid!"

"Spot on!"

Glancing up, Jones saw the two staff had disappeared, leaving them alone.

"How are you feeling about the big event?" Hugo asked.

"So nervous," she said. "But also looking forward to it. I just hope everyone else is as excited."

"I'm pretty sure they are," said Hugo. "It was buzzing in here last night. Lots of people talking about how happy they were for its return. And then all the young ones who weren't born when the last lights competition and party were held were asking lots of questions. I think tonight is going to be an enormous success."

"I just can't imagine what Rex is doing in there at the moment," said Jones. "And it appears everyone is in on it except me."

Hugo shook his head. "Not me, I have no clue."

Having finished the first course, the girl behind the bar refilled their glasses and took their plates. It wasn't long before the chef appeared with their plates of squid.

"I still can't believe you've done all this for me," said Jones.

"I had to have lunch too, you know," Hugo smiled.

"Well, what about them?" asked Jones, indicating the bar staff and chef.

"Don't worry about them, they're out the back eating the same as us!"

Jones laughed. Of course, Hugo looked after his team.

They ate quietly for a few minutes, enjoying the moment of peace, all alone.

"What are you doing for Christmas?" Hugo asked.

Jones stopped. She didn't quite know why he was asking but answered truthfully.

"I wasn't planning on doing anything," said Jones. "It's a hard year. I was going to stay home, maybe watch TV in my bed with a selection of my favourite foods."

Hugo nodded at this. "I can understand that."

"What are you doing? Are you going to see your family?"

"No, my family all live throughout the world, but none currently in Australia," he explained. "I was planning to go to my friends in Adelaide. A group of us have been doing Christmas together for a few years."

"That sounds nice," said Jones. The two of them seemed to know instinctively not to say any more. Although it seemed like the most obvious thing in the world for them to spend Christmas together, neither said anything. Jones was happy with that. Of course, she knew she wouldn't be spending Christmas alone. She had Autumn. They hadn't quite worked out the finer details, but, of course, they would be together.

Jones had already ordered the prawns, the Christmas pudding, and the Christmas Ham. She was planning croissants for breakfast, with champagne, and there would be mangoes and strawberries ready to eat throughout the day. Her favourite thing, an enormous pot of custard, would be prepared to go over the pudding and then eaten cold for breakfast on Boxing Day. They were going to alternate between being at the house and being at The Memory Bank, so Autumn could recharge throughout the day. And of course, there would be presents.

It wouldn't be the same for Autumn. It wouldn't be the same for either of them. But they would be together, and they would spend the time reminiscing about every other Christmas they had spent together.

Sipping his wine, Hugo looked at Jones. "I wonder what we'll do on our third date?"

Jones's heart immediately fluttered. She loved he was thinking ahead. "It's my turn to organise a date," she said. "Leave it with me."

Hugo smiled. "I look forward to it!"

CHAPTER 30

If she hadn't been on a date, Jones would have seriously considered picking up the plate and licking it. The pear tart with fresh whipped cream was delicious. She couldn't believe she'd never ordered it before.

Fortunately, her desire for just one more taste was interrupted by the arrival of Iris.

"We're ready when you are!"

"Oh, thank goodness. That was getting sickening," said Autumn, emerging through the window from outside.

"Perfect timing!" said Hugo. He stood and reached out his hand to Jones to help her up from her chair.

"Are you coming too?" Jones asked.

"If you'd like me to," said Hugo.

"Yes, please," she said. Hugo kept hold of her hand, and with Autumn leading the way, they followed Iris back to The Memory Bank.

Everyone was sitting on the edge of the stage, waiting. They all jumped up when Jones arrived. Rex stood on the stage, a sheet covering something quite large.

"Jones," said Prue. "You need to go up on the stage with Rex."

Hugo let go of her hand, and Jones, unused to all this attention, hesitated before taking the three steps onto the stage. Autumn floated up to stand opposite Jones.

"Would you please do the big reveal?" said Rex, indicating that Jones should lift the sheet.

Although she attempted a smooth movement, of course, the sheet got caught underneath one corner. Rex had to bend down and unhook it.

Both Jones and Autumn sucked in their breath, amazed at what they saw.

"The red button!" Jones said, mouth open, staring at Rex. "You found it?"

"I always knew exactly where it was," said Rex. "I've kept it in my shed for all these years."

"And it still works?"

"It sure does! Give it a go."

"Really?"

Rex nodded, encouraging Jones to push it.

She glanced up quickly at Autumn, tilting her head slightly.

Together, they stepped up and placed their hands over the button. But it was Autumn's hand that was placed closest to the button. Jones willed her sister to push it. No doubt the crowd in front was wondering why Jones was taking so long, as though her hand was stuck in mid-air. Finally, they both felt the energy rush through Autumn's hand and at that moment, to cover this amazing feat, Jones pushed down.

It was then the Christmas tree lit up with thousands of tiny fairy lights glowing amongst the keys. But not only that, Jones hadn't noticed someone had strung the ceiling with lights. They were in a giant wave formation, rippling across the room, with starbursts dotted throughout.

"Rex! How on earth did you do this? I wasn't out to lunch that long?"

Rex tapped his nose but then looked out at the garden. Standing there was a group of at least ten men and women, all grinning at Jones.

"Let's just say I roped in a few helpers, and we worked like a well-oiled machine."

"Oh, thank you!" said Jones. She couldn't help but give him a giant hug.

"I think your parents would have enjoyed this," he whispered in her ear. Jones looked into his face, tears in her eyes. She couldn't do anything but nod, and then pull back to survey the amazing work.

"Just imagine how good this is going to look when it gets darker," said Prue, snapping photos on her phone.

"Well, I'll turn them off now," said Rex.

Jones spun around. "Oh, why?"

"Because you Jones are going to press this button tonight when you open the proceedings," he said.

Jones clasped her hands together, holding them in front of her chest. "Oh, that's a brilliant idea!" From the corner of her eye, she could see Autumn beaming. She knew that she not only loved what Rex had created but was also buzzing with the fact that she had just pushed the button. Jones only hoped she could do it again tonight.

Rex flicked a switch, and all the lights disappeared.

Everyone went back to their work, but Autumn and Jones stood, staring at the Christmas tree.

"Do you think Mum and Dad really would have loved this?"

asked Autumn, looking up and around the room. "All of this?"

"I think so," said Jones, glancing at Autumn. "I hope so."

"Jones, I think we need to look in Granny's lockbox," said Autumn.

"What, now?" Jones said, frowning.

"Yes," said Autumn. "There's something niggling at me. Something I think we've overlooked."

As Jones walked towards the counter to get the key, she spoke under her breath. "About what? About the opals?"

"Yes," said Autumn. "The opals, Molly, Lorne, all of it."

"All of it?"

"Just get the lockbox and take it into one of the private rooms," said Autumn.

Jones did as Autumn wished, and soon they were sequestered in the small room.

"Find the one with the notes on the theft of The Lights, the opal earrings," said Autumn.

Fortunately, that one had remained on the top, so Jones could quickly find the relevant pages.

"Can you read out the part about Colin?" said Autumn.

The only person I think who would be so brazen to steal The Lights, or anything at all from The Memory Bank, is Colin Fletcher. He's the one that has regularly been in trouble with the police. Mostly for fighting when he was drunk, but is it such a stretch to say he wouldn't steal from us and whack Molly over the head when she caught him?

And I think I know exactly when he did it. I can remember talking with

Margot and Kitt and saw Colin talking with Lorne. Then Molly walked up, and not long afterwards, Colin walked away. I got distracted after that, but I wonder if Molly went after Colin, wondering what he was doing. Did she suspect something? She confronted him, and that was that. I've hinted as much to the police, but I just don't want them to discover that anything is missing. That would be a tragedy for us.

"There," said Autumn, pointing at the page, leaning over Jones's shoulder.

"Where? What?"

"The bit about Colin, Molly and Lorne," said Autumn. "They were all talking together."

"So?" said Jones. "They could have been talking about anything."

"Yes, but what if they were talking about The Lights? What if they were in it together?"

"What, Colin *and* Lorne and Molly?"

"No, just Colin and Lorne," said Autumn.

"So you want to approach Colin and see if he knows anything about the opals?"

"Gosh no!" said Autumn. "That would be way too risky."

"Why, Colin's pretty harmless."

"Is he? I wouldn't be so sure of that."

"What are you saying, Autumn?"

Autumn came down to sit in the chair opposite Jones.

"What I'm saying is," said Autumn, her hands pressed into the table, looking directly into Jones's eyes. "I think the theft of The Lights and the murder of Lorne Fox are connected."

Jones's jaw dropped! "Really?"

"Yes. I think that Lorne and Colin were in cahoots. And I think that Lorne did something to Colin that was finally brought to a head when we decided to recommence the Christmas Lights competition."

"And Colin confronted Lorne and killed him?"

"Or Lorne confronted Colin. Either way, things got aggressive and unfortunately Lorne came out on the wrong end of the stick."

"Underneath it you mean," said Jones. She fell silent, contemplating everything Autumn had said. Once again, she felt they were speculating wildly. Except this felt different. This was an eyewitness account. At least regarding the opals, The Lights. The concept of the two crimes being connected? Her mind was spinning.

"What do you think?" asked Autumn.

"Let's for a moment assume that the two are connected," said Jones. "Do you think that Lorne *and* Colin both broke into The Memory Bank? And then something happened between the two of them that has caused a rift ever since?"

Autumn nodded vigorously. "And that something could very well be Molly. Colin whacked her over the head and Lorne, her boyfriend, was furious."

"But why did Colin kill Lorne? If it was Colin who hit Molly, wouldn't Lorne want to kill him?"

Autumn sighed, nodding. "Yes, yes, you could be right. Maybe it was something else that caused the rift. Maybe Molly was just collateral damage. But what else could it be?"

Jones started flipping carelessly through their granny's diary, mulling over the problem. Colin and Lorne had decided to rob The Memory Bank. Somehow they knew valuable items were being stored there, *and* knew which box it was in. They decide to steal the items, including The Lights, and their Granny's opals, but it all goes wrong.

"The opals!"

"What?"

"That's the missing piece," said Jones. "Yes, Colin whacked Molly over the head. Yes, Lorne was furious at this. So, instead of giving Colin a piece of the action, so to speak, Lorne keeps everything for himself, as a punishment for Colin's actions."

Autumn flew out of her chair. "By Jove, I think you're right!"

"By Jove?" Jones had to laugh.

"Oh, let me get in character," said Autumn, spinning to reveal her detective outfit of trench coat and fedora.

"Okay, okay," said Jones. "But you think we might be on to something?"

"I certainly do," said Autumn. "Don't you? Don't you think perhaps Colin was trying to get the opals back?"

"But would Lorne still even have them? I mean, they weren't reported missing. He could have easily sold them."

"Yeah, you're right," said Autumn. "But it's something to consider, right?"

"It most certainly is," said Jones.

"Should we tell Christopher?"

Jones paused and closed her eyes. "I don't know," said Jones. "I don't think we've got anything. It's like we need to have Colin confess."

"Or catch him in the act?"

"In the act of what?"

"Of stealing the opals again, of course?"

"What are you talking about? The opals are long gone. We have no idea where they are, and we don't think Lorne still has them."

"But does Colin know that?" Autumn raised his eyebrows. "And the way he drinks these days, he could be made to believe almost anything."

"What would we get him to steal? And how would we get him to do it?"

Autumn shrugged. "We need to drop hints, perhaps. I don't know. I'm sure we'll think of something, but the thing is, we need to get him to confess. And an ambush doesn't sound like a bad way to do it."

CHAPTER 31

After returning the lockbox, Jones made her way out into the garden before she was promptly blocked.

"Stop!" said Atlas, two hands up in front of Jones's face.

"What are you doing?" Jones jumped back awkwardly.

"I've been told you are not allowed back here just yet," he said.

"Oh no, not another surprise!" said Jones.

"No, at least not quite like Rex's," said Atlas. "It's Hugo. He's setting up the bar, and he doesn't want you to look until it's ready."

Jones smiled. Of course. She nodded. "Alright, alright, I'll go find something to do then, shall I?"

"That is an excellent idea!"

Jones spent the next half hour pottering around, attempting to be helpful. It seemed everything was in hand. Rex was finalising the lights. Iris was arranging the awards table with Prue's oversight. Tara ensured the stage was set correctly, adjusting the lectern and arranging the banners of the various sponsors. Prue had tasked Atlas and Plum with arranging flowers.

Which is when Jones remembered what she needed to do. Granny's decorations.

"Plum, have you seen a eucalyptus branch anywhere?" Jones asked.

"Oh, well yes," she said. "It's over by the door. But I thought it must have been a mistake with the order."

"Not a mistake at all." Jones found the branch, along with a silver bucket and a bag of sand. It was everything she had requested of the local florist Karkalla Blooms.

Lugging the bag of sand over to the counter, she returned for the bucket and branch, ready to set up her countertop Christmas tree.

"Oh, the baubles!" said Autumn, floating over. "I'd forgotten about them." Autumn had changed out of her trench coat and was now wearing what could only be described as a tea dress. A delicate floral dress, with a flared skirt, and short French sleeves. She looked gorgeous, as always.

Jones lifted the bucket onto the counter after placing down a thick layer of paper to preserve the timber. She then, with much effort, carried the bag of sand and dropped it onto the counter.

"Are you ok with that?" said Autumn.

"I'm not entirely sure," said Jones, proceeding to cut the corner off the bag. Carefully, she tilted it over the edge of the bucket and let a small amount trickle in. When the bucket was secured with the weight of the sand, Jones lifted the bag and poured half of it in. She then took the eucalyptus branch, dug a well, and placed it in, before pushing the sand around to hold it. Finally, she poured in the remaining sand, and with only a little wobbling of the branch, the Christmas tree was in place.

Retrieving the box with the baubles inside, Jones took much delight in once again unwrapping them, and placing each one on the branches. Every few moments she would step back, glance over her styling work, and then make a few adjustments before the final bauble was in position.

"Well done!" said Autumn. "I love it!"

"It's just like I imagined!" Jones said, clasping her hands together. "But there's one more thing." From underneath the counter, she pulled out the family Christmas photo they had found in the decorations box. She propped it up next to the tree and stood back to admire her work.

"Perfection," someone whispered, sliding their arm around Jones's waist. She glanced up to find Hugo at her side. "Are you ready for your next surprise?"

"I'm not sure if my emotions can handle it," Jones joked.

"I think you'll manage." Hugo smiled, and taking her hand, led Jones to the garden.

Moving behind some of the garden dividers and larger potted trees, they weaved their way to the rear of the garden, with Autumn trailing behind. They moved into the larger open space, with a green lawn area, a paved patio, and a large awning that could be open and closed, depending on the weather. It was under this awning that Hugo's surprise was positioned.

"What do you think?" he asked.

"Is that a horse float?" Jones asked.

"It sure is!"

What Jones saw was amazing. A horse float, converted into the cutest little outdoor bar she had ever seen. The old timber float had been fully renovated, painted off-white, with the side panel of the bar the original timber, polished to a glowing honey colour. The top half had been cut and gas lifts pulled it up, positioned above a fold-out bar top. Finally, the whole thing had been decorated with fairy lights.

Around the bar, wine barrels and stools had been placed for people to sit at.

"Hugo, I love it! Where did you get it?"

Hugo stepped into the horse trailer and stood behind the bar. He began grabbing bottles and pouring them into a cocktail shaker.

"A friend of mind found it, and we've been restoring it for a bit over a month," he said.

"What, you mean you created this?"

"Sure did!" said Hugo. "Sybil's van inspired me. I thought I could do something similar, but wanted to tow it behind my car. After a bit of brainstorming, it became obvious. A horse trailer!"

"It's brilliant," said Autumn. "Gosh, I wish he could pour me a champagne right now."

Hugo shook the shaker, and then, pulling a ribbed cocktail glass from the shelf, poured the drink. It was a rosy pink, and he garnished it with a sprig of thyme.

"Created just for you," said Hugo, handing Jones the glass. "This is The Memory Bank cocktail."

Jones's eyes widened. No one had ever done something like this for her before. Her own cocktail. She sipped, and of course, it was delicious.

"Wow. What's in it?"

"It has gin, champagne, raspberries, soda water and," Hugo smiled. "Lilly Pilly cordial."

"Lilly Pilly cordial? I've never heard of it!"

"I've sourced it," said Hugo. "Well, I was able to order some Lilly

Pilly berries, and I found a recipe online. It's pretty easy, really."

"Oh sure, shipping in Lilly Pilly berries sounds so easy!"

"Well, they're not cheap," said Hugo. "But I'm thinking one day I'm going to plant a grove of them. I mean, Lilly Pilly Creek should have a ready source of Lilly Pilly Berries, don't you think?"

Jones nodded but was too busy taking another sip of her drink. "Should I be having this now?"

"Why not?" said Hugo. "It's still a few hours until we start."

"Live a little," Autumn piped in.

"What exactly is the time?" asked Jones.

"Quarter past four," said Hugo.

"Sybil should have arrived. I might pop out and check she's ok," said Jones. But she didn't move. She wasn't going to let a drop of the cocktail go to waste.

As she tipped the last of it down her throat with a flourish, she handed Hugo back the glass. Standing on tiptoes, she reached up and pulled his face down, giving him a quick kiss on the lips. "Thank you."

CHAPTER 32

"This *is* fancy!" cried Jones as she walked out to greet Sybil. Her entire van had been trimmed with silver tinsel, and all her paper cups were now Christmas-themed.

"It's taken forever!" said Sybil. "And this weather didn't help."

Sybil was looking rather flushed. Jones hoped her coffee cart idea wasn't a complete failure. She glanced at Sybil, who appeared to read her mind.

"Don't worry, I'm prepared for lots of orders of iced coffees and Frappuccinos."

"Frappuccinos? What are they?"

"Oh, you know, those American-style flavoured iced coffees piled high with cream," Sybil explained.

Jones nodded. "Well, I'd love to try one, but I've just had a cocktail."

Sybil laughed and Jones went on to explain, describing Hugo's horse float bar with much enthusiasm.

"Well, you sound completely smitten!" said Sybil with a wink.

"Smitten with the mobile bar?" said Jones, but she smiled, knowing exactly what Sybil was referring to. "Do you have everything you need?"

"Yep!" said Sybil. "Sure do. I'm going to close up for now, and pop home to get ready. I want to make sure I'm back in plenty of time. I bet there will be lots of people mingling outside before the doors open."

Jones glanced at her watch. "Gosh, you're probably right. We should all be getting ready. I might go inside and round up the troops."

"See you later!" called Sybil before pulling down the hatch and disappearing.

Jones went inside and found Prue, who was up on the stage, surveying the room, and checking her clipboard.

"How's it all going, Prue? Much more left to do?"

Prue looked up, and then, bringing her clipboard to her chest, addressed Jones. "Actually, I think we are on top of everything."

"Should we close up and let everyone go home and get ready?"

"Yes, I think it's that time,"

"Shall I let everyone know?" asked Jones.

"Allow me," said Prue. And with that, she walked over to the lectern, picked up a microphone and switched it on. With a tap, she tested the microphone before speaking into it.

"Attention! Attention!"

Jones watched as several people in the room jumped, not expecting Prue's voice to boom across the room.

"Bloody hell Prue!" cried out Rex.

"Attention everyone," she continued. "It is now four-thirty. Unless there are any last things to get done, it appears now would be the time for us to head home to get ready. We will meet back here at six-thirty sharp, so we can open the doors at seven. Do you all agree?"

"Agreed!" called out Tara.

"Agreed!" everyone else chimed in.

"Well, if you can all move on out the front door as quickly as possible so Jones can lock up. We need to ensure everything is secure."

The group quickly tidied up what they were working on and made their way out of The Memory Bank. Jones popped out to the garden to make sure there weren't any stragglers. Hugo and his team had already left, and the garden was empty. She locked the glass doors, and then after Prue had confirmed that everyone had left, the pair exited and Jones locked the main doors.

"See you back here soon," said Prue, and she headed off down Main Street.

"Do you want me to come and help you get ready?" asked Autumn.

"That would be amazing," said Jones. "I have no idea what I'm going to do with my hair. And I think I've chosen a really uncomfortable pair of shoes."

The sisters jumped into Jones's Mini and whizzed back to their childhood home.

Jones got into a cool shower and relished the water on her body. It wasn't long, however, before she turned the heat up and felt the warmth on her sore muscles. She had worked hard the last few days.

Before she had gotten in, Jones had laid her proposed outfit on the bed for Autumn to survey. "I have a feeling I may have gotten a bit carried away with the online shopping," Jones had said. She'd escaped to the bathroom before she could experience Autumn's full reaction.

When she returned in her dressing gown, wet hair bundled up in a towel, she nervously awaited Autumn's feedback.

"I love it! I love it! I can't believe this is what you chose, though?"

It was a short, white dress with long billowing sleeves, entirely covered in silver sequins. The dress wrapped around, and was low cut, with a belt and circular belt buckle. The shoes to go with it were potentially even more daring. Hot pink suede stilettos.

"Is it ok? Really? Or just wildly over the top?"

"It is absolutely over the top! It's perfection!"

Jones grinned but still wasn't convinced.

"But first the hair. What do you think?" Jones pulled the towel off, and let her wet hair drop to her shoulders.

"Keep it simple," said Autumn. "With that outfit. Blow dry, and then a few waves with the straightener. Sleek and stylish. It will be amazing."

Jones nodded. She thought she could manage that.

"And don't forget earrings! Have you got any silver hoops?"

Jones had no idea but went to find her jewellery box, dumping it out on the bed so Autumn could see what she could find.

Attempting to be as quick as possible, but without messing things up completely, Jones dried her hair and then ran the straighteners through. She was happy with the slight waves she had created and bent over to blitz her head with the hairspray before focusing on her makeup.

She decided to go with a slightly smoky eye, flushed cheeks, and, of course, bright pink lipstick.

Returning to the bedroom, Autumn clapped with excitement. "Oh yes! Now it's time to get dressed!"

It was a bit of a struggle to get the dress on straight, but she was very glad she hadn't chosen a dress with a back zip. Putting the belt in place, she stood in front of the mirror, pulling the skirt down a little.

"Are you sure it's not too short?"

"Of course not!" Autumn enthused. "Now the shoes!"

This was going to be the trickiest part. She had made sure to insert some cushioning before she wore them. With a tug, the shoes were on, and slowly she stood.

"It has been a very long time since I wore heels!" Jones tentatively walked towards the mirror.

"Wait!" Autumn flew in front of Jones to stop her. "The earrings!"

Jones turned back to the jewellery box. "Did you find any hoops?"

"Yes, I'm pretty sure there are some at the bottom," said Autumn.

She was right. Jones didn't even recall buying them.

"Not quite as big as I would have liked," said Autumn.

"They are more than big enough!" said Jones as she pushed them into her ears.

It was now time to review the outfit choice. Walking to the mirror, it surprised her to see a pleasant reflection.

"Stunning," said Autumn.

Jones looked nothing like herself. No quote t-shirt. No cardigan. No linen shorts. But she was happy. Autumn was right. Tonight, she looked stunning.

"I just hope I can walk up on stage without tripping over!"

"Oh, you'll be fine. Is your speech all ready?"

Jones nodded and walked over to her bureau, where some notecards were sitting. "I'm keeping it short. It's Prue's night tonight."

"Well, I'd be a little worried that outfit might upstage her," said Autumn.

Jones laughed. "I doubt it! What are *you* wearing?"

"I've been working on this all week, and I think I've finally nailed it."

With great drama, Autumn closed her eyes, lifted her head to the ceiling, and raised her arms. Somehow, a shadow rapidly passed over her from top to bottom. Autumn was transformed.

"Oh Autumn!" said Jones.

Autumn was, of course, dressed in a red dress, almost burgundy. The skirt was full, with tulle that rippled across and carefully picked out with sparkling beads. The top was one-shouldered, with a translucent sleeve. Her hair was piled high, red curls tumbling, and she had gone for a darker make-up style than usual. She completed the outfit with simple gold jewellery and statement red stilettos.

"You like?" she asked, twirling.

"Absolutely! I have no concept of how you do it, but this is the best yet."

"If only everyone could see us together," said Autumn. "We would blow their minds."

Softly, Jones said, "We sure would."

"To the ball!" Autumn cried and linked her gossamer arm through Jones's.

"Hang on," said Jones. "Let me just put my sneakers on."

"What?"

"Well, I'm not walking in these." Jones held up one of the pink shoes.

"Yep, ok," said Autumn. "But hurry up. It's just after six."

"Okay, okay," said Jones. "But what are we going to do about Colin?"

"I think those cue cards are the key," said Autumn.

"Really?" Jones stood and picked up the cards from beside her.

"Yes," said Autumn. "And the opals."

"You are going to have to spell this one out for me," said Jones.

"Grab your things, and I'll explain the plan as we walk."

CHAPTER 33

Jones had to admit, she felt good as she strode down the street in her white sneakers and glittery dress. Autumn floated next to her, dress swirling. Autumn was right. If Lilly Pilly Creek could see them both, the pair would have made a dazzling entrance.

"Ok, so, what's the plan?"

"Now, hear me out," said Autumn. "It might not work, of course, but I just have a feeling."

"Alright, alright, spit it out."

"So, all of this is premised on the fact that Colin is still looking for the jewellery, The Lights."

"Uh, huh."

"In your speech, I think you should say something cryptic that gets Colin thinking and makes him take dramatic action."

"What sort of dramatic action?"

"He tries to steal the opals again!"

"You've totally lost me," said Jones.

"Right, I'll spell it out from start to finish, and then you can critique."

"Go ahead," Jones extended her arm out in front, giving Autumn the floor.

"Ok, so, in your speech, you say something like 'the thing that you have been looking for all these years was right here all the time.' I think you could wangle that in somehow?" Autumn shrugged. "Anyway, this will get Colin's mind ticking over. Hopefully, he hasn't already drunk too much, but just enough for the inadequate logic of it to make sense only to him. He realises the opals must be back in The Memory Bank, and he decides to break in, again."

"I get where you're coming from, but the whole thing sounds a little flimsy," said Jones. "What if he doesn't break in tonight? How will he get a key? And what lockbox will he break into?"

"I admit we need to fine-tune the details, but I've had a few ideas," said Autumn. "First, it's up to us to direct him to the lockbox somehow."

"So, he could find a piece of paper that says the opals are in a certain lockbox?"

"Maybe," said Autumn, pausing. "Or he'll presume it would be in a lockbox owned by Lorne. So maybe we make a fake list that includes Lorne and his lockbox number."

"But he won't be able to just pull the lockbox out," said Jones. "He'll need a key."

"A fake key!" said Autumn. "We set up the small safe to contain only fake keys that don't fit any current lockboxes."

"But when are we going to do this? The party starts in less than an hour!"

"You're right," said Autumn. "Ok, what about just one key?"

"One key?"

"Yes, but it's labelled as Master Lockbox Key," said Autumn.

"One key to open them all?" Jones joked.

"Yes! Colin won't know it's a fake."

"Ok, that might just work," nodded Jones. "And I presume you're going to keep an eye on Colin and alert me when he's making his move."

"Yes, but I did have one more idea," said Autumn.

"Oh? And what would that be?"

Autumn floated out in front of Jones, turned to face her, and stopped.

"We let Christopher know what we have planned."

"Christopher! Oh, he is not going to go for this," Jones said, shaking her head.

"He might! He might if *you* explain it to him."

"No matter how I explain it to him, I doubt he'll approve."

"I think we need to try," said Autumn. "We need Christopher with you when you catch him in the act. Colin could get violent. We don't want you getting hurt. Plus, we need the police to witness it all. Otherwise, the whole thing will just look like a stupid drunk guy accidentally making his way into the lockbox room."

Jones shook her head. This whole thing sounded ridiculous. Were they taking The Eldershaw Sisters Detective Agency a little too seriously?

"But not only do we need him to get caught in the act," said Jones. "We need him to confess to stealing the opals in the first place, *and* to assaulting Molly and murdering Lorne. How on earth is that going to happen?"

Autumn shrugged. "That, I'm afraid, is up to you. You're going to have to sweet talk it out of him. With my help, of course."

"Oh Autumn, I don't know about this," said Jones. "It's one thing for us to drop a hint surreptitiously in the speech and see if Colin bites. But to get Christopher involved? This means having to explain our ridiculous theory that the opal theft and the murder are connected. I just don't know."

"Jones, I think we're going to have to leave that to Christopher. He has proven to be very intelligent, and also very trusting of your instincts. He might just surprise you."

"I'm not so sure," said Jones, shaking her head.

"Let's not worry about it now," said Autumn. "You need to get those heels on!"

She was right. They were just in front of the Lilly Pilly Pantry, and about to cross the road to Hugo's and The Memory Bank. It wasn't graceful, but Jones managed to get her sneakers off and heels on without catastrophe.

"Let's do this," said Jones.

She crossed the road and suddenly heard a loud wolf whistle.

"What the!" said Autumn, but then they both burst out laughing. It was Sybil, leaning on the end of her van, clearly appreciating Jones's outfit.

"Loving the look, Jones," she said, waving her hand in a zig-zag as she looked Jones up and down.

"Why thank you, Sybil," said Jones, attempting a very wobbly curtsey. "You look amazing too!"

Sybil had a tinsel crown on top of her piled-up silver hair. She wore a long green dress with white flowers, and the whole thing was lit up with fairy lights.

"And are you ready?" Sybil asked.

"I think so!" said Jones. "But I'd better get in there. You know what Prue's like."

"That I do," Sybil smiled, climbing into her van to prepare for the crowd that was soon to arrive.

Jones wasn't sure what to expect when she walked into The Memory Bank, but she was blown away by what she saw. Soft Christmas music was playing. The lights were low and dotted around the room were lamps, glowing warmly in the space. Vases of flowers were everywhere, and vintage chairs were grouped around the room. Yes, Jones had seen all of this as it was being placed, but the way it had come together, well, it made her a little emotional.

"Wow," Autumn breathed.

"I know," said Jones. "And we haven't even turned on the Christmas lights yet."

"Jones! You look amazing!" It was Iris. She rushed over to Jones and gave her a huge hug.

"Thank you, Iris," said Jones. "You look gorgeous too." Iris was wearing a lilac dress that appeared to be an original from the fifties. It suited her perfectly.

"Thank you, thank you," said Iris. "Now you need to come with me."

Iris took her hand and pulled Jones over to the stage. The members of The Progress Association were mingling, along with Atlas and Plum.

"Oh, Jones!" said Plum. "You're a bombshell!" Plum herself was wearing a purple satin dress, mid-calf length, with magenta ballet flats. As always, she looked stunning.

Jones smiled but tried to ignore the stares and compliments. "What's going on?"

Atlas stepped forward, holding something in his hand. It was the photo from the newspaper when the giant red button was first installed.

"We are going to recreate this photo!" he said proudly.

"Oh, that is a brilliant idea," said Jones, and yet her throat caught on the last word, and she found her eyes brimming with tears. The appreciation she felt for this group of people, along with the sadness of knowing her parents and grandparents were missing this, almost became too much. Waving her hands in front of her face, as though that was going to stop her tears, she climbed onto the stage.

Atlas positioned everyone based on the photo, with the help of a professional photographer who had been arranged for the evening. They even managed to get Rex, Colin and Plum close to their original positions. "Although Plum, can you make sure we see your face this time?" he joked.

Jones was on the opposite side, placed in the same position as her father. Glancing at Autumn, her sister glided up and stood where their mother had been.

"Atlas, you need to be in the photo too!" called out Jones. Atlas feigned refusal, but quickly jumped on the stage and positioned himself with the group. Jones placed her hand on top of the button, and she felt Autumn's hand on top of hers.

"Don't accidentally press the button, Jones," Prue joked, although Jones knew there was an element of earnestness in her comment. Jones winked at her.

"Looking at me!" called the photographer. "Smile everyone! Hooray, you've finally made it! Smile!"

The group beamed as the photographer snapped away.

"I think we got it!"

There was a sudden burst of clapping and everyone looked up to see that Sergeant Schmidt had arrived, applauding them all. He was wearing his uniform, but the jacket was trimmed with silver tinsel. Everyone laughed at his entrance and made their way off the stage. Except for Prue and her clipboard, who made sure she had the best vantage point.

"Go and talk to him!" hissed Autumn. "We don't have time to hesitate."

Jones rolled her eyes but made her way over to Christopher. He was trying to conceal his glances, but Jones knew he was noticing her dress.

"Hi Jones," he said. "Everything ready?"

Jones smiled. "Yes, I think so. But ah, could I talk to you about something? Away from the group?"

"Certainly. Are you ok?"

"Yes, yes, I'm okay," said Jones, and she led him behind one of the velvet stanchion ropes that had been set up to block visitors from going into certain areas of The Memory Bank. She took Christopher into the lockbox room and closed the door, Autumn casually sliding straight through.

"Are you sure you're ok?" he asked.

"Look, I've got a crazy hunch and an even crazier plan, and I'm hoping you can help me?"

"Of course," said Christopher. "Are you planning some secret for tonight?"

"No, well, kind of," said Jones. "But it's not what you think. I think I've worked out who killed Lorne."

Christopher's brow furrowed. "You have?"

"Yes," Jones nodded. "And I need your help to have them reveal themselves."

He tilted his head, clearly unsure about what Jones was saying. She ploughed ahead anyway, telling him the plan she and Autumn had come up with.

"I know it sounds ridiculous," said Jones. "And you can say no. But do you think it's worth a shot?"

Christopher turned and started pacing the room. He was not one to jump into something without thinking it through thoroughly.

"We don't have time for this!" said Autumn. "If we're going to get this done, we have to get ready. Set up the key box, and print the fake list of names. Come on!"

Jones glanced at Autumn and raised her eyebrows, shrugging. There was nothing she could do.

"If he doesn't agree, we're going out on our own anyway," said Autumn. "Otherwise, we might miss our chance."

"What if it does work," said Christopher. "But he doesn't attempt to get into the lockbox tonight? What if he tries another day, and you're constantly in danger?"

"Aw," said Autumn. "See, he's worried about you."

Jones ignored her and continued. "Look, he wouldn't be able to get in the lockbox room normally. It's usually locked. And of course, we would be leaving the small safe open tonight, and locking the actual keys away. But normally there's no way he could access that either." Jones looked at Christopher, whose face was stern. "On a normal day, there's no chance of anything happening. Tonight is the night."

Christopher shook his head but said, "Okay, I think you're right."

"Yes!" said Autumn, punching the air.

"So, what do we need to do?" he asked.

"Leave it with me," said Jones. "You go and wander around like nothing is out of the ordinary. I'll get the scene set and report back."

"Excellent work, Detective," Christopher said with a grin.

"Ha, ha, ha," said Jones. "Now scoot!"

Christopher left the lockbox room, glancing back with a smile before making his way into the main party area. Jones shut the door and turned back to Autumn.

"Are you sure Hugo's the one?" asked Autumn. "I mean, Christopher is just so adorable."

"Shut up Autumn! We have work to do."

"If you insist," said Autumn. "So what do we need to do?"

"Lock away all the real keys in the big safe. Set up the master key in the small safe. Prepare a list of fake lockbox names and numbers. How much time do we have?"

"The doors open in twenty minutes," said Autumn, poking her head through the wall to look at the clock.

"Twenty minutes! I think we're going to need help."

Jones raced out, looking for Atlas.

"Atlas, please, don't ask questions about what I'm going to request from you," said Jones.

Atlas shrugged. "Sure, what do you need?" Jones sighed with relief. She knew she could rely on Atlas. Quickly, she described the fake list of names and lockbox numbers she needed, and Atlas headed off to his office to get it sorted.

Next, Jones pulled out the small safe from behind the counter and grabbed all the current keys. She raced to the larger safe in one of the rear rooms of the bank and safely stored them in there. She then took an unused key that was kept there.

"Okay, so I need to put a tag on this that says 'Master Lockbox Key'. Right?"

Autumn nodded. "Yep, try to make it obvious. I think Colin will need a bit of hand-holding."

Jones laughed a little and found a hanging price tag that they used on some shop items. In large black letters, she wrote its label, and then, with twine, tied it to the key.

"So, where's the best spot to put the safe that isn't obvious, but would be easy to find if you were looking for it?"

"I think just under the counter, right where you would stand to serve customers," said Autumn.

Jones agreed, and placed the safe there, leaving the door

intentionally ajar. "It seems so ridiculous that anyone would fall for this," said Jones.

"Well, if anyone will, it's Colin."

"All set?"

Jones jumped. "Oh Prue, you scared me!"

"What are you doing huddled over here?"

"Just tidying up a few things," said Jones. "What do you think? Are we all ready?"

"As ready as we'll ever be," said Prue, clutching her clipboard to her chest. "But yes, I think everyone has done a brilliant job."

Jones glanced at Prue's clipboard. "Prue, you wouldn't happen to have a spare one of those?"

"What, my clipboard?" She held it out in front of herself.

"Yes," said Jones. "I mean, a spare one here? By any chance?"

"Actually, I do," said Prue. "I have spares of everything. Did you want to borrow it?"

"Yes please," said Jones.

"Follow me!" Prue led her over to a large cane basket that she had tucked away behind one of the shelves. In it was all manner of things, including one clipboard.

"Thank you, Prue!" Jones went to walk off.

"Jones," said Prue. "Meet me at the door at two minutes to seven, and no later!"

Jones nodded and hurried off toward Atlas.

"As you requested," Atlas said, handing her a small pile of printed pages.

"Thank you, Atlas!" Jones took them and slid them onto the clipboard. "Now, Atlas, just so you know, if you see anyone sneaking behind the velvet ropes, please don't worry. I've spoken to Christopher, and he and his team will be patrolling this area. So you can leave any problems to them."

"Good idea," said Autumn.

"No worries," said Atlas. "I think I have enough jobs from Prue, anyway."

"Oh, no!" said Jones. "You're meant to be enjoying yourself this evening, not working!"

"It's ok," said Atlas. "You know I'm happy to help. And most of it's not much. I won't miss the fun."

"As long as you're sure," said Jones. "If it gets too much, I will happily have a word with Prue!"

"Oh, I know you would," Atlas smiled cheekily, recalling the time Jones dramatically escorted Prue out of The Memory Bank. Prue had crossed the line, trying to buy the building they currently stood in.

Jones rushed to the lockbox room. She placed the clipboard on the table, hoping it wasn't too obvious. Then, leaving the room, she pulled the door closed but didn't lock it.

"Do you think that's enough?" said Jones.

"Who knows?" shrugged Autumn. "Now, don't forget the key part of the plan."

"What?" Jones's eyes bulged, no idea what she had forgotten.

"Your speech!" said Autumn. "You need to add the new line."

It was five minutes to seven. Jones was cutting it fine, but she rushed to her handbag, scribbled the line in the only place that it would work, and then, slinging the small handbag over her shoulder, went to meet Prue. She was puffing slightly, but she made it.

"So, we open the doors. Hugo's staff will be on the floor with drink trays and letting everyone know where the bar is. Quarter past seven, the Lilly Pilly Pantry team will bring nibbles around and let everyone know where the grazing tables are. Seven thirty, we make our way over to the stage, ready to officially open the event at seven forty-five, and start the award presentations." This tumbled out of Prue's mouth and all Jones could do was nod.

Prue glanced at her watch, and then up at Jones. "Away you go!"

CHAPTER 34

Jones took out the large, old-fashioned key from her purse and placed it in the lock. She twisted, removed it and then, with her heart beating, opened the door.

The crowd outside all started cheering and clapping. Jones was shocked but grinned, and then without saying a word, stepped back, swinging her arm to the side and ushered everyone inside.

Wren slid past Jones, a tall woman in a tuxedo at her side. She gave Jones a quick hug but conveniently managed to avoid formal introductions due to the crowd behind her. Jones wouldn't forget.

Mr Manowski was looking dapper and tipped his hat as he strolled inside.

Malcolm and Davina Anderson congratulated Jones as they snuck through. Their son Harris followed closely behind, smiling.

Jed of the Haunted Cellar fame smiled at Jones as he walked in. Her stomach clenched, hoping Harriet Treasure was the only ghost he could see.

Even Clancy Tupper, with his walking stick, managed to sidle in, unable to make eye contact with Jones.

It was as though the whole of Lilly Pilly Creek had arrived. Peering above the crowd, it pleased Jones to see a long line for Sybil's coffee van. There were also groups forming as they realised not everyone was going to fit inside The Memory Bank at one time.

Iris and Atlas stood on either side of the door, attempting to track the numbers. Hugo's team was at the ready, handing out beers and wine. Rex was greeting people at the entrance to the garden, encouraging them to head outside. Tara was no doubt out there, assisting with the drinks at Hugo's horse float bar.

Jones wandered through the room. Everyone was coming up to her to say how amazing The Memory Bank looked. They were so pleased that both the Christmas Lights Competition and most especially, the party, had resumed. She watched as group after group stood in front of the key-covered Christmas tree and took photos. She couldn't quite believe it had all come together.

Now, if only their Eldershaw Detective Agency scheme came together as successfully.

"Why don't you go grab yourself a drink," Autumn whispered.

Jones nodded. "Yes, maybe just one," said Jones. "And Autumn, I know we'll have Christopher positioned near the lockbox room during the speeches. But you'll be watching as well, right? You'll come and tell me if Colin heads that way?"

"Of course," said Autumn. "I'll watch your speech, and then I'll be glued to Colin's side."

"Where is he at the moment?" asked Jones.

Autumn floated above the crowd, scanning.

"Leaning on the wall near the stage," said Autumn. "He looks so cute. He's wearing a bow tie!"

Jones shook her head. "Can you believe he killed Lorne?" she whispered before heading out to Hugo's bar.

"Ah, the lady of the hour," said Hugo, as Jones managed to get to the counter through the milling crowd.

Jones shook her head. "I don't think so," said Jones. "But I could certainly do with a drink before the presentations start."

"A signature cocktail?" Hugo asked.

"No, no," said Jones. "Much too strong when I have to stand up and speak in front of people! Just bubbles, please."

Hugo poured the wine into a tulip champagne flute and handed it to her. "On the house," he said. "How long until the presentations?"

"As per Prue's schedule, they will start on the dot of seven forty-five," said Jones.

"Well, I'll ensure I am there by seven forty-four at the latest!"

Jones smiled, took a sip and raised her glass in Hugo's direction as he turned to serve the line of people waiting.

Glancing out over the garden, she was thrilled to see so many people enjoying the warm evening. Fairy lights flickered everywhere, people were laughing and chattering, and even if she did say so herself, the garden looked amazing.

As if by destiny, Jones turned and spotted Flick, standing alone underneath a tree she had never seen before. It had pink berries all over it.

"Flick, what is this gorgeous tree? I don't remember you bringing it in?"

Flick turned to her and smiled, quickly glancing up at Hugo. "I snuck it in just before you arrived tonight. With some help."

"What do you mean, you snuck it in? What is it?"

"I thought Hugo would have told you!" Flick was grinning now.

"Hugo?" Now Jones was confused.

"Well, it's a Lilly Pilly tree!"

Jones gasped, and Autumn had obviously been listening because she flew over to hover next to Flick.

"Is it? Oh wow! I know Hugo was talking about getting some, but I didn't think he meant in here."

"It was a surprise," said Flick. "He was asking me questions about growing them, and I told him I'd seen one at a stockist of ours. He insisted I buy it for your garden."

"Now Christopher doesn't stand a chance," said Autumn. And Jones had to agree. A guy who buys you a tree. How could anyone else compete?

"What's the time?" she asked Flick, who glanced at her watch.

"Nearly seven thirty," she said.

"Oh, right, I'd better get to the stage," said Jones. "Thanks for coming tonight, Flick. You should be so proud of the garden."

Flick nodded but appeared unable to speak. Jones squeezed Flick's hand and then headed towards the stage.

The Progress Association was mingling around, except for Colin. Jones couldn't see him anywhere.

"I sent him off," said Prue, rolling her eyes. "He's already had a few, and he was going to be no help whatsoever. I told him to hang near the door and help round up the crowd when I get up on the stage."

"Good idea," said Jones.

"Now, does everyone know what they're doing?" The group nodded, but of course, Prue still went through the run sheet, reminding everyone of their jobs. Iris and Tara were to stand at the awards table. Rex needed to be ready by the main power switch in case anything went wrong with the red button push. Atlas was in charge of the music. Plum was going to be guiding award winners on and off the stage, directing them to the official photographer after accepting their award.

And Jones was going to be up on stage at the beginning, welcoming everyone to The Memory Bank. After that, she hoped, she could leave the stage and be ready to take down a killer.

Jones shook her head at the thought. The likelihood of that ever happening was so remote. She needed to focus. Prue was signalling her.

As the clock ticked over to seven forty-five, Prue nodded at Atlas, and he turned the music volume up loud. The crowd hushed, and glanced around the room, before their eyes settled on Jones, her dress shimmering, as she walked up onto the stage under the beam of a spotlight.

Jones paused behind the lectern, waiting a few moments for the crowd to gather and hush. Out of the corner of her eye, she saw people moving in from the garden. She glanced down to see Hugo to the right of the stage, and Autumn floating towards the rear of the room. Jones smiled, turned back to her notes, and took a deep breath.

Jones gave a slight nod to Prue, who signalled Atlas to lower the music.

"Good evening everyone. It is my honour and my pleasure to welcome you to The Memory Bank. After thirty years, we are once again thrilled to be celebrating The Lights of Lilly Pilly Creek."

The crowd broke into applause, and there were even a few cheers. Jones spotted Sybil in the crowd, who gave her a huge thumbs up.

Jones smiled and returned to her notes.

"Reflecting on the years since the last Christmas Awards Party, many things have changed, in Lilly Pilly Creek, and my own life. I know if they could be here today, my grandparents, parents, and of course my sister Autumn…." the crowd murmured, looking up at Jones, many of them smiling. "They would be so proud of all the hard work the Progress Association committee has put in to relaunch the Christmas Lights competition, and to put on tonight's event."

There was a round of applause before Jones listed the committee members and thanked them all.

"The Memory Bank has been a special part of Lilly Pilly Creek for over forty years. In that time, we have evolved and grown, but at the heart of everything we do is protecting the memories of the town, the stories of Lilly Pilly Creek. For myself, I have returned to this town only recently. Although not for happy reasons, being able to step into my sister's shoes," Jones kicked up one foot, which she knew Autumn would appreciate. "And becoming the newest custodian of The Memory Bank, I have learnt how important memories are."

Jones paused and looked around the room, seeing the smiling faces of many friends and customers.

"We may leave this town, we may leave Lilly Pilly Creek, to seek new adventures. Although some of us don't return, we will always have our memories." Jones glanced at Autumn, suddenly worried their clue would be too cryptic. She decided to try and catch Colin's eye before glancing down again.

"For those of us who do return, it may just be that what you've been seeking all these years has been in a Memory Bank lockbox all along."

Jones glanced at Colin, who had a strange look on his face. She then looked out into the crowd, stunned. They had broken out into applause. There were hoots and even a wolf whistle, which she knew was from Sybil. Jones was surprised. Whatever metaphorical meaning they had taken from her last line, it was beyond Jones. Still, she beamed as she looked down on these people who had supported her.

"Now we have something very special for you." At Prue's signal, Atlas rolled out the stand holding the giant red button.

"Just before the last Christmas Lights Awards Party, thirty years ago, the Progress Association of the day, which included Colin, Rex and Plum, presented this red button to my parents. I want to thank Rex," Jones extended her arms towards Rex at the side of the stage. "For surprising me with not only this button but what you are about to see."

Autumn flew over, and with their hands together, they pressed the button.

The crowd gasped as the tree and the ceiling lit up. The room was a murmur as they took in the spectacle.

Prue walked over, hugged Jones, and took her place at the lectern.

"Let's give one more round of applause to Jones Eldershaw, our host for this evening."

Prue and the crowd clapped as Jones walked off the stage. She felt her knees wobble as she returned to the ground. Hugo walked over to her and gave her a hug and a kiss. They stood together at the side of the stage, arm in arm, watching Prue commence the awards ceremony.

Jones had to admit she didn't hear a word Prue spoke. She was too busy enjoying the comfort of being so close to Hugo. She was also concerned about what may be going down at the rear of the Bank without her knowledge. Jones knew Autumn would come and get her as soon as she was required, but she couldn't help but wonder how long that might take.

Prue began by announcing the award for best Roadside Stall Lights Display. A lady by the name of Peggy Hart who ran the Bouquets and Buckets Flower stall, bounced onto the stage, thrilled with her win, and the trophy she was handed. She spent a few moments thanking everyone she had ever met before Prue managed to usher her off the stage and into Plum's care.

Just as the next award was to be announced, Jones saw a blur of red coming rapidly towards her.

"It's not Colin!" Autumn cried. "Colin isn't the killer!"

CHAPTER 35

Jones looked up at Autumn, confused.

"Quick! Come see!"

Jones excused herself from Hugo, fortunate she didn't need to make up an excuse as any explanation would have interrupted Prue.

Autumn was floating back and forth, desperate for Jones to follow her. Jones did her best to be discreet, slowly making her way to the counter, before slipping around the back and towards the lockbox room.

"Is anyone following me?" Jones whispered.

"No," said Autumn. "But you need to hurry. Stand back at first. Just watch."

The door to the lockbox room was open, but not wide enough for Jones to see anything. Autumn went up and, placing her hand on the door, managed to push so it slowly moved open without alerting the person inside.

"Can you see?" Autumn asked, rushing back.

At that moment, Christopher walked up. Jones put her finger to her lips. He nodded and stood beside her. Jones pointed, and together they walked closer to the door. They stood to the side and peered in carefully. They could see who was inside, and it was not who they expected.

"Oh...my....gosh!" Jones mouthed dramatically to Christopher, who looked equally shocked.

"Molly Shepherd!" said Autumn. "Can you believe it!"

They turned back to the door. Just because Molly was inside didn't necessarily mean she had anything to do with Lorne's death. In fact, at this stage, it made no sense. She was the one who'd been attacked. Did she know what Lorne was doing? Was Colin even involved? Jones's mind was racing.

They watched Molly. She was holding the key Jones had set up for her to find. But instead of looking at the list that was clearly in view, she was going along, putting the key into random locks, attempting to open them.

"This is going to take forever," said Autumn. "For goodness' sake, Molly! That whack on the head has really done something to you."

"Do something," Jones tried to say out the side of her mouth. She tipped her head to the side, willing Autumn to understand.

Autumn frowned, knowing Jones was trying to tell her something. She looked back and forth between Jones and Molly and then looked around the lockbox room.

Suddenly, she flew to the clipboard with the list of names and placed her hand over it. She'd understood. Jones willed her to make the pages flutter, to grab Molly's attention.

It wasn't long before Jones saw the corners wiggle, and then finally, they made a distinct flutter sound. Both Christopher and, fortunately, Molly looked towards the notes. Christopher brushed it off, but Molly did not. She walked straight over to the list, and then, realising what it was, began flipping through the pages, clearly looking for a name.

Molly folded four of the pages back. Jones knew on the fifth page, not too far down, was Lorne's name. Lockbox number 562.

Quickly, Molly rushed over and placed the key in the lock. It opened. This was not a shock to Jones or Autumn. Molly was thrilled. Tugging, she pulled out the lockbox and turned around. As she moved to place it on the table, Jones stepped into the room.

"Hello Molly," she said.

Molly shrieked and dropped the box on the table with a bang.

"Oh Jones, you scared me," said Molly. She smiled at Jones, but her face went red, her hands shaking.

"I was just wondering what you were doing?"

"Oh, ah, well," Molly clenched her fist and took a deep breath. "I ah, noticed this, ah, this lockbox door was open, and I thought I'd better take a look for you. You know, after what happened last time," Molly raised her eyebrows.

"What exactly *did* happen last time, Molly?" Jones asked.

"You, you know," she stuttered. "You know what happened."

"Do I? Because I have a feeling I haven't been told the full story, and I was hoping you might fill me in."

"The full story? I got whacked on the head and left for dead. That's the full story."

"Ah, that's right. Lorne whacked you on the head and left you for dead, didn't he?"

"Yes, that's right," said Molly. Jones smiled at her. Molly's eyes then bulged. She realised what she'd said.

"So it *was* Lorne," said Jones. "It was you and Lorne, in cahoots to steal my Granny's opals, wasn't it Molly?"

Jones paused, staring at Molly. Molly looked to the ground, swaying slightly. "I uh, I uh don't know what you're talking about."

"Yes, you do Molly," said Jones. "Lorne was a nasty piece of work, though. Wasn't he. He changed his mind about something, didn't he, Molly? Something went wrong, and Lorne, being Lorne, wasn't going to let anyone stand in his way. Even if it was his girlfriend. Even if it was you."

Molly kept her eyes on the ground but shook her head.

"Keep going Jones," said Autumn.

Jones was feeling very unsure of herself. She wasn't a police interrogator. She could only imagine what Christopher was thinking, but as yet, he hadn't made his presence known.

Jones decided to change tack. She wanted to be a little more comforting to Molly. More her usual self, and see if that got Molly talking.

"It's ok Molly," said Jones, slowly walking to her.

"Be careful," said Autumn.

Jones ignored her sister. She knew Christopher would step in if anything happened. She put her arm around Molly's shoulders.

"It's ok Molly. It wasn't your fault, was it? Did Lorne decide he wanted all the jewellery for himself? Did he see what was really in that box, and decided he didn't want to split it? Was that it?"

Molly shook her head.

"No? He was still planning to share it with you?"

Molly nodded.

"Ask her if she chickened out," said Autumn.

"Well then, it must have been you. You decided at the last minute you didn't want to go through with it. Is that right?"

It was very slight, but Molly nodded. Autumn sucked in her breath, knowing they were close, at least to the first confession.

"You asked him to stop and put it back, didn't you?"

Molly nodded again.

"But he didn't listen to you. Lorne ignored your pleas. You tried to grab him, but he whacked you over the head, with, with….."

Jones glanced up and looked at Autumn, her eyes wide, desperate for Autumn to help her.

"The lockbox!" cried Autumn. "He whacked her on the head with the lockbox!"

"With the lockbox," said Jones. "He whacked you over the head with a lockbox! How dare he!"

Molly whimpered and staggered, moving towards the only chair in the room. She flopped down into it and lay her head on the table.

"Lorne is a horrible, horrible person," said Jones. "It's not your fault he stole all the jewellery and assaulted you. He's been allowed to get away with it for all these years. But why didn't you report him, Molly? Why didn't you tell the police?"

"Because I forgot," said Molly. "I forgot all these years. I pushed it away."

Jones was patting Molly's shoulders, calming her, encouraging her.

"Of course you did," said Jones. "But then you started remembering. Didn't you? What was it? When you found out we were restarting the lights competition?"

"I think so," said Molly. "I started having nightmares. I'd blocked it from my mind for all these years. But then I remembered. I saw Lorne, the fury in his face, just before he hit me. And I remembered about the jewellery. I remembered he had taken the jewellery, even though I'd begged him to stop. That I'd changed my mind. But he still took it, and didn't give a single piece to me."

"That's it," said Autumn. "That's why she killed him! Because he assaulted her *and* stole from her."

"He stole from you? He stole from you and assaulted you? How dare he! How dare Lorne do that to do? I hope you confronted him. Did you, Molly?"

"Of course I did!" Molly said angrily. "Of course, I confronted him, that lying swine."

Jones glanced up quickly, looking for Christopher. She could see him, still standing at the side of the door. She presumed he was recording everything.

Jones walked back to the side of the table, so Molly might lift her head, and she and Christopher would both be able to see her reaction as she spoke.

"He was an awful human being," said Jones. "You didn't deserve to be treated so horribly!"

"Of course I didn't," said Molly. "All these years, he'd left me behind, stolen from me. And just when my business was struggling, when I needed help, he refused."

"You asked him for help?" Jones asked.

"Yes," said Molly. "All I asked for is some money. The amount he would have owed me for the jewellery he stole. It was our plan. *I* was the one who'd gotten the box number out of Mrs Eldershaw. *I* was the one who slipped the key from the safe when Mrs Eldershaw was distracted. He didn't care. Couldn't have cared less about me or about what he'd done to me."

"You're telling me, even all these years later, he felt no guilt for what he'd done to you?"

"None at all," said Molly.

Jones shook her head. "Unbelievable! I don't know what I would have done. I think I would have snapped. You had every right to snap. You had every right to hurt him like he'd hurt you. Gosh, wouldn't it have been perfect if you'd been able to whack him over the head as he'd done you?"

"Nice touch," said Autumn.

"But you didn't have a lockbox with you in the nursery, did you? What did you have? What could you grab?"

"The shears," said Molly. "The shears were the closest things."

"Oh, they would have been perfect! That solid heavy metal of the blades would have done a lot of damage. Did they Molly?"

Molly let out a cry before exclaiming. "Yes! I whacked him and whacked him just like he whacked me! Lorne Fox is evil. Ask anyone in this town. Not a single person misses him! Not one!"

"Not one," said Jones. "Except his daughter. Except Flick."

Molly began to sob, her face in her arms on the table again.

"I'll take it from here, Jones," said Christopher, walking into the room.

"Molly," said Jones. "Just one last question."

Molly's sobs quietened, but she didn't respond.

"Was it you that sent those letters?"

"Mmmm," Molly said quietly.

"Why?" said Jones. "You told me it wasn't you. Why did you send them?"

Molly slowly lifted her head and turned to look at Jones.

"To distract you," she said. "I knew with your history you couldn't help but meddle. Knew you would get too close to the truth. "

Christopher took her arm and got her to stand. Molly continued to stare at Jones.

"I thought you'd be too worried about the letters and the ghosts of the past to bother with the present."

CHAPTER 36

Jones ended the evening sitting up in the horse box bar with Hugo. Christopher had discreetly handcuffed Molly and, with help from Constable Partridge, walked Molly out of The Memory Bank. Not many guests would have seen, but it didn't take long before gossip was rippling through the crowd.

Fortunately for Prue, the award ceremony had been completed, and the grand finale, the Lilly Pilly Christmas Lights of the Year Award had been presented to the Quinn Family.

"They had this amazing display set up in their paddock of corrugated iron Kangaroos, pulling Father Christmas's sleigh," Jones, who had been on the judging panel, explained to Hugo. "With a mob of koala elves, and the man himself wearing a blue singlet and a cork hat. They'd even created a giant sign saying 'Merry Christmas Lilly Pilly Creek!' It was brilliant."

Hugo had poured Jones one of her signature cocktails, and when the crowd started to disperse, and fewer drink orders were coming in, Jones gave Hugo a very quick rundown of the arrest of Molly Shepherd.

"You are kidding me," he said. "Molly was not only involved in the theft, but she killed Lorne? I can't believe it!"

"Neither can I," said Jones, sipping her cocktail. "We were entirely convinced it was Colin."

"Well, he does fit the part," said Hugo. "But I'm pleased to say he passed out a while ago."

"Well, I suppose that is good," said Jones. "Colin was harmless after all."

"Were you happy with the evening?" asked Hugo, his hand on Jones's knee.

"To be honest," said Jones. "I didn't see much of it. Most of my time was spent manipulating Molly into confessing to a crime."

"Crimes," said Hugo, sipping his own cocktail. "And you weren't manipulating her. You were coaxing the truth out of her and, by the sounds of it, you did an amazing job."

"We might have to wait and see what Christopher says," said Jones. "I may have stuffed up everything."

"Christopher would have stepped in earlier if he thought you were doing anything wrong," said Hugo. "But what is it with you and murders?"

Jones raised her eyebrows as she took a large gulp of her cocktail. "I have absolutely no idea," she replied. "Hopefully, this is the last serious case I'm involved in."

"No way!" said Autumn, who had glided over after taking a turn around the party, no doubt eavesdropping on everyone talking about Molly. Jones smiled but didn't look up. Autumn was right. She may not want to be anywhere near another murder, but solving cases was certainly fun. This one was just a little too close to home for her liking.

Prue walked up to the bar. "How are you, Jones? I heard about Molly. Is it true you got her to confess?"

How everyone had come to that, albeit correct, conclusion was beyond Jones. But it was the superpower of a small town.

"Kind of," she shrugged. "But Christopher was right there. I wasn't doing it alone."

"We're all just flabbergasted," said Prue, shaking her head. "It's almost ten o'clock. It's probably a bit earlier than I expected, but most people have moved outside. I'm wondering, do you think we should call it a night?"

"I'm certainly ready to finish up," said Jones. "But maybe the committee might want to hang out here for a bit. Have a few drinks and debrief?"

"That sounds lovely," said Prue.

"Oh, and invite Sybil in, if she's still here," said Jones.

Prue happily took charge of ushering everyone out of The Memory Bank. The committee gradually made their way to the stools around Hugo's horse float bar. He poured drinks for everyone, a number happily accepting one of The Memory Bank specials.

"Thanks for the Lilly Pilly tree, by the way," said Jones, leaning into Hugo as he came up to sit on a stool next to her.

"Oh, you saw it!"

"Yes, Flick told me all about it," said Jones. "It's gorgeous. And the first of many, perhaps?"

"Yes, I wonder if you could grow seedlings from the fruit?" Hugo pondered. "We could start our whole orchard, from the one tree."

Jones noticed, but didn't comment on Hugo saying 'our' orchard. It appeared that Autumn was too busy eavesdropping to have heard it. Jones rested her head on Hugo's shoulder. She took the time to appreciate the gorgeous evening, the group of people around her, and the fact she had someone by her side whom she could see a future with.

The next moment, Jones felt a buzzing, and realised the phone in her handbag was ringing. Pulling it out, she saw it was Flick.

"Hi Flick, is everyone okay?"

"Yes, we're fine," said Flick. "A bit of a shock, but no, that's not why I was ringing. I was just wondering, are you still at The Memory Bank?"

"Yes, there's a group of us in the garden."

"Is there any chance you might come to the front door and let me in? I've got something to show you."

It surprised her, but of course, Jones agreed. With Hugo who wasn't going to let her answer the front door alone, and of course Autumn, they went to Flick.

"Hi Flick," said Jones. "Come in. I'll just lock the door behind us. After the evening we've had."

"Well, that is kind of why I'm here," said Flick.

"Oh?"

"Yes. Everyone was whispering at the party, so I left early to go home and be with Mum. But Christopher rang me and told me everything."

"Of course," said Jones.

"And well, obviously, I'm relieved and shocked and very confused at the moment. But it also reminded me of something." Flick turned to the purse she was carrying and flipped it open.

"This," said Flick. Out of her purse, she pulled a key. A lockbox key.

"Is that yours?" asked Jones.

"I suppose it is now," said Jones. "But it was in Dad's things. I didn't know what it was. Didn't think much of it with everything that's been happening."

"I can imagine," said Jones.

"And of course, I'm so sorry. I had no idea Dad was the one that broke into The Memory Bank. That he attacked Molly." Tears streamed down Flick's face.

"Of course you didn't," said Jones, putting her arm around Flick.

"It's just, I don't know what would be in this lockbox. All of his papers were in a safe at home. And I think any family history stuff is with my uncle. I was wondering….." Flick looked at the floor.

"Yes?" Jones asked.

"Well, I don't want to guess," Flick said. "Do you think we might open it? Now? Tonight?"

Jones glanced up at Hugo and they shared a small smile.

"Of course Flick," said Jones. "Follow me."

"Hugo, you can come too," said Flick, when she noticed him hesitating.

They walked over to the lockbox room, which Jones had, of course, locked when Christopher removed Molly. She unlocked it and brought Flick in.

"Take a seat," Jones said, indicating the very chair that Molly had recently sat in. "I'll get out the lockbox and leave you to it."

"Oh no, I want you to stay," said Flick. "I think you're meant to stay."

Jones had no idea what Flick was referring to and imagined she was just feeling shaken up by the evening's events.

Unlocking and pulling out the box, she placed it in front of Flick. Jones handed the key back to Flick to unlock the box itself.

Jones and Hugo stood back, but, of course, Autumn hovered over Flick's shoulder. Jones tried to catch Autumn's eye, and when she did, she indicated that Autumn should move away.

Slowly, Flick turned the key, pulled it out, and lifted the lid. She started sobbing.

"Flick! What is it?" Jones was a little concerned. After discovering everything her father had done, her mind raced with the possibilities of what was inside.

"Come," gulped Flick. "Come here and look."

Jones looked up at Hugo and then walked over to the table. Autumn came with her, and together they peered over Flick's shoulder.

"The opals!" Jones cried. It was her turn to shake. She quickly knelt next to Flick, stunned.

"Oh my gosh," said Autumn. "I can't believe it."

"What is it?" Hugo asked, walking over to look.

There, in the bottom, completely by themselves, were a pair of opal earrings. Their Granny's earrings.

The Lights.

CHAPTER 37

Just under a week later, on Christmas Day, Jones got up early and walked to The Memory Bank.

It had been decided that Jones would spend the morning with Autumn, eating the croissants and coffee, and satisfying herself with a glass of champagne, seeing as Sybil's coffee van would be closed.

In the afternoon, she'd been invited to spend Christmas lunch with Neha, her husband, and Plum. Autumn insisted she go. She tried to explain to Jones that days and times were very different for her now. She wouldn't be lonely. She would enjoy her afternoon, especially knowing they were still together, and able to spend one more Christmas Day with each other.

Hugo had said he could change his plans, but Jones insisted he go spend the day with his friends. It was still a bit early, she thought, for them to spend Christmas together. However, she did ring Hugo as soon as she woke up that morning to wish him Merry Christmas.

"I was thinking I might drive back to Lilly Pilly Creek tonight," he said. "What do you think?"

Jones smiled into the phone. "That sounds lovely," said Jones. "I've got some prawns in the freezer and ham in the fridge which are no longer being eaten today. Maybe you wouldn't mind helping me out?"

"Not at all," Hugo laughed. They hung up, confirming they would touch base sometime after lunch.

Jones got ready, today wearing some pale blue pants and a short-sleeved white shirt with brown slides. No quote today. She grabbed her handbag and sunglasses and carried a large picnic basket with her. Jumping into the Mini, Jones grabbed the steering wheel and smiled, excited she was spending Christmas morning with her sister.

Autumn was waiting out the front of The Memory Bank. She was wearing a red tartan skirt and a green silk singlet with strappy heels.

"Merry Christmas!" she called as soon as she thought Jones could hear. Jones assumed no one would be watching and waved wildly at her sister.

Once inside, they headed directly to the garden and Jones lay a tablecloth out. She then spent time setting a beautiful breakfast table, complete with silverware, napkins, champagne glasses, and the platters she had prepared.

"I've just done the croissants with jam and cream," Jones explained. "There was no way to keep them warm."

"Not a problem for me," said Autumn. "I wouldn't notice even if they were hot!"

Jones laughed. For a moment, she had forgotten that she was to be the only one devouring this food. She set two places just the same, and even poured two mimosas, mixing sparkling wine with pineapple and mango juice for a Christmas twist.

"This is just perfect," said Autumn.

"Hang on!" said Jones. "One more thing."

Out of the basket, she pulled two Christmas bonbons.

"Oh, yay!" said Autumn.

"Is there any chance you could pull them?" Jones asked.

"I have absolutely no idea," said Autumn. "But let's give it a crack.

Oh, haha. Get it. A crack!"

Jones smiled, appreciating that Autumn's joke would be equal to the quality of the joke inside the very bonbon she held out to her.

Autumn reached out her hand and placed it around the bonbon.

"I'm not sure I can do this," said Autumn.

"Well, let's just give it a try," said Jones. "You hold it and I'll pull."

Jones was very gentle at first, but then she felt a bit of force around the bonbon so tugged harder. Autumn had her eyes closed, focusing. Jones gave another quick tug and 'pop!'

"Oh, it worked!" squealed Autumn. "That's amazing!"

"Another one?" asked Jones, picking up the second bonbon.

Autumn shook her head. "No way," she said. "If I try that, I won't have enough energy for breakfast. You do it."

Jones cracked it, and emptied both of their contents, the most important part being the tissue paper Christmas hats inside.

There was a blue and an orange one. Jones picked up the blue one and popped it on.

"Oh, that orange will clash with my hair," said Autumn. Jones, slightly confused, went to pull hers off but at that moment, Autumn shook her head, and suddenly on top of her auburn hair was a green Christmas hat, in exactly the right style.

Jones laughed! Christmas had now truly begun.

Together they read the bonbon jokes as Jones sipped her mimosa, spread jam and cream on her croissant, and savoured the sweet bites of mango. They laughed and chatted, and spent a decent amount of time, once again, discussing the fate of Molly Shepherd.

They had been told she was currently in remand, waiting for a hearing. Christopher had said it was not looking good, not with the recorded confession, and some witnesses that finally decided to come forward after all of these years. It seemed between a select group of Lilly Pilly Creek citizens, it was well known that Lorne and Molly might have been in the whole thing together. But they didn't dare cross Lorne Fox. And because their grandparents and parents hadn't mentioned the theft, and Molly had decided, whether by force or otherwise, not to press charges, it seemed there hadn't been anything the police could do.

"Now, before I leave for lunch," said Jones, as she was coming to the end of consuming the spread in front of them. "There is one thing I thought we should do together."

"Oh, yes?"

"I thought we might return The Lights to where they belong," said Jones, pulling out a small jewellery box from her handbag.

"And where is that?" asked Autumn.

"Why, right here, of course," said Jones. "The lockbox."

Autumn smiled. She knew Jones was exactly right.

"In Granny's lockbox?" Autumn asked.

"The very one," said Jones. She stood, carrying the box and her second mimosa with her. Jones took the key from the safe, and together they went into the lockbox room. She pulled out her Granny's lockbox and placed it on the table.

"Can you imagine what Granny would think," said Autumn. "Knowing The Lights, her opals, were back after all these years?"

"I know!" said Jones. "I think she would be pretty proud of us."

Jones lifted the lid and carefully placed the jewellery box securely inside. They both stared at the box for a moment. Jones glanced up at Autumn, who nodded. Jones placed the lid back down and locked it.

"Do you know what you need to do now?" said Autumn, as Jones went and returned the lockbox to its slot.

"What?" Jones asked, looking up.

"I think you need to get a journal. One of the journals we sell."

"Oh? Why?"

"Because I think you need to continue the tradition. I think you need to start writing journals, just like Granny did. And you can start with the story of The Lights of Lilly Pilly Creek."

SIGN UP TO MY NEWSLETTER

Thank you so much for reading The Lights of Lilly Pilly Creek. If you enjoyed the book and would like to be notified when new books in the Lilly Pilly Creek Ghost Mysteries series are released, or other titles, I would love it if you would sign up to receive my newsletter. Every now and then you may receive exclusive free bonus material, as well as my latest news or when titles go on sale. If you would like to sign up please visit my website

abbielmartin.com

ABOUT THE AUTHOR

Abbie L. Martin is a South Australian author who lives with her family in a small town very similar to Lilly Pilly Creek. She has been dreaming of writing and publishing since she was a child, and when she reached her forties, finally decided to take the leap. Whilst also running a business with her husband, and juggling life with three children, Abbie loves nothing better than peace and quiet with a good book and a glass of wine, preferably an Adelaide Hills sparkling.

BY ABBIE L. MARTIN

The Lilly Pilly Creek Ghost Mystery Series

Book 1 - The Ghost of Lilly Pilly Creek

Book 2 - The Bride of Lilly Pilly Creek

Book 3 - The Lights of Lilly Pilly Creek

www.ingramcontent.com/pod-product-compliance
Lightning Source LLC
Chambersburg PA
CBHW070546120726
47909CB00007B/2259